A DEADLY DROP

By Diana J Febry

COVER DESIGN BY DIANA J FEBRY

PROOFREAD BYSJ, PROOFREADER & COPYWRITER

CHAPTER ONE

Duncan Thomas took a moment to admire the sunset through the floor-to-ceiling windows. He enjoyed the daily reminder of his grand romantic gesture, which never failed to boost his ego. Oh, to be young and frivolous! He stood where his wife had watched the sunrise as a child and at the exact spot where he had proposed to her. Back then, they had huddled for warmth in a draughty, derelict barn surrounded by dusty cobwebs. Now it was an architectural marvel. People consistently underestimated him and the lengths he would go to achieve his ends, then and now.

He turned to walk to the main hall, where his wife bent over the local newspaper at the central counter. He sat opposite her, and said a cheery, "Good morning."

Not taking her eyes from the newspaper article, Pat said, "Is it? And why are you up so early? I expect you'll be wanting coffee?"

"I can get it myself, dear. No need to trouble yourself." Craning to see what Pat was reading, Duncan asked, "What have you got there?" His jaw clenched when Pat looked up. Her face was lined, but her eyes held the same passion and intensity she'd had in her twenties.

"An absolute bag of crock is what this is. I'm going to put a spanner in their works." Pat furiously jabbed the newspaper with her forefinger. "Over my dead body, will they get away with this."

Sighing, Duncan asked, "Get away with what, dear?"

"That gormless child Rhianna Garland has been made our local rural officer."

"Oh dear," Duncan said, struggling to feign much interest. "I'll go and get that coffee. Do you want a refill?"

When he returned with two mugs of fresh coffee, Pat was frantically scribbling notes in her notebook, oblivious to his presence. He placed her mug beside the newspaper and settled down to enjoy his coffee.

"I think my sister is behind it."

Putting down his coffee, Duncan asked, "Now, why do you think that?"

"Because that stupid girl isn't devious enough to shoehorn herself into that position by herself. I'm contacting the press about it."

"Make sure you have your facts straight before you do. You don't want to get yourself into trouble," Duncan gently warned.

"Oh, I will." Looking up, Pat said with steely determination, "Trust me, I will get to the bottom of this and expose her devious scheming."

"Look at the state you've got yourself worked up into," Duncan said. "It's not good for you. I bet your heart rate is through the roof."

Pat pulled up her sleeve to check the reading on the smartwatch Duncan had bought for her after her last little spell. "It is a little high."

"Why don't you put the newspaper away a moment, and we can have a chat about something less stressful. See if we can get that level down a little."

Putting down her pen and pushing her reading glasses to the top of her head, Pat said, "Duncan Thomas. If I didn't know you better, I would say you were up to something."

"Not at all, my lovely. I've woken early on this beautiful morning, and I thought having a relaxed breakfast with my beautiful wife would be a pleasant start to the day."

"Oh, get away with you. You really are a stupid, old fool," Pat said. "It's cold, wet and miserable out there."

CHAPTER TWO

DI Fiona Williams pulled up outside the twenty-four-hour convenience store, leaned back in the car seat, and closed her eyes. Supper with her parents had been typically tricky and draining. It was the worst she had seen her father, and it was clear they had reached a point where something had to be done. Her mother, remaining stubbornly oblivious to the rapid deterioration, couldn't stop the inevitable. Somehow, she had to persuade her mother to see reason and accept that changes were needed. A joint approach would work best, so she needed to get her brother, who had always been the favourite child, on side.

Fiona opened her eyes to check the time. Her tiredness, combined with the winter darkness, made it feel later than it was, and it was still a reasonable time to call her brother. Except, the meal with her parents had left her emotionally drained, and she wasn't sure she had the energy to give it her full attention.

Things were relatively quiet at work, so this would be a good time to take a week's leave. Tomorrow, she would apply for a week's holiday to give her time to discuss the situation with her brother and parents properly. She could squeeze in giving her living room a lick of paint. It was looking more tired and jaded than she was. Satisfied and relieved she had a plan, she forced herself out of the warm car into the icy cold.

She caught sight of her reflection inside the brightly lit store. She looked as frazzled and rundown as she felt. She grabbed a pint of milk, a bar of chocolate, a bottle of wine and, on impulse, a frozen pizza. Whacking it in the oven tomorrow would be far easier than cooking something complicated. The healthy diet and lifestyle could wait another week. Head down, already imagining herself curled up on the sofa with her chocolate and wine, she headed for the door. She was nearly out of the store when she heard a familiar voice.

"Hey, Fiona. Wait up."

Fiona's heart rate went up a notch. Stefan. The last person she wanted to see at any time, let alone when she looked and felt half-dead. If she had to see him, she would prefer it to be when she had a full armour of makeup, a cute dress, killer heels and looked amazing. Not with dull, blotchy skin and dark rings under her eyes. Pretending she hadn't heard him, she continued through the door and quickened her pace. She nearly made it to her car, but when juggling her shopping to retrieve her car keys, she dropped them in a puddle. Cursing under her breath, she put down her shopping to retrieve them.

"Here, let me," Stefan said, scooping up the keys, and making Fiona jump as she hadn't realised that he had followed her from the shop. He pressed the fob and opened the rear passenger door. Without asking, he picked up the shopping bag and placed it on the car seat.

Fiona kicked herself for being too slow to react. If she had been less tired, she might have been quick enough to grab the bag away and say she was doing just fine by herself. If Stefan wasn't such a liar, his posing as a knight in shining armour and his automatic assumption that she needed his help when she didn't, wouldn't be so annoying. Now, she knew better than to fall for his fake chivalrous act.

Closing the rear car door, Stefan said, "You haven't returned my calls."

Edging towards the front of the car, Fiona replied, "No. I've been busy and …"

"Could we meet up for a drink and a chat one evening? Or a morning coffee if you prefer? We have things to talk about. Clear the air."

Knowing she sounded ungrateful and crabby, Fiona reached for the car door, and said, "Maybe, when I'm less busy."

"This weekend?" Stefan said, moving closer to the driver's

door.

Fiona hated the part of her that felt like a flustered schoolgirl wanting to set a date. The only plus to the encounter was she felt hot and flushed rather than freezing cold. Her phone rang, saving her from replying. Pulling it out of her pocket and checking the screen gave her the excuse to make her escape. "Sorry, I need to take this."

She eased herself into her car seat, listening to the call. Instantly alert, her thoughts spinning, she said, "Urgent call. Gotta go."

Holding onto the car door, Stefan said, "How about Sunday? 8 o'clock at the Shipp."

Pulling the door closed, Fiona said, "Maybe, whatever," and started the car engine. As she pulled away, she spotted Stefan's parked car on the other side of the road. Why hadn't she seen it earlier? If she had, she wouldn't have stopped. She could have coped with black coffee in the morning. An attractive brunette sitting in the passenger seat curiously looked back at her. Fiona quickly looked away to concentrate on the road and not her illogical, fierce feelings of jealousy. Why should she care about the girl who was unfortunate enough to be spending time with the last person on earth she wanted anything to do with?

Once around the corner, she called DS Phil Humphries on her hands-free. "I'll swing by in ten minutes. We've a suspicious death. Can you be ready to leave … Okay if we take your car?"

CHAPTER THREE

Humphries was leaning against his car when Fiona drove into his street. She twisted awkwardly to grab the bar of chocolate from her back seat before transferring into his car. Opening the wrapper, she said, "I need an energy hit. Do you want to share?"

"So long as you don't tell Tina. We're keeping our weight down for the big day."

Handing over half of the chocolate bar, Fiona said, "You've still got a few months to duck out."

"Are you serious? Her mother would hunt me down and kill me."

"You know what they say about girlfriends turning into their mothers," Fiona teased.

Refusing to bite, Humphries asked, "What do we know about this death?"

Fiona's mind momentarily drifted off. She was sure she would never turn into her mother. She took a bite of chocolate and tuned herself back to work mode. "Husband returned home to find his wife had fallen down a set of stairs and called an ambulance. When the paramedics arrived, they thought the injuries were inconsistent with a fall, so they called it in. That's all I know, other than it's in Willbury."

"Whereabouts in the village?"

"I'll direct you once we get closer."

Fiona waited until they entered Willbury, which was little more than a few ancient cottages and barn conversions straddling a pot-holed, narrow lane that linked two larger villages. "When you come to the signpost at the other end, there's a track on your left which leads to the house."

Humphries turned by the sign and stopped the car, looking up an uneven, muddy track thinly covered with chippings. "Thanks. Now, I know why you wanted me to drive."

"It's only a short distance." Fiona pointed. "Look, you can see the lights up there."

"Up, being the operative word," Humphries said, selecting first gear. Peering up at the lights that appeared to hang in the air, he added, "It's at least half a mile away." As they slowly bounced over ruts and splashed through water-filled potholes, he muttered, "There goes the tracking and suspension."

As the incline became steeper, the surface gradually improved and finally turned to deep gravel, which rattled against the car's metalwork. While Humphries ground his teeth, Fiona said, "The views from up here must be magnificent."

"Shame it's dark, or that would have made all the difference," Humphries replied sarcastically. "Next time you ask me to drive, the answer will be no."

They drove behind a high bank that shielded the house from the track. When they emerged on the other side, they saw they were the last to arrive. They parked up behind the other vehicles and crunched across a gravelled path to the front door guarded by a constable Fiona recognised. "Hi, how's the new baby doing?" she asked, taking the clipboard from him to sign.

"Very well, thank you. Sleep is overrated, so I hear." Turning to point, he added, "Protective gear is over there, and all the action is at the back of the house."

Handing the clipboard to Humphries, Fiona asked, "Which team is here?"

"Tracey Edwards is leading the SOCCO team and Dr Gibson."

"Thanks. We'll get kitted up and join them."

Donning the protective gear, Fiona said, "I'm pleased we've got Edwards and Gibson. Both are experienced and easy to deal with, even if Gibson can sometimes be abrupt. Hopefully, we'll be done and dusted and home for the evening news."

"Abrupt? That's one word for him. I would use rude and

pompous, myself," Humphries said.

"Maybe, but he's always efficient, and it's good that he speaks his mind and doesn't waste time."

"I bet they all drove here in company vehicles," Humphries moaned.

Fiona rolled her eyes, but said, "Look, sorry about the car. If it turns out to be a case, I'll drive next time."

"I just wish you warned me," Humphries mumbled, as he followed Fiona. "I was settling down for a night in front of the television when you called. It wouldn't be so bad if the weather would hurry up and improve. We're approaching spring, but it still feels like the middle of winter."

Half listening to Humphries moan, Fiona led the way through a hallway into an open space with an impossibly high ceiling, incorporating a generous reception, dining and living area. Two opposing walls were floor-to-ceiling windows, while the two other walls were covered with modern artwork. Colourful rugs covered the stone floor. Although lacking antlers and stuffed animals, Fiona thought it had an old hunting lodge vibe. She could imagine a fire raging in the fireplace and a celebratory feast displayed on a massive table, weighed down with flagons of beer and chunks of meat.

"Not exactly cosy, is it? It's freezing in here," Humphries said. "I hate to think what it's like up here in really cold weather."

"I bet the views are stunning in daylight. I expect they have a cosy snug to curl up in on winter nights. It sounds like everyone is through there," Fiona said, indicating an open door in the far wall.

Beyond the door, they found a large kitchen where Edwards was talking to one of her team. The modern stainless-steel appliances were shiny and spotlessly clean and wouldn't look out of place in a high-end restaurant. Two easy chairs on either side of an intricately carved, tall, stone fireplace clashed with the kitchen's sterile functionality.

"Hi, Fiona. Humphries. The body is through there," Edwards said, pointing to an archway. "Best stocked wine cellar I've ever seen."

Fiona and Humphries passed through a pantry area and came to a steep set of stairs leading downwards. Although only dimly lit, there were handrails on both sides. Despite this safety precaution, a woman in jeans, jumper and waistcoat lay at the bottom in a pool of blood with Dr Gibson crouched by her side. The woman's twisted neck made it clear they were far too late to be of any help.

Fiona turned to Humphries. "See what Gibson has to say. I'm going to see if the husband is still here."

Humphries ducked his head to descend the narrow steps while Fiona returned to the kitchen. "Can I speak with the husband?"

"Yes," Edwards said. "Come with me, and I'll show you where he is."

Edwards led the way back to the central hall where they had started. From there, she led Fiona through a side door, and along a long, glass-covered walkway. If Fiona's sense of direction was correct, the views would be of the open farmland behind the building, but all she could see were snatches of her own reflection against the darkness outside. "Off the record, what are your initial thoughts?"

"I spoke to the paramedics when I first arrived," Edwards said. "From a medical point of view, they were both convinced it was no accident. The victim sustained a massive blow to the back of her head which does seem inconsistent with the way she has fallen. But so far, we've found nothing to suggest there was a struggle before her fall, and there's no sign of a forced entry at the front of the house. That said, the back door was unlocked with the key in place when we arrived."

Passing through a door on their right into a corridor with doorways on either side, Fiona asked, "Could the husband have unlocked it after he arrived?"

"He's an odd one, but that's for you to discover," Edwards said, opening the third door along. "I'll leave you to it."

After the chill of the corridor, Fiona was instantly drawn to an open fire crackling in the fireplace of the small room. A man, whom she judged to be in his late forties or early fifties, sat huddled in a white, police-issue jumpsuit cradling a mug of coffee behind a desk. The pallor of his skin matched the grey of his receding hairline but barely distracted from his good looks. The two lurcher-type dogs sprawled on the fireside rug, briefly lifted their heads to consider her before snuggling back down and closing their eyes.

After stepping into the centre of the room, she spotted a uniformed constable sitting in an easy chair tucked into the corner by a bay window. After acknowledging the constable with a nod, Fiona said, "Hello, Mr Thomas. My name is DI Fiona Williams. Do you mind if I ask you some questions?"

The man looked up warily and gestured to two hardbacked chairs by the window. "I guess. What's going on out there?"

"The officers are working hard to establish what happened here this evening," Fiona said, pulling out a chair and sitting. Although Duncan looked dishevelled, he appeared remarkably relaxed for someone who had just discovered his dead wife. It was too soon to jump to the obvious conclusion, but something about him seemed wrong. Looking around the room, she sensed the chaos and clutter of books and paperwork was staged. The piles of books and files were neatly aligned, and the room was as spotlessly clean as the kitchen. There wasn't a speck of dust anywhere. "Does anyone other than you and your wife have access to the house?"

Duncan shook his head. "No."

"A cleaner, perhaps?"

"I don't think we would like that. Strangers touching our private things. And Pat loved to clean. She liked everything to be in place."

The victim may have been obsessive about order, but did anyone love to clean? Could a discarded dirty cup be sufficient to spark a violent argument between a couple when one of them craved neatness? Interestingly he said we. A force of habit, or could he be the one who insisted on privacy, cleanliness and order? "Do you have any children?"

"We were never so blessed," Duncan said. He removed spectacles from a case on the table and cleaned the lenses. "Don't you want to ask me about this evening?"

"Yes, of course," Fiona said. "I understand you came home to find your wife at the foot of the cellar steps. Is that correct?"

"Yes. She must have fallen while going down to collect a bottle. It's obvious, isn't it? Why are there so many people here?"

"I've already said, Mr Thomas. They're trying to establish what happened. Where were you coming home from?"

"Duncan. My name is Duncan."

"Okay, Duncan. Can you tell me where you were this evening?" Receiving a blank look in return, Fiona asked, "Have you been at work today?"

"Yes, of course. It's Thursday," Duncan said with an exaggerated eye roll. "Where else would I be? I came home from work and found my wife had fallen down the cellar stairs. What more can I say?" Sensing Duncan's defensiveness, one of the dogs dragged itself up and positioned itself protectively by his chair.

"I need a few more details," Fiona said. "Could you talk me through, step by step, what time you finished work and what you've done since?"

After another dramatic eye roll, Duncan slowly said, as if talking to a young child, "I finished work at the usual time. Five o'clock. I stopped for a couple of drinks in the Rattlebone before driving home. When I arrived home, I was surprised to see the dogs outside by themselves. They tend to take themselves off after rabbits if left unsupervised. I called the dogs and walked into the house with them, calling out Pat's name. The house had an empty feeling. I felt that straight away." Duncan looked up and asked, "Is any of this relevant? Don't you want to write it down?"

Fiona shook her head. "A statement will be prepared later, but for now, if you could continue to tell me what happened."

Duncan scratched the dog's head before continuing, "I stood outside the front door a while, trying to work out why I had a strange feeling that something was wrong. When I opened the door, the dogs ran past me, through the kitchen and headed straight to the cellar."

"Was the door locked?"

"Yes. It locks automatically when shut."

"How about the back or any side doors? Do they lock the same way?"

"No. We tend to leave the back door unlocked when we're in," Duncan said, starting to rise. "Shall I go and check?"

"Don't worry about that now," Fiona said. "Could you continue with what happened after you entered the house?"

"I followed the dogs, and that's when I saw Pat at the foot of the steps. I called the dogs away and locked them in here. Then I rang for an ambulance."

Fiona frowned. "You didn't go down to check on your wife's condition first?"

"Pat," Duncan said with an annoyed sigh. "Her name is Pat. Why aren't you using her name?"

Fiona nodded an apology. "You didn't check on Pat before calling the ambulance?"

"No," Duncan replied defensively. "I called from here. I thought it would save time."

"Then what did you do?"

"I shut the dogs in this room and hurried back to the cellar. I intended to go down, but I froze at the top of the steps, feeling queasy. I'm not good with the sight of blood, and I worried that if I fainted, there would be no one to open the door for the paramedics."

"Did you think of propping open the front door before going down to check on your wife's condition?" Fiona asked. "Or checking whether the back door was unlocked?"

Duncan shook his head. "I don't know what I was thinking, other than I didn't want to go down there. I was too preoccupied with trying to process what I'd seen to think about anything else. The next thing I remember is being in the entrance hall and hearing the ambulance arrive. I let them in and poured myself a glass of wine. They seemed to be down there a long time. I assumed they were doing medical things, and it was best I kept out of their way. That's when other people started to arrive. Someone took my clothes and sat me in here. That's about it, really." Duncan lifted the mug to his lips but put it down straight away. "This is cold."

The constable leaned forward in her chair as if to get up. "Would you like me to make you another?"

"Could you be so kind," Duncan said, holding out the mug. "I don't suppose you could get me a glass of wine instead?"

The constable caught Fiona's eye as she reached for the mug. "I'll make us all a strong coffee."

When the constable left, Fiona asked, "Where do you work?"

"In Tilbury. I have a small office there. I'm an architect."

"Whereabouts?"

"In the High Street, a couple of doors down from the Beaufort Inn."

"Were you there all day?"

Duncan shook his head. "I had a meeting with a client at three o'clock and returned to the office a little after four. My secretary was there with me until five o'clock. I left shortly after to meet a friend at the Rattlebone."

"We will need to speak to your secretary and friend later," Fiona said. "What's your friend's name?"

"Graham White. I'll get his number."

While Fiona made a note of Graham's number, she asked, "Do you remember what time you left the pub?"

"No, but it was after seven and already pitch black when I reached my car. I was annoyed as I had hoped to catch the end of The Archers on the radio. It was just finishing, so I switched it off. I expect there's some way I can catch up with what happened, but I'll probably pick up the storyline easily enough if there isn't. Do you know if Radio 4 does a catch-up service?"

"I'm sorry, I don't."

Fiona didn't know the estimated time of death, but she calculated that if Duncan had driven straight home from the Rattlebone, he would have arrived shortly after half past seven.

They lapsed into silence, watching the flames in the fireplace. Duncan gave the impression of a bumbling professor mixed with a little boy lost, but it felt like an act. She would keep an open mind, but a marital argument turned violent, followed by a push down the stairs was the obvious explanation for the evening's events. Finally, she asked, "You do realise Pat is dead?"

"I had rather assumed," Duncan said airily. "I suppose that's what this is all about. You always look at the husband first, don't you? They've already muttered something about processing me down at the station like a belly of pork."

"We will need to eliminate you from our enquiries," Fiona replied, before they were interrupted by the constable returning with three mugs of coffee. As the coffees were handed out, Fiona said, "This is a beautiful house. Did you design it yourself?"

"Of course," Duncan replied, his face animated for the first time. "The barn was Pat's favourite place as a child. She loved to sit up here to watch the sun go up and down. When we married, it seemed the obvious place to build our home, and I designed it to have a perfect, unobstructed view of the sunrise and the sunset."

"You were lucky the landowner was happy to sell you the plot of land," Fiona said, stirring her coffee.

"Not really. It belonged to my father-in-law, who was happy for me to take her off his hands and move up here. The barn was his wedding gift to us. When he died, the farm was shared equally between Pat and Natalie, so now we also own the surrounding land. She still lives in the farmhouse."

"Who? Natalie?"

"Yes. Pat's sister. She never married or moved out of the family home."

"I see," Fiona said, putting her coffee to one side. "You said earlier that you didn't go down to the cellar to check on Pat. Have you been down there at any point this evening?"

"No. I told them when they insisted on taking my clothes. All rather pointless it seems to me, as they will obviously find traces of Pat on my clothes and traces of me in the cellar from earlier,"

Duncan replied.

"By earlier, when do you mean?"

"I was in the cellar yesterday, and I kissed my wife goodbye this morning before I left for work," Duncan replied. "Do you know how long they will keep me for *processing*? Only, I have a busy workday tomorrow."

"I'm sorry I don't, but you might find you want to reschedule your plans for tomorrow. Probably for most of next week as well."

"I have meetings arranged, so that won't be possible."

Fiona struggled to work him out. Was it delayed shock? Surely at some point, the seriousness of the situation would creep into his consciousness. "I have a couple more questions for you. Once you've answered them, I'll see if they're ready to take you in."

"Thank you. That's most kind."

"You poured yourself a glass of wine after the paramedics arrived," Fiona said. "Where did you get the bottle from, if you didn't go down to the cellar?"

"We always have a couple of bottles floating around the kitchen."

"So, why do you think Pat went down to the wine cellar this evening?"

"I expect she was looking for something particular," Duncan replied, as if that should be obvious to Fiona. "She enjoyed cooking and could be very pedantic about matching the wine to the dish."

"Or maybe she had a visitor?" Fiona suggested. "Was Pat expecting someone to drop by today?"

"I don't think so. I'm sure she would have mentioned it if she was. We're rather out of the way up here. We don't get many surprise visitors. People don't tend to pop in on the off chance that one of us would be in."

Fiona handed over her notepad. "Could you jot down a list of Pat's friends who might visit?" While Duncan was writing, she asked, "Other than pouring the glass of wine for yourself, did you move or put anything else away?"

"Move? Put away? I don't follow you."

"I noticed there was nothing out on any of the counters in the kitchen. No cookery books or utensils or anything else to suggest she was planning to cook a meal."

"Oh, I see," Duncan said, creasing his forehead in thought. "No. Everything is as I found it."

"Did she have a mobile phone?"

"Of course. It was in the kitchen drawer where she always keeps it, and your people have already taken it."

"Was there a television or a radio on when you came home?"

"I haven't been in any of the rooms to check, but I don't think so. Pat was never one to sit around in front of the television. She spends her day outside with her horses and dogs or in the garden. Inside, she likes to cook," Duncan said, handing back the notepad and pen.

Fiona looked down at the short list of friends. Considering the spotless kitchen with no cookbooks in sight, she wondered if Pat was waiting for someone to arrive before starting to prepare an evening meal. "Can you think of anybody who would want to harm Pat?"

"No, not really. We live a quiet life."

"Not really?"

"Her views upset some local people in the past, but it all died down. They may not be happy with the situation, but they've accepted it."

"Sorry, can you explain this situation?"

Duncan sighed heavily before saying in a bored tone, "When Pat inherited the land from her father, she banned the fox hunt and stopped the pheasant shoots that used to be held here. She was a vegan and very outspoken about conservation and blood sports. Not a popular stance to take around here, but not something worth killing her over."

Knowing how toxic the subject of hunting was, Fiona wasn't so sure. "Do you share her views?"

"I'm a city boy, born and bred. I left that side of things to her," Duncan replied. "I was shocked by how unpleasant the reactions were at the time, but I don't involve myself in village matters."

"Not even to defend your wife?"

"Pat was a formidable woman when roused, quite capable of defending herself. She was always the forthright one with the brains. Her sister was the pretty one."

"Do you have the names of the people who took such issue?"

"No," Duncan said dismissively. "It wasn't my concern. Pat dealt with it all."

"How about you? Have you any reason to wish Pat harm?"

Duncan gave Fiona a piercing stare, before saying, "It's not something I've ever considered, no."

"Have you argued about anything recently?"

"No. I don't believe we have."

Fiona noted the odd phraseology. You know if you've had a disagreement. "How would you describe your marriage?"

"Oh, very average, I suppose."

Fiona thought Duncan's reaction to his wife's death was the most unaverage one she had encountered and had the feeling their marriage was also far from average. Depending on the forensic evidence, their relationship would be the starting point of any investigation. "Well, that will be all for now, but as the investigation progresses, I will want to speak to you again. Would you mind if I take a look around the house before I leave?"

"It's already swarming with strangers, so I don't see why not."

Fiona found Humphries chatting in the kitchen. "Has the cause of death been established?"

"Technically, the fall down the stairs broke her neck," Humphries replied. "But she sustained a heavy blow to the back of her head, moments before."

"Could it have been caused by the fall?"

"Gibson says not. They're looking for a potential weapon. Something heavy and solid."

"Have they an estimated time of death?"

"The paramedics thought she had been dead for at least an hour when they arrived shortly after eight. Gibson doesn't disagree with them, but he will give his estimate in his report.

On a plus note, we should be able to ascertain the exact time she died as she was wearing an expensive smartwatch. It will need to be unlocked to retrieve the data. Gibson said his team will deal with it. The time of death could be different to the fall, but any unusual activity will show up."

"An exact time of death will be helpful, but can the technology be relied on? I think I'd prefer to work with whatever estimate Gibson gives," Fiona said. "The time is important as Duncan says he was in the Rattlebone with a friend until shortly after seven."

"Then a precise time could prove crucial," Humphries said.

"If accurate," Fiona replied. "Anything else?"

"They have separate bedrooms," Humphries said.

"Interesting, though I'm not terribly surprised. The husband is rather detached from reality."

"Do you think it was him? There's no sign of a forced entry," Humphries said. "Although, the back door was unlocked with the key in place."

"Too early to say. It could have been a visitor or an intruder. I'll have another word with Edwards and check she's okay with us looking around the rest of the house. Then we may as well leave them to it. Bright and early start in the morning."

"If my car makes it back down that track," Humphries grumbled.

CHAPTER FOUR

The first room Fiona and Humphries entered was a large drawing room. A huge fireplace dominated one side of the room, with seating and low tables paying homage to it. Heavy drapes were closed across French windows. Fiona pulled a section back and stared into the inky blackness. Over her shoulder, she asked, "What are your first thoughts?"

"This room is used for entertaining, or should I say impressing, rather than everyday use," Humphries replied.

"Agreed, but I meant the case generally."

Humphries shrugged, looking around the room. "The husband returned home to find supper wasn't on the table and hit his wife harder than he intended."

"The husband's reaction was strange, and I suspect the relationship was too, but I think it's too soon to focus solely on him."

"What do you think the two of them did up here?" Humphries asked. "I wouldn't like to be so isolated. They couldn't even pop out to a pub without driving."

"Enjoyed each other's company," Fiona said. "I gained the impression they liked their privacy."

"And the place is big enough to avoid each other's company if they didn't," Humphries said.

"Duncan said Pat had some run-ins with the local hunting fraternity in the past. That may be worth looking into."

"If it wasn't the husband, the lack of a forced entry suggests it was someone known to her," Humphries said. "Someone she felt comfortable enough around, to turn her back on them and walk toward the cellar steps."

"A friend comes around, and you decide the visit warrants collecting a fresh wine bottle," Fiona surmised. "Would you get the glasses out first? There was nothing out in the kitchen."

"Possibly, but not necessarily."

"So, the guest follows her through the kitchen ..." Fiona continued.

"Which suggests a friend who knows the layout," Humphries said. "Or the husband."

"She is relaxed about being followed. Maybe they were chatting. Then, out of the blue, whack." Fiona turned, and asked, "What do you think she was doing before her guest arrived? This place is pristine, with nothing out of place. It looks ready for a *Home and Country* photo shoot. So, what was she doing? Standing and staring into space ..."

"Why standing?"

"All the kitchen chairs and stools were tucked away." Waving her arm around the room, Fiona said, "All the cushions in here are freshly plumped."

"So, she wasn't waiting in here or in the kitchen," Humphries said. "Let's try another room."

Closing the door behind them, Fiona said, "Everything tidied away could suggest she was waiting for someone to arrive, rather than being caught by surprise."

"That, or someone cleared up after themselves before leaving."

The next room was more what Fiona was hoping to find. Three two-seater settees surrounded a coffee table facing a television. Bookcases lined the walls, and an old-fashioned writing desk was tucked into the corner. Fiona lifted the lid to reveal neat compartments for paper, pens and envelopes, although nothing suggested it had been recently used.

Dotted around the room were a few black-and-white family photographs interspersed with some high-quality wildlife shots. Looking closely at a striking picture of fox cubs, Fiona said, "These are incredibly good, but they aren't professional prints as there are no signatures."

"Do you think Pat took them?"

"I'll ask Duncan the next time I speak to him. These aren't lucky shots. Someone has sat for hours watching and waiting for the perfect moment, and they've been taken with quality equipment." Looking around the room, Fiona said, "There's still nothing to indicate what she was doing before her visitor arrived. Everything in here is just as neat and tidy."

"She could have been waiting outside?"

Admiring a close-up shot of a badger, Fiona said, "True. At least this room gives us some insights." She checked a selection of book titles, an eclectic mix of gardening and wildlife books, classical novels and plays, obscure autobiographies, westerns and romance novels. "Let's have a quick look at the other rooms."

The remaining downstairs rooms yielded nothing of interest. Upstairs, all four bedrooms were doubles with ensuite bathrooms. Without checking the wardrobes and bathroom cabinets it was hard to tell which were Duncan's and Patricia's and which were guest rooms. "Well, we now know they were equally obsessively tidy," Humphries said. "Have you seen enough?"

"For now, yes."

CHAPTER FIVE

Fiona arrived at the station early the following morning to read through the overnight reports while it was quiet. Once the office started to fill, she called Humphries, DS Abbie Ward, DC Andrew Litton and DC Rachael Mann to the corner of the room, where she had set up a whiteboard. As they took their seats, she said, "I was called out to a suspicious death last night at Field Barn, on the edge of Willbury, with Humphries."

"On the edge, being the operative word," Humphries whispered to Abbie, who giggled.

Ignoring the aside, Fiona continued, "A woman in her fifties, Mrs Patricia Thomas, was discovered at the bottom of her cellar steps by her husband, Duncan."

Abbie looked around, and said, "Is this it? The five of us?"

"For now, yes. Several officers are involved in DCI Hatherall's operation, which I believe will be wrapped up soon," Fiona said. "Time will tell if our team needs to be increased."

"Is it possible she simply fell?" Rachael asked.

"A blow to the back of her head suggests otherwise, and last night, forensics found traces of blood on the base of a metal ornament made from horseshoes and a recent effort to clean it. The victim's husband confirmed it was theirs, and it was found where it was usually displayed in the main hall area. Samples are being tested for a match, but it looks likely that it was the murder weapon. Any early thoughts?"

"That suggests the attack wasn't premeditated," Abbie said.

"Not necessarily. The attacker could have been a previous visitor who knew the ornament was there and planned to use it," Andrew said.

"It could be either," Fiona said. "We also don't know if the person went there planning a confrontation or whether an argument escalated from an innocent comment."

"You're already ruling out the husband?" Abbie asked.

"Absolutely not. His reaction to his wife's death was strange. He claims he never went down into the cellar to check on his wife's condition before or after calling for an ambulance. So far, this seems to be supported by the forensic evidence. He may have been in shock, but when I spoke to him, he was more upset about missing an episode of The Archers than the death of his wife." Fiona gave a dismissive shrug that belied the fact that Duncan's reaction had kept her awake half the night. "Or it could simply be that Duncan Thomas is a strange man. Last night he seemed so disconnected that it crossed my mind that he might have a medical condition."

"Like autism?" Rachael suggested.

"Some mild form of it, possibly. He's an architect with his own firm, which takes training and intellect. It also involves good people skills. I plan to talk to his secretary, along with the client he visited yesterday and the friend he went to the pub with after work. So, by the end of the day, I should have a feel for the type of man he is, and a confirmed alibi for the time of death. Humphries, are you okay to work with me today?"

Humphries nodded and muttered a comment audible only to Abbie. Whatever it was, it caused her to smile. Fiona inwardly cringed, wondering if she was the butt of a joke. "Abbie and Rachael, can you find out what you can about Pat Thomas and check for any history of domestic violence? Her sister, Natalie, lives in the family farmhouse in the village. Details are in the crime log. She's as good a place to start as any. Her husband told us that Pat annoyed the local fox hunt by banning them from her land. That wouldn't have gone down well in the area. See what more you can discover and what will happen to the farmland now."

"I thought I recognised the name Pat Thomas," Abbie said. "She made the local press last year. A terrier boy hit her on camera, and she pursued a successful assault charge against him."

"Terrier boy?" Fiona asked.

"A term they use to reinforce rank," Abbie said. "They're adults employed by the hunt, primarily male. They block up all the known fox dens in the early hours of the morning before a hunt and then follow the hunt on quad bikes armed with spades and a box of terriers. If a fox goes to ground in a den they missed, they dig it out and send the terriers down after it."

"That's barbaric! I thought they only followed an artificial scent these days," Rachael said, shuddering.

"That's what they want you to think," Abbie said, rolling her eyes. "If they are trail hunting as they claim, then why are the terrier boys there?"

"Do you know what his sentence was?" Fiona asked.

"A slapped wrist and a couple of pints bought for him down the pub, I expect," Abbie replied.

"Find out for sure," Fiona said. "Let me know if he warrants being brought in for questioning. After speaking to Natalie, find out what other people in the village thought of her anti-hunting stance, and whether there were any other issues. Their home, Field Barn, is remote, and the only access is a track from the end of the village. Ask if they've recently seen any strangers in the area or heading up the track to the house. Unfortunately, there are no security cameras at Field Barn, but something could have been picked up on someone else's camera, so remember to ask."

"Will do," Rachael said, making a note of Fiona's requests.

"Andrew, can you see what you can dig up on this assault charge and whether the man has a record and keep us updated on the forensic details as they come in?" Fiona asked. "Pat's phone was found in a drawer where she usually kept it, and I've asked for the records to be accessed as quickly as possible. The village only has about sixty residents. Run a check on them to see if anything comes up."

"Do you want me to do a financial check on the husband?" Andrew asked.

"Yes, make that a priority."

CHAPTER SIX

Thomas Architectural Services was a small, glass-fronted office with a flat above. Humphries had called ahead, so they knew Duncan's secretary, Karen Hayes, would be waiting for them. A smartly dressed, trim woman with her hair neatly tied into a bun looked up as Fiona and Humphries approached the door and waved them inside. She locked the door behind them before disappearing into a side room to make them a coffee. Fiona and Humphries took a seat to wait, idly flicking through the obligatory glossy brochures showing the company's past projects.

The cups and saucers rattled in Karen's shaky hand as she placed them on the desk, spilling coffee. "Oh, silly me. I'll go and get some kitchen towels." She shot to the back room before Fiona could stop her.

When Karen returned looking flushed, Fiona took the roll of kitchen towels from her. "Why don't you sit down, Miss Hayes."

"Oh, yes, of course," Karen said, still flitting about behind her desk. "Yes, sit down. That's what I'll do. First, I'll switch off the phones. They've been ringing like crazy this morning." Once finally seated, she said, "You'll probably think me guilty of something at this rate, but I'm so nervous. I've never spoken to the police before. I was always blamed for things at school because I had a guilty face even though I wasn't responsible. It's just the way I am, you see," she said, blinking her eyes, begging for understanding.

"Try to relax," Fiona said, wiping the base of her cup and handing the kitchen paper to Humphries. "We're only here to ask a few questions. We don't bite."

"No, no. Of course, you don't. It's just me and my nerves. Although I didn't know Mrs Thomas, the news of her sudden death has upset me," Karen said in an anxious rush. She took a deep breath, and asked, "How can I help you?"

"We need confirmation of Duncan's whereabouts yesterday. Did you see him?"

"Why, yes, of course," Karen said, before rushing through her recollection of Duncan's movements. "He arrived in the morning at nine o'clock on the dot as usual. He worked through some paperwork before he popped out to lunch at twelve. After lunch, he prepared himself for a meeting with a new client who is considering building an extension. He left shortly before three and was back again shortly after four. He asked me to help him to carry some files up from his car. Then it was five o'clock. I need to leave on time as my mother expects me home at a certain time. She becomes distressed if I'm late. When I left, he was finishing up his report." Looking relieved she had finished her spiel, she sipped her coffee.

"And that was at five o'clock?"

"Yes, that's the time I always leave," Karen said. "I quickly finished what I was doing and left."

Fiona looked at Karen's long-sleeved top. "Do you wear a watch?"

"No, I rely on the office clock up there," Karen said, indicating the large wall clock with a nod. "I remember now. It was Duncan who pointed out the time."

"Is that usual?" Fiona asked. "For you to lose track of the time and Duncan to remind you?"

"Not usually, no. But Duncan knows how upset my mother becomes if I'm late. He's always been very understanding about her."

"How long have you worked here?"

"A little over five years. I feel awful about … Oh, you don't need to know about that."

"Know about what?"

Tracing the raised pattern on her coffee cup, Karen said, "Well,

I was thinking of leaving. I've already drawn up a list of positions to apply for. But now, with what's happened, I don't know if I should. How will it look if I up sticks and go, so soon after his wife's death? People will think me dreadfully callous. Some might even think I had something to do with it."

"And did you? Have something to do with her death?" Humphries asked.

"Good gracious, no. I only met her once. She seemed perfectly harmless, although I understand she had some unpopular views. Not that they would bother me. I wouldn't be capable of harming anyone," Karen finished with a nervous laugh.

Fiona didn't think Karen was capable either, but she was intrigued to know why she was so anxious. "Do you enjoy working here?"

"It's very convenient. I live around the corner, so I can walk here and go home for lunch."

Fiona interrupted, "Do you go for lunch at the same time as Duncan?"

"No, we stagger leaving in case someone comes in. Mr Thomas takes his lunch in the café four doors down between twelve and one. I take a little over half an hour when he returns. I normally have a cup of tea and a sandwich with my mother. With her health failing, I like to be able to check on her. Duncan has always been very good about me popping home at other times if there's ever been a problem. Sometimes, I'm not sure if he would notice if I popped out without telling him. But I always do, of course. To be polite."

"Did you pop out at any time yesterday?"

"No, I was here all day. Other than lunch, of course."

Fiona estimated the drive to Duncan's home would take fifteen minutes. His lunch hour gave him plenty of time to return home if the estimated time of death turned out to be earlier than they thought. Karen nervously played with her sleeve, and her anxiety was starting to put Fiona on edge. She thought Karen would probably lie for Duncan if asked, even if it made her uncomfortable. "Why are you thinking of leaving?"

"Partly because of the money. Everything is becoming so expensive I hardly make ends meet, and it's not the same now. Not without Harry."

"Harry?"

"Harry Cavanagh. He worked here up until a few weeks ago. I don't know why he left. Duncan came in and announced he had moved on, and could I clear out his drawers and put everything in a box. Which I did, of course. I left the box by the door, and in the morning, it was gone. Which was a shame as I wanted to say goodbye to him properly."

"This happened suddenly? Without any warning?" Fiona asked. "Have you spoken to Harry since?"

Karen gave a sad shake of her head. "I know I shouldn't have, but I had Harry's personal number, so I rang him several times. He didn't answer or call me back. It was very silly of me, but when I heard there was a murder, it did cross my mind it was Harry. He was always so full of life and joking about, trying to cheer me up. It seems strange he doesn't want to speak to me, now. I thought we were friends as well as work colleagues. But then, he's one of those people who makes everyone feel special." Sighing, she added. "He always made time for people, friends and strangers alike, and he made being here fun. It's so dead without him." Karen slapped her hand over her mouth and looked like she was going to cry. "Oh, goodness. I shouldn't have said that. Boring would be a better word."

"It's okay. Don't worry about it," Fiona said, exchanging a look with Humphries. "Could you give us Harry's telephone number and address?"

"I suppose that's okay. With you being the police and everything," Karen said, opening a drawer in her desk. "I have it all written down here." She flattened a piece of paper covered in spidery handwriting on her desk and neatly copied the details. Handing them over, she asked, "If you speak to him, could you ask him to call me? Just so I know he's doing okay."

"I'll ask him when I speak to him," Fiona said, tucking the slip of paper into her pocket. "How did you get along with Duncan?

You said he was reasonable about you needing to pop home from time to time."

"It wasn't all the time. Just sometimes when my mother rang," Karen said defensively. "Duncan is okay, but he's not exactly talkative. I wouldn't say he was creepy or anything like that, but he is odd, and sometimes that is uncomfortable."

"In what way?"

"It's hard to say exactly. When it's only us, it's like being here by myself. Small talk is beyond him. He doesn't see the point of talking if the conversation doesn't have a purpose. He doesn't like the telephone. He'll make calls when he has to, but if the phone rings he won't answer it, even if he sees I'm already on a call. And some clients are offended by his manner. Their reaction sets off my anxiety. Sometimes they give me pitying looks, like I must be stupid to tolerate him. Harry used to smooth everything over and charm everyone. I don't know what will happen without him here."

"Duncan might employ somebody else to replace him."

"Maybe, but it won't be the same," Karen said sadly.

"Did Duncan ever talk about his wife?"

"Duncan doesn't chat. Not like normal people do. He asks me to do work things, but he doesn't *chat*."

"Is he ever aggressive or impatient?"

"Duncan? Good Lord, no. Quite the opposite. He's always very calm and controlled," Karen said. "Like I said, boring."

Walking to the car, Fiona tried the number for Harry Cavanagh. Before they reached her car, she passed the slip of paper to Humphries. "He's not answering, and we're due to meet Graham White in ten minutes, so we haven't time to swing by first. Ring the station and ask for a welfare check on him."

Half-listening to Humphries' telephone conversation, Fiona pondered Harry's sudden disappearance and whether it was connected to Pat's death. Pulling up outside White Estate Agency, she asked, "What were you chatting about? Are they happy to do the check?"

"Not really, and if we insist, it will be given low priority.

Their records show they've already made one visit, following a concerned call from none other than our Karen."

"Strange she didn't mention it."

"According to the file, when they visited, there was no one home, but also no sign of a disturbance at the house. The officer spoke to a neighbour who said he saw Harry leaving with a suitcase a few days earlier, which was nothing unusual as he regularly spent time away. The neighbour assumed that he travelled for work. No further action was taken other than advising Karen."

"We need to find him," Fiona said. "Call Andrew and ask him to see what he can find out about him."

CHAPTER SEVEN

From the passenger seat of Abbie's car, Rachael asked, "Have you ever joined the hunt with your horses?"

"No, never," Abbie replied. "I hate people's misconceptions about horse riders. We're not all stinking rich, and not everyone with horses supports hunting." She softened her tone, and said, "My two are dressage horses. They would be horrified by the prospect. It would be like asking a ballerina to play rugby. Fiona always assumes I rub shoulders with *that* type of person, though. Which, for your information, I don't."

"Point taken, but you do have background knowledge which Fiona knew would be helpful."

"If we discover anything, she'll take over and claim all the credit."

"I didn't get along with her when she first arrived, but she's always been fair to me and gives credit where it's due."

"Yes, well, she hates me," Abbie said. "DCI Hatherall put us working together once, and she threw me out of her car. Didn't you hear about it?"

"No! When was that?"

"It might have been when you were on maternity leave."

"What happened? It doesn't sound like her."

"Long story. She accused me of something I hadn't done, and she's never properly apologised. I'll tell you some other time." Abbie pulled off the lane onto a short private drive. "It looks like we've arrived."

Looking up at the substantial farmhouse, Rachael said, "One person lives here? Alone? How the other half live. It must be worth millions."

"If you'd read the file then you would know it was the family home and her parents left it to her when they died. Chances are most of the rooms are locked up and never touched," Abbie said. "As neither sister has children, I expect it will end up going to some distant relative. They'll turn up and quickly realise their good fortune has a massive catch. They won't be able to afford the extensive work needed to make it habitable, and a Londoner will snap it up."

"Do you think it caused ill feeling between the sisters?" Rachael asked. "I would be livid if my parents left their home solely to my brother."

"Possibly."

Both women studiously ignored the brace of pheasants hung next to the front door while they waited for it to be opened. Abbie was about to ring the bell a second time when the door was partially opened by a tall woman with dark hair flecked with grey, tied back in a ponytail. Despite her mud-splattered jeans, tatty jumper and lack of adornments, she was what Abbie's mother would call a handsome woman with strong features.

"Are you the police officers I was told to expect?" When Abbie nodded, she swung open the door and beckoned them inside. "Natalie Godwin. Follow me."

They walked along a dingy corridor. The stone floor was mud-ingrained and littered with empty boxes and the occasional strand of straw. The bare, beige walls had possibly been white once. It was colder inside than it was outside, causing Rachael to shiver.

They entered a large and pleasantly warm kitchen heated by an Aga and an open fire. A casserole simmering on a hot plate perfumed the air. As well as the sturdy kitchen table that would seat ten, there was a sofa and an armchair by the fire alongside a small library of books. In the corner lay an assortment of Labradors and terriers. Abbie thought Natalie probably spent most of her time in this room when at home and didn't bother heating the rest of the house to save money.

"I've made a pot of tea and some bacon sandwiches. Sit yourselves down at the table." As Abbie and Rachael pulled out chairs, Natalie pulled open the aga door and said, "I hope you're not vegans. If you are, I'm afraid I'll struggle to feed you. Black coffee or a glass of water, maybe."

"Thank you very much, but you needn't have gone to so much trouble," Abbie said, as the inviting aroma of bacon wafted over, causing her mouth to water. She wondered how Fiona would handle the situation, as she was a vegetarian. She probably would have irritated Natalie by saying a glass of water would be fine. She really didn't know why Hatherall put so much faith in her. Maybe, he would take over the case. That would wipe the smile off Fiona's face. "We're sorry about the death of your sister."

"Are you? That's good of you," Natalie said, carrying over the teapot, shortly followed by mugs and a serving plate piled high with sandwiches. "Milk and sugar are on the table. Well, come on. Tuck in." As Abbie and Rachael bit into their sandwiches, Natalie said, "Einstein was highly intelligent, even for a pig. The day I was due to take him to the abattoir, he escaped and led me a merry dance around the village."

Rachael instantly returned her sandwich to the plate while Abbie swallowed her mouthful, feeling torn. She didn't like the idea of eating a named animal, but it was the most delicious bacon she had ever tasted. Suspecting Natalie was testing them, she forced the image of a cute farmyard pig with a curly tail from her mind. Instead, she thought of Napoleon in *Animal Farm*, cleared her throat and asked, "Were you and Patricia close?"

"Patricia? Oh, you mean Pat. Dad used to call her little Patti," Natalie said. "We rubbed along okay when we were children, but we were like chalk and cheese from day one. She was always a little different and thought herself better than everyone else. Most of her information came from books, but she was always convinced the grass was greener everywhere else. She flittered from here to there, always supporting random causes while never finding the utopia she was looking for. I stayed on here to make the farm work and later to nurse our parents, and over time we grew even further apart."

"Is that why sole ownership of the farm passed to you?" Rachael asked.

Natalie shook her head. "It was only this house. The farmland was left to us jointly. Knowing we could never agree on the best way to manage it, we decided to split the land equally."

"So, what will happen, now?"

"Her share of the farm will pass to Duncan. Keeping the farm from outsiders while one of us was still alive was the one thing we agreed on. I just hope my dippy sister didn't later change her mind and leave everything to some new age refuge somewhere. Our father would turn in his grave if he saw what she's done to his prize farmland. Her ridiculous ideas have made us a laughing stock around here."

"What would happen if Duncan died as well?" Rachael asked.

Natalie frowned, thinking over the question. "It's not something I've ever considered. As my sister was younger, I always thought I would go first."

"Did you see much of each other?" Rachael asked.

"It's unavoidable in such a small village." Sighing, Natalie continued, "It's no secret that we didn't see eye to eye on many things, but we were always civil to one another in public. We even exchanged Christmas cards occasionally. But my goodness, she was frustrating to deal with. I suppose, in a strange way, I'm going to miss locking horns with her."

"Did your disagreements ever become physical?" Rachael asked.

Natalie threw back her head and laughed. "I hate to disappoint you, but no. Our main weapon was a prolonged silence." She shook her head, and added, "I had best check on the herd of horses that she allowed to roam freely over her place. See if any of them are salvageable with some schooling. I was planning to take a casserole over for Duncan, anyway. Someone needs to keep an eye on him to make sure he's looking after himself. That's what family is for, after all. Despite everything, you're still there for each other in a crisis. Keep it in the family, is what our mother used to say. Don't go airing your dirty laundry in public. I think a lot of people would be better off if they followed that advice, including people who should know better, like certain members of our royal family."

Warming towards Natalie and her no-nonsense attitude, Abbie asked, "When was the last time you saw your sister?"

"To talk to? That would be a couple of weeks ago. But I've seen her from a distance on other occasions. I don't think she saw me, but I saw her only yesterday. One of my dogs ran after a deer over her way, so I had to go near the track to call it back."

"Where was she, and roughly what time was this?" Abbie asked.

"In her front yard, and it was sometime in the afternoon. After lunch, but before supper. Sorry, I can't be more accurate as I don't wear a watch."

"Did you see anyone else in the area?"

"No, not a soul. Pat isolated herself up at the Field Barn. She only has herself to blame for being killed up there by some random lunatic. Did they take anything of much value?"

"We're still looking into what happened," Abbie said. "Can you think of anyone local who would want to harm your sister?"

"I can think of several people who may have thought about it, but no one who would follow through on their thoughts. We're simple country folk around here who quietly get on and deal with whatever life throws at us. Generally, with a cheery smile, or at least a grimace that could be mistaken for one. That or wind. I had assumed she disturbed a robbery. Is that not the case?"

"We're keeping an open mind," Rachael said.

"How about the young lad charged with assaulting her recently?" Abbie asked. "Do you know if he still held a grudge?"

"Phil Lovell's boy? I expect he's forgotten all about it by now. You know how young people are. The hunt paid his fine, and most people around here were on his side. That prosecution was vindictive and a complete waste of everyone's time, if you ask me. Pat provoked Fred, and she was the adult in the situation."

"Fred Lovell? Is that the name of the person who assaulted her?"

"Yes. Well, I think he kept his father's name. He lives with his mother over in Sapperton."

"Did your sister ever fear there might be some comeback over the incident?" When Natalie shrugged in reply, Abbie asked, "Are people still talking about it?"

"Good gracious, no. All water under the bridge. People have more important things to worry about around here. When you live and work in the countryside, there's always something new that needs dealing with, especially if you have livestock."

"Do you know if anything else was bothering your sister recently?" Rachael asked. "Did she have any concerns about her safety?"

"If she did, she never said anything to me. Not that I would have expected her to. We passed the time of day and exchanged the usual - how are you? – without listening to the reply, if we bumped into one another, but that's about it. And don't go asking me who she might have confided in. No one I know, that's for sure. Her people weren't the same as my people if you know what I mean. If she didn't disturb a robbery, are you sure she didn't die in some stupid accident? She's always been very clumsy."

Not answering the question, Abbie said. "You can't think of anyone with a grudge against your sister who may have acted on it?"

Natalie furiously shook her head. "If it was murder rather than an accident, and it wasn't a random stranger, it was most likely due to a fallout with one of her fellow protestors. That's where I think you should concentrate your investigations rather than poking about in the village. Those anti-hunt people are dishonest and untrustworthy, and they're completely eaten up by jealousy. They pretend to be caring and kind, but underneath, they're a violent, bitter lot with chips on their shoulders a mile long."

"Would you know where we could find them?"

"Good Lord, no! I wouldn't waste my time on such horrid people. I have a few trusted friends in the village, but other than that, I keep myself to myself." Natalie finished her tea and asked, "Is Duncan in a terrible state?"

"I've no idea, but he'll have an officer with him."

"It should be family at a time like this. Well, I'll find out for myself once the casserole is cooked through, and I take it over to him," Natalie said. "I assume that won't be a problem?"

"No. I'm sure he'll appreciate your kindness," Abbie said. "Does he have family of his own?"

"If he does, they're not on speaking terms, as far as I'm aware. Are we done here?" Natalie asked. "Only I would like to get on."

Rachael shot Abbie a quizzical look before asking, "Can you tell us where you were yesterday afternoon and evening?"

"Me! Good gracious," Natalie said, looking shocked. Recovering herself, she said, "I suppose you have to ask these questions. As I've already told you, I was chasing after one of my dogs in the late afternoon. Once he was recaptured, we walked home, and I brought the horses in before supper and bed."

"Could anyone confirm that?"

"Only the dogs and horses."

"Thank you for your time and the sandwiches. We can see ourselves out," Abbie said, standing to leave. "That's all for now, but we may need to contact you again."

Natalie started to clear away the plates, saying, "You know where to find me. I'm always here or hereabouts."

CHAPTER EIGHT

Humphries stopped at the window of White Estate Agency to look at the houses for sale.

"Thinking of selling your flat?" Fiona asked.

"Not straight away, but we were going to look at trading up next year when we're more settled. It's always good to keep an eye on prices and what's available."

"Let's not keep Graham White waiting. You can ask to be put on the mailing list when we've finished interviewing him."

"I already am," Humphries said, tearing his eyes away from a reasonably priced three-bed cottage in Alderston that had taken his fancy.

Fiona's phone rang. "It's Peter. I had better take it, so you can drool over expensive houses for another five minutes." She took a few steps away before answering the call. "Hi, Peter. How are you and that secretive project you're working on?"

"That's why I'm calling. I understand the woman who died last night had some recent run-ins with the local hunt."

"Yes," Fiona said. "We're still talking with family and friends, but I will need to speak to them."

"I'm afraid the hunt is out of bounds for the next few days."

"What! One of them may be responsible. An employee assaulted her last year, and he was successfully prosecuted. I can't exclude them from my investigation."

"You need to trust me on this one. You know I wouldn't ask if it wasn't important. It will only be for a couple of days. All I ask is you delay speaking to them for now and keep well clear of Fred Lovell."

"Fred Lovell?" Fiona asked.

"The lad who assaulted her."

"If we find evidence linking him, or any of the other hunt members, to the murder, then I'll need to interview them straight away. I can't just ignore their possible involvement."

"Do you have that evidence, now?"

"No, but ..."

"I'm only asking you to hold off for a few days. If something does come up that dramatically changes things, we can discuss it again. Can you make sure all your team know?"

Fiona was annoyed by the blanket restriction, but without concrete evidence to indicate any of the hunt members were involved, she had no option other than to agree, although she intended to speak to him later about it. When she called Abbie, they were already on their way to Lovell's address, and it took a while to calm her down. Fiona told her about Harry Cavanagh to lessen the pain and asked her and Rachael to focus on finding him.

When Fiona walked to the front window to update Humphries, his response was predictable. "Typical. Rich people can always rely on their friends to protect them."

"I don't think it's a question of protection. I could be wrong, but it sounded to me more like there's an ongoing investigation. Maybe that's what his secret project is all about," Fiona said. "Although, I don't intend to leave it there. I will speak to Peter about it as soon as we return to the station."

Inside the estate agency was a row of three desks. A young, heavily made up and perfumed woman was taking selfies of herself at the only occupied desk. She reluctantly put her phone away and rose to greet them, "Can I help you?"

"We're here to see Graham White," Fiona said, resisting the urge to sneeze as the perfume tickled her throat.

"Are you selling or buying? I could help you?"

Fiona held out her warrant card, stepping back from the wafting perfume. "We rang ahead. He was expecting us."

"Oh, yes, of course. He rang a few minutes ago to say he was held up in traffic because of a bridge closure. He's going to be ten minutes late. Can I get you a drink? Tea, coffee, hot chocolate?"

"A glass of water would be good," Fiona replied.

"Nothing for me, thanks," Humphries said. "I was looking at one of the properties you have for sale. Lilac Cottage, out in Alderston. Has there been much interest in it?"

"Yes, there has. Properties like that will always be in demand, whatever happens to the general market. Two couples are currently bidding against each other for it. I expect an offer to be accepted by the end of the week, if not today. Are there any others that interest you?"

"No, it was only that one."

"I'll go and get that water. Please take a seat." When she returned with the water, she hesitantly said, "So, you're here about the murder?"

"What murder would that be?" Humphries asked.

"Umm, I assumed there was only one. Pat Thomas."

"Do you know anything about it?"

"Not really, no. Is it true she was tied up and thrown down the stairs like a bag of rubbish after she was tortured and killed?"

"Where did you hear that?" Humphries asked.

"It's what people are saying." She was saved from saying more by Graham White's arrival. She stood and said, "These police officers are here to see you."

"Thank you, Angela. We'll go through to the back," Graham said, gesturing the way to Fiona and Humphries. "Not very salubrious, I'm afraid, but we'll have some privacy. I see you have a glass of water. Can Angela get you anything else?"

"We're fine," Fiona said, as they followed him through to the tiny staff area, where a sofa and a table were wedged between filing cabinets and a photocopier.

Graham invited them to sit on the sofa while he pulled out a hardbacked chair from the corner. "I'm not sure I'm going to be able to help you much, other than as a character reference for Duncan, but please, fire away."

"Where were you yesterday, earlier in the day?"

"Me?" Graham said, looking alarmed. "I was showing clients

around houses. I can give you a copy of my diary entries if you like."

"That would be useful," Fiona said. "Where were you when you finished looking at houses?"

"I met up with Duncan in the Rattlebone, as I'm sure you know. As we're occasional regulars, the landlord will vouch for us. Duncan left after two drinks. I stayed on for another as I had spotted an old friend."

"What time did you meet?"

"It was supposed to be just after five o'clock, but I was running late after failing to resolve a sale issue. It was gone six by the time I arrived. Duncan had already bought our drinks and was sitting at our usual table doing the crossword. When I apologised for being late, he admitted he had also arrived late. I did wonder if he was being polite as he had completed half the crossword."

"He may have started it earlier in the day," Humphries suggested.

Graham shook his head. "The paper belonged to the pub. When I sat down, he returned it to the rack. Plus, he had drunk half his pint."

"Do you remember what time Duncan left?"

"I wasn't watching the time, but at a guess, I would say around seven o'clock."

"How long have you known Duncan?" Humphries asked.

"Since forever, it seems. We met shortly after he moved to the area, so probably twenty years. Once you get past his manner, he's a straightforward person to work with. He knows his stuff, and I've always trusted his judgement when it comes to property and business generally. It's just dreadful about Pat. He's going to struggle to cope without her. An absolute tragedy. What was it? An intruder?"

"It's too early to say," Fiona said. "How did Duncan seem in the pub? Did he seem nervous or agitated about anything?"

"Not at all. He was his usual talkative self." Graham stopped and smiled, before adding, "Sorry, I'm being sarcastic. Duncan doesn't do small talk. We talked about the progress of a project we're both involved in. A small development of homes just outside Sapperton. After that, we talked about the housing market and how far we thought property prices would fall before recovering."

"Do you think they will recover quickly?" Humphries asked.

Before Graham could reply, Fiona glared at Humphries, and asked, "Did your conversation with Duncan touch on anything personal? How he was feeling, or his plans for the weekend? Anything really that might give us some insight into his state of mind."

"No, it was all work-related. That's standard for Duncan. He's a very private person," Graham replied. "If it helps, I would say he was very much his usual self."

"Which is?"

Graham scratched his head, thinking. "He's hard to read. Reserved, relaxed but alert."

"Did he ever discuss his wife and his marriage?" Fiona asked.

"Not really, but it was obvious that he was completely dependent on Pat."

"So, they were a close couple? Happy together?"

"I suppose," Graham said.

"You only *suppose* it was a happy marriage?" Fiona asked.

"It's not something we ever discussed, but Duncan seemed okay with his home arrangements," Graham said carefully. "When we meet, we mostly discuss work matters. Very occasionally, the topic may stray to politics, golf or rugby, but rarely personal matters."

"Yet, you say he was dependent on his wife."

"Duncan was a brilliant architect. He could visualise and draw what his clients wanted, even before they knew what they were looking for. He could foresee the potential difficulties and how to overcome them in an instant. Confront him with any building or planning problem, and he would have an imaginative solution. He was also one of the most astute businessmen I've ever met," Graham said. "Dealing with everyday life is another matter, and his people skills aren't always as they should be. But underneath, I found him to be a thoroughly decent person. Chances are, if he was born today, he would have been given some sort of label that would have limited his achievements. That's what's wrong with the youth of today, if you ask me. Instead of leaving them to develop at their own rate, they are labelled and placed into boxes."

"We'll leave that discussion for another day," Fiona said, not wanting to be sidetracked. "Duncan's secretary gave the impression he was professionally dependent on an employee called Harry Cavanagh. Would that be a fair assessment?"

"More total rubbish from that stupid woman! Duncan only employed her to be kind because of her mother's health," Graham said. "That's the sort of person he is. Always thinking of others."

"So, he wasn't dependent on Cavanagh?"

"The idea's laughable. He managed before without him, and I'm sure he will again. I would have done the same thing in the situation, and a lot more. You can hardly blame the man."

"Situation?"

"Oh, dear. I've rather gone and put my foot in it. I assumed from your questions and mentioning Karen, that she told you. She was always over-friendly with Cavanagh."

"Told us what?" Fiona asked.

"You're going to find out sooner or later, so I may as well spill the beans. Pat and Harry had an affair. When Duncan found out, he sacked Harry and gave Pat an ultimatum. Me or him – you can't have both. As they were still together and Harry disappeared, I assumed Pat decided to stick with the marriage. I can't imagine living with Duncan was always easy, but still. Not someone your husband employs. But this was weeks ago. I don't see how it could relate to Pat's death."

Fiona was rethinking her conversation with Duncan. He had issues expressing himself emotionally and suppressed feelings of hurt and betrayal often had explosive consequences. That could explain his wife's fall. If Harry was also harmed, it would be harder to explain away as a spur-of-the-moment action. "Are you sure about this relationship?"

"I've had to read a little between the lines," Graham admitted. "One day Duncan told me about the affair, and the next, he said Cavanagh was no more."

"Do you know where Harry is or how we could contact him?"

"Sorry, I wouldn't know where to start. He was always too polished and slick for my liking. Harry was all window dressing. The exact opposite of Duncan."

"You've no idea where he might have gone?" Fiona asked. "You can see why we are keen to speak to him?"

"Not really, no. Unless you think Harry is responsible for Pat's death."

"Or Duncan is responsible for his," Humphries said.

"Whoa. I meant he stopped working for Duncan. Not that he's dead. I'm sure he's alive and well somewhere. And you can't possibly be suggesting Pat's death was part of some twisted crime of passion," Graham said.

"After a husband discovers his wife is having an affair, the lover disappears, and the wife is killed," Humphries said. "It seems a perfectly reasonable suggestion to me."

"No, Duncan would never. I can assure you, here and now," Graham said, his voice rising, "he did not kill Pat or that despicable man. He isn't capable. I have known him for years. He's gentle and kind. If you think that there's a connection to the affair, then you should be investigating Harry. He worked alongside Duncan for several years, and all that time, he was seeing his wife behind his back. That takes a certain type of person, don't you think? You must conclude from how he behaved that Harry is someone quite capable of looking after himself and other people's wives."

"Is this opinion your own, or one you share with Duncan?" Fiona asked.

"Duncan didn't express an opinion. He told me in his usual matter-of-fact way what had happened. I'm going on the facts, and the few brief times I met Harry."

"Was the affair yesterday's topic of conversation?" Fiona asked.

"No, I've already told you. We discussed business. Duncan told me about the affair and Cavanagh leaving a couple of weeks ago. He didn't mention it again, and I didn't ask for details."

"Do you know who Harry's friends are, or the places he likes to visit?"

"Sorry. If pushed, I would say expensive, swanky places."

"How well did you know Pat?" Fiona asked.

"She attended a few social occasions with Duncan, so I've only met her as part of a crowd. She struck me as an intelligent woman, passionate about animal welfare. Her views were sometimes controversial, and I understand they made her an outcast in the village. Thinking about it, she may have been equally dependent on Duncan. That could be what drove her to have an affair."

"That's a strange comment to make."

"What I mean is, Pat seemed to be a very passionate woman. Duncan is a good man, but I can't imagine he was very receptive to Pat's emotional needs. I don't think he would know where to start."

"Cold, in other words."

"No. I'm not explaining this very well. Duncan would have provided stability and companionship, but he wasn't someone to understand deep feelings. He might have listened, but I doubt he would have had any empathy. Or passion." Graham blushed. "Oh, dear. I don't think that's exactly what I mean, either."

"It's okay. We have the gist of what you're saying, and you've confirmed you were with Duncan from just after six to seven o'clock," Fiona said. "If you could give us a copy of yesterday's diary entries, that's all we need for now, but we may need to speak again as our enquiries continue. Before we leave. Are you married?"

Graham opened and shut his mouth in surprise a few times before saying, "I'm not, but I really can't see the relevance."

CHAPTER NINE

In the car, Fiona asked, "What did you think of Graham's defence of Duncan? It seemed to be more than just standing up for his friend."

"I agree, but his criticism was more interesting. I wasn't sure where he was going when he said Duncan wasn't emotionally attuned to others," Humphries said. "I had the impression he was talking from personal experience. Do you think there's more to the friendship?"

"It's worth considering," Fiona said. "Can you check to see if Dr Gibson's preliminary report is in and the estimated time of death?"

After checking, Humphries replied, "The cause of death is confirmed as a broken neck sustained in the fall, and it would have been instantaneous. He's given a window of between four and seven o'clock, which ties in with the paramedics saying she had been dead for at least an hour before they arrived. The paperwork for the smartwatch to be unlocked has been completed, and the full autopsy is set for tomorrow afternoon."

"Take a look at the diary entries. Where was Graham during those hours?"

Reading the photocopied diary pages, Humphries said, "He had back-to-back house visits for most of the day until five o'clock."

"They'll all have to be checked from four o'clock," Fiona said. "As Peter is being so obstructive about the hunt, I'll see if I can persuade him to release Eddie Jordan to help us out. He can concentrate on Graham while we continue with Duncan. Even if Duncan's afternoon client confirms the time of their meeting, he doesn't have a solid alibi for five to six o'clock. He could have nipped home in that time, or he could have paid someone else to kill his wife."

"If he paid someone, there will be a trail somewhere," Humphries said.

"Then Andrew will find it," Fiona said. "I admit I was hoping the time could have been later – after he returned home. This affair worries me, especially as Duncan didn't mention it last night, and Cavanagh seems to have disappeared."

"The time is only an estimate, and Duncan could have made it home a little earlier. I haven't met Duncan yet. Do you think it was him?"

"I don't know," Fiona said. "What would you do if you came home from work and found Tina at the foot of the stairs to your cellar?"

"I don't have a cellar," Humphries pointed out, deadpan. "I live in a flat, so it's all one level."

"Very funny. But come on. What would be the first thing you would do?"

"After turning the light on, you mean?" Humphries replied.

"Be serious."

"I would go down the stairs to check how badly injured she was, then take things from there."

"I'm sure that's what most people would do. Yet, Duncan didn't. He locked the dogs away and called for an ambulance from his study. He didn't even go down to his wife while waiting for them to arrive. His excuse was that he doesn't like the sight of blood, but there wasn't that much. Why wasn't he down there trying to save her life?"

Humphries shrugged. "That doesn't necessarily mean he killed her. From the top of the stairs, it did look like she was probably dead."

"Only probably, and he didn't say that when he called for an ambulance. He said there had been an accident, which suggests he didn't know how badly she was injured," Fiona said. "And don't forget, by the time we arrived, her death had been confirmed by the paramedics. Even if he thought she was dead, wouldn't he want to spend his last moments with her?" Fiona asked, pulling over to park outside Lisa Bouchard's place of work, Duncan's afternoon client.

Lisa was a practical, sensible single mother of two boys. She planned to extend her home to include a self-contained annexe for her mother. She had found Thomas Architectural Services online and hadn't previously met Duncan. She confirmed he arrived outside her home at three o'clock and stayed for about an hour. Back in the car, Fiona and Humphries checked the distances between Lisa's house, Duncan's office and Field Barn, and agreed he couldn't have detoured and returned to his office by shortly after four.

"If everyone is telling the truth, the only time Duncan can't account for is between Karen leaving him alone in the office at five and Graham meeting him in the pub just after six," Fiona said.

"Other than the half-drunk pint and the crossword puzzle," Humphries said. "If there was no traffic and he risked a speeding ticket, he still couldn't do it in less than ten minutes. That doesn't leave him much time to enter the house, throw his wife down the stairs, and wipe down the ornament he hit her with before walking casually into the pub, ordering a pint and picking up a newspaper to wait for his friend. Doable in theory, but hard to pull off in practice."

"He could have left the cleaning up for when he was waiting for the ambulance to arrive," Fiona said. "It would neatly explain why he didn't go down to the cellar." She started the car, and said, "The Rattlebone does food all day. We'll get something to eat there. We can ask the landlord if he remembers Duncan arriving, and whether he seemed his normal self before we head back to the station for the afternoon briefing."

After they ordered their food, a pumpkin katsu curry for Fiona and a chicken wrap for Humphries, the landlord said he couldn't confirm the time, but he remembered Duncan coming in and sitting by himself, waiting for Graham to arrive. "We were really busy, but I can't remember anything unusual about his behaviour or how long he had waited."

"Is he a regular in here?" Humphries asked. "Popular?"

"Tolerated rather than popular and not someone I take much notice of. I couldn't care less either way about fox hunting, but most of my customers are pro-hunt."

"We weren't aware he had ever expressed a view," Fiona said.

"I'm not sure if he did, but we all know who he's married to."

"Did it ever cause an issue in here?"

"I like to keep the peace. I made it clear to Duncan from the start that if he brought his wife in with him, she should keep her opinions to herself. Not like the Beaufort over the road. They banned them outright."

"And did he do as you asked?"

"To the best of my knowledge, his good lady wife, God bless her soul and all that, never stepped a foot inside here, and if he had an opinion on the matter, he kept it to himself."

"Any of your locals threaten him or his wife anyway?"

"They didn't in my earshot. And if you're asking for my opinion on whether one of them killed Pat Thomas, my answer is no. Some of them might talk the talk with a beer inside them, but they wouldn't have the guts to do anything. Anyway, it looks like your food is ready."

When they'd finished eating, the landlord came over to collect their plates. "Was everything okay?" When Fiona and Humphries assured him that the food was fine, the landlord fiddled with the empty plates he had piled on one side of the table before sitting down. He leaned across the table and quietly said, "I've been debating with myself whether to tell you or not."

"Tell us what?" Humphries asked.

"It's probably not important, but I was always surprised Duncan and Graham maintained their friendship after ..."

"After what?"

The landlord looked around the nearly empty bar before leaning in closer and saying, "There was some bad feeling between Pat and Graham."

"Go on," Fiona said, wondering if Graham's mention of

the affair with Harry was to divert their attention and not accidental as he had claimed.

"Pat's parents owned a cottage in the village they used to rent out. Her mother asked Graham to sell it when Pat thought she was of unsound mind. He sold it to his son at a price far lower than its value. Pat threatened all sorts of legal action." The landlord stood and collected the plates. "I just thought you should know."

◆ ◆ ◆

Fiona headed for Peter's office, deep in thought. The relationships between Duncan, Pat, Graham and Harry were interesting and held all sorts of motivations for murder. Complicated webs of jealousy, betrayal and hatred were commonplace in small towns, and while they didn't always lead to murder, they needed a thorough investigation. Besides the complete lack of forensics, nothing about Pat's death suggested a professional, premeditated hit. A moment of passion by an inexperienced killer seemed far more likely.

Fiona's mind constantly returned to the lack of a struggle which strengthened the likelihood of the killer being a known neighbour. The identity of the killer lurked somewhere in the couple's past. The more complicated it was, the harder it would be to solve the murder.

As Duncan confirmed they rarely locked the house in the day if they were in, she couldn't discount the possibility that a stranger had wandered in and taken Pat by surprise before disappearing without a trace, never to return. Yet, Edwards had found a frustrating lack of evidence putting anyone else at the scene other than Pat and Duncan. Without forensics, such a person would be hard, if not impossible, to trace if no one had spotted them in the area. The house-to-house enquiries might produce a suspicious vehicle near Field Barn that evening and, if they were lucky, the registration number. But when had she ever been that lucky? And why would Pat head to the cellar for a quality bottle of wine for a complete stranger?

As she neared Peter's office, Fiona focused on her reasons for wanting to interview the hunt members. A logical cause of the fall was that an argument had escalated and ended in a blow and a push. Someone requesting that hunting be resumed on Pat's land and her flatly refusing was a possibility. Unfortunately, it threw up the same problem as a random stranger. Would Pat have considered anyone from the hunt worthy of a drink, let alone a quality one?

She knew questioning hunt members without solid grounds could prove controversial. It was increasingly obvious that trail hunting was a smoke screen, and fox hunting had continued since the ban, and the subject had become toxic. Pat's assault during the previous season was not an isolated incident. Skirmishes and arrests at hunt meets were becoming the norm. There was huge public support for the ban to be properly enforced, yet the authorities failed to act. It didn't help when the local MP was recently filmed following the hunt.

With a determined look on her face, Fiona knocked on Peter's door. There was no response, so she opened the door to find an empty office. A passing constable noticed and told her that Peter had left the station about an hour ago and wasn't expected back that day. Annoyed, she returned to the incident room to prepare for the briefing.

CHAPTER TEN

Stewart Harding pulled off his work boots inside the porch and lined them up neatly. He was a creature of habit. Out the door at six every morning, coffee break at eleven, ate his packed lunch at one and was at the entrance of the Suffolk Arms, the only pub in the area that wasn't posing as a fancy restaurant with fancy prices to match, by opening time every evening. Two pints and then home to his wife for tea. Only today, he was worried. He liked things to be black and white. He worked hard, instilled discipline into his two adult children, paid his taxes and had been faithful to his wife, Claire, throughout their long marriage. Everything ticked, and in the correct box was his way. Grey areas were too taxing.

"Is that you, Stew? What are you doing home at this time of the day? Has the pub burnt down or run out of beer?" Claire asked, wiping her hands on a tea towel. "Supper won't be ready for another couple of hours."

"I didn't feel like the pub this evening," Stewart said, sitting at the kitchen table.

Claire gave him a concerned look and felt his forehead. "That's not like you. Are you feeling okay?"

Resting his elbows on the table, Stewart said, "I'm fine. How about a cuppa?"

"The kettle's on," Claire replied. Pulling out mugs from the cupboard, she asked, "Have you heard the news about Pat Thomas? People are saying it was no accident. It was murder! Fancy that around here."

Stewart dropped his head into his hands. "Not you as well. That's all I've heard today. It seems the whole village stopped by to gossip about it."

"Well, it's something worth gossiping about, don't you think?" Claire asked, placing two mugs of tea on the table. Receiving no reply, she said, "Before I forget. You've another job lined up once you've finished at the Saunders. Dave Rogers called this morning. A section of the garden wall has collapsed behind the Old Manor. It's partially blocking the Drum pathway. I said you could see to it in a few days."

"I should get to it the day after tomorrow."

Claire watched her husband as she drank her tea, wondering what on earth had happened. It must be something serious for him to alter his routine. Her imagination ran wild with all the possibilities. What could be more intriguing than murder in the village? She had telephoned both their children to tell them about the murder, so she knew they were okay. Finally, she put down her mug, and asked, "So, what's bothering you? I can't remember the last time you didn't pop into the pub on the way home."

"Oh, just something on my mind. I wanted to think it through before listening to all the daft talk. You know, decide what's for the best on my own."

Claire frowned. "Something I could help with?"

"Happen you could," Stewart said, putting down his mug.

"Well? What is it?"

"It's probably something and nothing. It's just that yesterday I went to check on a stone wall for the woman before I went to the pub."

"What woman?" Claire asked before realisation dawned. "You mean Pat?"

Stewart nodded. "Being a short distance from where I was working on the top road, I walked over. When I was leaving, I saw her sister hurrying along the track to the house. There's always been bad blood between those two. She had a face like thunder, so I stepped back behind a tree so she wouldn't see me. I didn't fancy being on the wrong end of her temper. She can be a cruel woman, that Natalie, when the fancy takes her. No wonder she ended up single. She was a pretty enough thing, but no one wanted to take on those black moods of hers."

"So?"

"People are saying Pat was whacked across the back of the head and thrown down the stairs in the early evening. Well, I can tell you, she was fit and well shortly after five o'clock when I saw Natalie heading in that direction."

Claire put down her mug. "You're saying Natalie killed her sister?"

"Now, don't you go putting words in my mouth. I said she was on the track that leads up to the house, not that I saw her go in there."

"This was as you were leaving?" After Stewart nodded, Claire said, "That means she could have been the last person to see Pat alive."

"The same could be said of me," Stewart pointed out.

"Oh, I see, yes. But what reason would you have to kill her? Especially if she was offering you work. Whereas that sister of hers. She's never forgiven Pat for barring access to the hunt."

"So, what should I do? Forget about it, or should I contact the police to tell them I was there and what I saw? I don't want to get dragged into the middle of something that has nothing to do with us. On the other hand, I don't think I could sit in the pub listening to all the gossip and theories and not say anything. All and sundry reckon they know what really happened, but I possibly do. I feel it's my duty to say something."

Claire sipped her tea, considering her husband over the cup's rim. In all their married life, she had never doubted his honesty. Not once. He might not be the best-looking or the most exciting of catches, but she knew exactly where she was with him. Normally, she could set her watch by him and predict his reactions to just about everything. The worry would grow like a cancer inside him if he stayed silent. His skipping the pub showed what a dilemma the decision was for him.

She didn't like the thought of shopping a neighbour to the police, but Natalie wasn't exactly neighbourly. She was friendly with the wealthy families in the village but looked down on the likes of them. A few years back, Claire had asked if she could erect a small plaque in the churchyard in memory of her father, who had been the verger for over thirty years. Natalie had loudly shouted down the suggestion as tacky, barely stopping short of claiming it would lower the tone of the village and devalue their homes. As usual, Natalie had gotten her way, and the plaque for her father was never mentioned again. The snub still hurt.

Claire carefully put down her mug. "Finish your tea. We'll go to the station together. And how about we stop off at the chip shop on the way home?"

The tension left Stewart's shoulders as he acknowledged his wife's decision with a nod of his head. "I also saw Brendon Murphy as I was walking back."

"Brendon? What was he doing out there?"

"What do you think? He had his gun with him and his supper in the bulging bag over his shoulder," Stewart said. "He was coming out of those woods that Pat fenced off to let nature take its course."

"Which direction was he headed?"

"Back to Hinnegar Woods with his catch."

"If he wasn't anywhere near the house, I don't think there's any need to tell on him. He obviously had nothing to do with Pat's death, and he could be done for poaching. We wouldn't want that, would we?"

"Pat would have gone spare if she knew."

"Pat won't be going anywhere anymore," Claire said. "Drink up your tea, and we'll get going."

CHAPTER ELEVEN

Fiona looked around the incident room, and asked, "Anyone know where Humphries is?"

"A couple came in saying they had information about the murder," Andrew said. "He's gone down to talk to them."

"Interesting. Let's hope they have something useful for us." Checking the time, Fiona said, "Rather than hold things up, I will run through what I discovered with Humphries today. Hopefully, he will have finished downstairs by then, and he can update us." She had just finished explaining that unless the current estimated time of death was well off the mark, Duncan had an alibi for most of the afternoon and early evening, when Humphries joined them.

Pulling out a chair and rolling it along to join the others, Humphries said, "It seems Pat Thomas was alive and well shortly before five-thirty. That's when Stewart Harding estimates he left Field Barn. He had met her after finishing work nearby to discuss repairing a collapsed stone wall behind her property."

"Can I assume that was Stewart Harding who came in to see us?" Fiona asked.

"Yes. Pat called him yesterday morning to arrange the meeting. He didn't go into the house, but if she had a visitor, she didn't mention it, and only her truck was parked outside. He walked around the house to the rear garden to inspect the fallen wall, and he didn't see anyone inside. He left fifteen minutes later to walk back to collect his van from where he had been working earlier in the day."

"Strange he didn't drive," Fiona said. "It's quite a long trek up there on foot."

"He was repairing another stone wall in what he referred to as the top field. It was only two fields away by foot, but if he had driven, he would have had to circle back into the village to follow the track up to the house. Chances are he wanted to protect his car's suspension."

"Can you show us on the map the route he took?"

Humphries studied the map pinned on the board before pointing out the route. "It makes sense that he walked."

"Duncan called the paramedics at quarter to eight, a little over two hours after Harding says Pat was alive. The paramedics arrived at Field Barn at twenty-past-eight, and they thought Pat had been dead for at least an hour, probably longer. Did anything about Harding strike you as suspicious?" When Humphries shook his head, Fiona said, "Complete a background check on him before we take his word as gospel."

"Will do, but there's something else," Humphries said. "As he was walking back, he spotted Natalie Godwin walking across the track near Field Barn."

The meeting was interrupted by the buzz of Fiona's phone. Looking at the screen, she said, "I have to take this. It's Dr Gibson." Ending the call, she looked up and said, "He stands by his estimated time of death as being anywhere between four and seven o'clock, but he's received a report from the tech company. Pat's watch stopped reporting her vitals at twelve minutes past six. I'm not entirely comfortable with relying on the watch's data, but it does tie in with everything else. As it suggests that Pat died less than an hour after Stewart was there and her sister was seen heading in that direction, either of them could be the killer."

"Or saw the killer," Andrew said.

"Just to clarify," Humphries said. "Natalie was crossing the track a short distance away from the house, not heading towards it."

Before Fiona could comment, Abbie said, "That ties in with what Natalie told us. She was in the area and saw her sister in the yard, but she didn't go up to the house. One of her dogs had run off across the track, and she was looking for him."

"Stewart did say Natalie looked angry," Humphries said. "That's why he ducked out of sight when he saw her."

"Did either of them see anyone else in the area?" Fiona asked.

Humphries shook his head. "Stewart didn't."

"Natalie didn't mention seeing anyone, but to be fair, she was probably focused on looking for her dog." Abbie went on to describe Natalie as straightforward and helpful. Although they wouldn't know the contents of Pat's will for a few days, Natalie wasn't expecting to benefit financially from her sister's death. Abbie also confirmed they had been unable to locate Harry Cavanagh but had a couple of contacts to follow up on.

"Tomorrow, can you specifically ask Natalie if she saw anyone?" Fiona asked. "Then, concentrate on finding Harry Cavanagh."

When Abbie and Rachael nodded, Fiona continued, "We know Duncan was in his office at five o'clock and in the pub by six o'clock. If we work on the time scale Gibson has given, it's tight, but we can't rule him out completely. Did you get the chance to look at Duncan's financial records, Andrew?"

"He voluntarily gave access to his bank accounts, and there are no unusual payments. It's mainly household bills and regular meals out. Also, unless he has a second phone we don't know about, there's no suspicious activity there. Same for his emails, and he's not active on any social media sites," Andrew said. "Also, this is probably irrelevant but worth mentioning. When they collected Duncan's clothes the constable noticed he was covered in old bruising."

"Was he asked about them?"

Andrew nodded. "He claimed he was knocked over by one of the horses."

"Duncan was in the pub at the time of death," Humphries said. "Can we eliminate him as a suspect?"

"Only if we rely solely on the watch's data," Fiona said. "Gibson gave a longer window of time."

"But still," Humphries protested. "It's more than cutting it fine, even if he had his foot down the entire drive back to the pub."

"I said it was tight," Fiona repeated. "Andrew, could you look at Graham White, the local estate agent, tomorrow? It's possibly nothing, but Pat had a dispute with him over the sale of a cottage belonging to her mother. See if there's anything there or in his background worth delving deeper into."

"We can ask Natalie about the sale," Rachael said.

Jotting notes on the board, Fiona said, "Duncan remains on the suspect list and finding Harry Cavanagh is a priority. We also need to take a closer look at Stewart Harding and Natalie, and the antagonism over hunting."

"Why would Harding have volunteered seeing Pat if he was responsible?" Humphries asked.

"Maybe he thought he had been seen by Natalie, so it was better to offer an explanation before she mentioned it," Fiona said.

"Having interviewed her, I don't think Natalie's a likely suspect," Abbie said. "Although they disagreed over hunting and farming generally, relations were cordial. She admitted they weren't close and wasn't exactly in floods of tears, but she's taken it upon herself to console Duncan and check on Pat's horses."

"Maybe, she's feeling guilty," Humphries said.

"It's only a theory, but I don't think we're dealing with something premeditated," Fiona said. "It's possible an argument escalated, and the person struck out in frustration, not intending to kill. We know there's a history of disagreements between the sisters, and she was seen near the house shortly before the attack."

"A detail she volunteered," Abbie said.

"Because she had been seen by Harding, and he was likely to say something," Humphries said.

"Which works both ways," Abbie said.

"Except, he had just been given work by the victim and had no axe to grind."

"According to him," Abbie fired back at Humphries.

"It's not a competition," Fiona said. "They are both people of interest because of where they were. Go back over their statements to check they didn't see or hear anything else unusual. And ask Stewart for his views on fox hunting."

"When we could be talking to hunt members who had a long-running dispute over access to the land," Abbie said.

"I'm not happy about the situation with hunt members being off-limits any more than you are. DCI Hatherall isn't in his office, but I intend to speak to him before the end of the day. If I can't get hold of him over the phone, I will swing by his place on my way home. Unless anyone has anything more to add, we'll leave it there and finish on time for a change. We've some busy days ahead of us."

After everyone had left, Fiona tried to get hold of Peter one final time on the phone. At this rate, she could see herself spending her evening camped on his drive. She was about to hang up, when Peter answered, "At last! Can we talk about Fred Lovell and the other hunt supporters? I need to speak to them in connection with my murder enquiry."

"Have you a time of death?"

"Between four and seven o'clock, probably shortly after six o'clock, but why is that relevant?"

After a brief pause, Peter said, "I can confirm Lovell is not your man."

"You sound very sure about that," Fiona said. "It's almost like you know exactly where he was at that time. Is he under surveillance, by any chance?"

"You didn't hear that from me."

"How about the other hunt members?" Fiona asked. "Any one of them may be involved."

"You're going to have to be more specific. Are you talking about hunt staff or followers?"

"It would be someone who felt they had some say about the land the hunt covers, so probably an employee."

"The master, field master, whipper-in, groom, kennel staff? Although to be honest, some of the casual foot followers can be just as fanatical about hunt traditions and their right to hunt."

"When did you become such an expert? What's going on?"

"I can't tell you," Peter replied. "Why do you think the murder relates to the hunt? You can't have ruled out the husband already."

"The husband is odd, but he has a reasonably good alibi. The victim made an enemy of the hunt by banning them from her land. I understand that it was prime hunting territory, whatever that means, and it has seriously inconvenienced them. Plus, there's the successful action against Lovell for assault. A blanket ban on us approaching any of the members is hampering our investigation, and vital evidence could be lost through the delay."

"I can't promise anything, but I may be able to tell you something more by tomorrow."

"Morning or afternoon?"

"Are you in the station?"

"About to leave for home."

Don't mention this to anyone. Nothing is definite, but there's a chance I could beat your early morning alarm call. How does that sound?"

"Intriguing," Fiona replied, wondering what Peter was up to. A dawn raid on the kennels sounded unlikely unless something else was going on. She'd never considered the financial side of hunting, although it clearly attracted wealthy individuals. Could it be a front for a drug racket or money laundering? "How much money does a hunt make?"

"Full membership is over £4000 a year, and members still have to pay an additional £80 every time they go out. Then there's a multitude of fundraisers and, wait for this, government grants. They even received Covid payments."

"Really," Fiona said, as surprised about Peter's sudden knowledge of hunting matters as anything else. It was more money than she thought, but there wouldn't be fantastic profits if they were paying all those wages. She shuddered to think how Humphries would react if he knew how much people paid for their jolly jaunts around the countryside in fancy clothes. "I'll look forward to your call in the morning."

CHAPTER TWELVE

Peter ended his call with Fiona and wearily looked up at the hallway clock. If he was going to be woken at silly o'clock in the morning, he should try to get some rest. Although he wasn't expected to be there, he felt guilty about not joining the team on the raids, and he was going to make sure he was waiting in the station to interview the men when they were brought in.

Unless there were any last-minute dramas, technically, his role was complete. Dewhurst had made it clear that his job was to oversee and liaise with other stations and the RSPCA, so the raids happened simultaneously. Across the country, while some officers would be catching the terrier men blocking up fox dens, others would be entering their homes with the animal welfare officers to seize dogs and other evidence. Keeping the operation secret had been a mammoth task, but miraculously they had succeeded.

The more optimistic and naïve officers thought the operation was a good start on cracking down on illegal hunting activities. The shrewd ones thought the same as him, that the planned morning raids were little more than a PR stunt and there wouldn't be any change in policing policy. The terrier boys were at the bottom of the food chain. Going after them was not only unfair, but in his view, likely to be a complete waste of time and taxpayers' money in the long run. It was the countryside equivalent of taking a handful of minor drug dealers off the street while leaving the drug lords untouched.

So what if they drove around in the early hours, blocking up fox dens in areas where a hunt was due to meet in a few hours? The dens would be empty. That was the whole point. When the foxes returned, they wouldn't be able to go to ground, so would have nowhere to escape once the hounds caught their scent. While blocking a den with an animal inside was illegal, it was perfectly legal to block an empty den. A junior legal assistant could successfully argue that there was no case to answer. His only hope was he could persuade the terrier boys to admit the hunt employed them and told them which dens to block.

His biggest issue with fox hunting was the arrogant way they flaunted the law. They carried on as if there was no ban and made no attempt to hide that they were breaking several laws. Every hunt day started with free drinks and nibbles for everyone. Empty beer cans were thrown by the drivers of quad bikes as they carried on drinking while they sped around country lanes chasing the huntsmen. The same was true of the car followers, and the horse riders regularly sipped from their hip flasks throughout the day. By late afternoon quad bikes were parked up outside pubs. Their often-injured terriers were left in small wooden boxes attached to the front of the bikes, and muddy shovels were propped on the back. Parked next to them would be a row of mud-splattered Land Rovers and horse boxes. He had heard of an occasion where a man drunkenly stumbled out of a pub to drive a lorry full of horses. And yet, the force never considered sending a patrol with a breathalyser kit out. It seemed the idea had never crossed their minds.

Before his involvement in the operation, he had at least thought there was some skill involved. He had since learned the romantic image of man's knowledge of the countryside being pitted against the wily fox in a fair fight was a complete myth. Like their nonsensical claims to be pest control when foxes weren't even registered as vermin.

The hunt ensured everything was stacked in their favour to ensure their rich London clients had a good day out. Out of season, the terrier men encouraged, fed and protected the foxes to keep the population artificially high in areas where hunts operated. Some were almost as hand reared as pheasants.

When he moved into his cottage in Topworth, an area known

as Saturday Country, he had feared he would be surrounded by pro-hunt supporters. He had been surprised to discover most of his neighbours either 'sat on the fence' or were sick to death of the disruption the hunt caused every weekend. Some were prepared to complain openly, but he was disheartened by the number who hated the hunt but felt too intimidated to speak out. Everyone agreed the police force was in the hunt's pockets and he found their viewpoint hard to deny.

So far, the nationwide surveillance of the activities of the terrier boys had gone suspiciously smoothly, and none were aware they were being watched. The hunts seemed to employ a certain type of person. Ones who knew their place in society and would slavishly follow orders without question for a few crumbs from their master's table. On a hunt day, they were thuggish enough to be set on the hunt objectors like a pack of dogs while the hunt members went off to have their jollies. Many of them had a record of violent behaviour offences. Peter almost felt sorry for them, but having seen the barbaric actions they performed for the hunt it was hard to have any sympathy.

Fiona's theory about the murder of Pat Thomas being related to her banning the hunt from her land was interesting, but if she was correct, he would have to watch her back. There was a good reason hunts were left alone to carry out their illegal activities, and it certainly wasn't a lack of intelligence. Once the raid was over, he would ensure anything relevant was passed on to her, and he would help her as much as possible.

The terrier boys could all be accounted for on the day of the murder, so they weren't directly involved. If a hunt member was responsible, it was someone higher up the pecking order.

Accepting it would be a waste of time going to bed as he wasn't even remotely sleepy, he settled into his favourite armchair and scrolled through Netflix, looking for something that would entertain him or send him to sleep. He wasn't too concerned about which.

CHAPTER THIRTEEN

Peter unfolded himself from his armchair when his phone rang. Bitterly regretting his decision to stay downstairs in the chair rather than go up to bed, he moved across the room in a half-stoop to grab his phone and car keys. He rotated his back before slowly standing upright as Eddie Jordan told him the raids had all gone to plan. Heightened activity had been noted at all the hunt kennels following the arrests and seizures. Peter smiled at the thought of them being the ones frantically looking for an escape route for once. His fear was that they would find one.

Fred Lovell and Mike Cole had been caught red-handed blocking up foxholes as expected, and it was all on film. Officers were still finishing up at both homes. Lovell's three terriers and a lurcher were found to be in good health and in the care of his girlfriend. Terriers belonging to Cole had been taken by the RSPCA officers. All three were judged to be underweight with untreated, extensive scarring to their faces. One was missing a part of its jaw. They were found in metal dog cages in the garden, without any soft bedding or water. Not illegal, but in the current cold weather, indicative of their views on animal welfare.

"Now, for the bad news," Eddie said. "Lovell called Peggy Crayston, the solicitor who handled his assault charge and isn't talking to anyone until she arrives. Crayston has also offered her services to Cole, and we have to wait to interview him as well. So, you may as well go back to bed for a few hours. I'll let you know when Crayston arrives to see her clients."

"Damn. Did either of them say much beforehand?"

"As soon as we arrived, Lovell stuck to no comment, and Cole followed suit. I guess he did learn something from the assault charge."

"I'll have a coffee to wake myself up a bit and then come in to read through the reports. Do you know if any of the other forces have completed their interviews?"

"Not yet. If I hear something, I'll let you know."

Peter thanked Eddie and moved to the kitchen to make coffee, feeling very tired and old. Waiting for his coffee, he leaned on the counter and looked out of the window. Outside, it was still dark, but the full moon glistened on his frosty lawn and lit up the For-Sale sign outside his neighbour's empty house. The owner had already moved back to France. It was going to be another bitterly cold day.

He arrived at the station at the same time as Lovell's solicitor, Peggy Crayston. She looked bright-eyed as she hurried across the car park in heels and an expensive wool coat. He watched her disappear inside before extracting his stiff body from his car seat and grabbing his flask of proper coffee. The brown liquid that spluttered out of the station machine wouldn't keep him awake, let alone alert.

He was sitting at his desk reading the file notes when he sensed someone hovering nearby. He looked up to see a very sheepish Eddie and knew things were unravelling. "What's happened?"

"The landowner is on his way in to give a statement. He's claiming he asked Lovell and Cole to block up the fox dens on his land when he knew they would be empty to deter the foxes that have been hanging around his chicken coop."

"Marvellous," Peter said, pushing himself away from the desk. "Make the interview last as long as possible. Oh, and check he actually does keep chickens and where his coop is situated. Any hesitation or discrepancies, and I think an inspection may be necessary."

"There's more, I'm afraid." Eddie swallowed before continuing. "Due to the forecast of a hard frost, the hunt decided last night to cancel today's meet."

"Like hell they did!" Peter fumed. "It's only a light frost, and they don't head off until after eleven when they've had a drink and it's thawed. I take it there was also an oversight in communicating their decision, and people were only told this morning."

"Got it in one."

"There's hardly any point in me interviewing Lovell and Cole as I already know their answers."

"Sorry, sir."

"No worries. Can you check whether this charade is being repeated by the other hunts?" Returning his attention to the files, Peter said, "I'll prepare myself to go through the motions of wasting another hour of my life."

"At least we've shown the hunts we are serious about ensuring they keep within the law."

"There is that," Peter replied, thinking the opposite. He picked up his phone and called Fiona.

CHAPTER FOURTEEN

Fiona was in bed contemplating whether to stay where she was in the warm or to take a quick run before work when her phone rang. She was surprised to see it was Peter calling. He was more of a night owl and rarely surfaced before daylight.

"I've got Lovel in custody. If you can be here in half an hour, you can join me in the interview room."

"What's he been brought in on?"

"Blocking fox dens on the morning before a hunt, but the landowner and the hunt have provided him with the perfect defence. You might catch him off guard if you ask him about Pat Thomas before the solicitor has told him what to say."

"Hang on. You told me yesterday that you were sure he wasn't involved in the murder."

"He couldn't have been as he was under surveillance, and we know exactly where he was, but if a hunt member was involved, he might have heard something."

"I should make it in time. Will you be leading the interview?"

"I'll start and at the end hand over to you. I'll see you shortly."

During the interview, Lovell gave the replies Peter had expected. He was out blocking the dens at the request of a local farmer when he knew the dens would be empty. He would never send his terriers to double-check they were empty, and he believed the scarring to his friend's dogs' faces was caused when they became caught up in barbed wire a while back. Peter ran through his questions keeping his expression impassive, as Lovell denied he had ever broken the law when employed by the hunt.

Peter leaned back in his chair, and said, "One thing I can't understand is why the hunt pays you to be present with your terriers during the hunts. If they are following an artificial scent, why do they need you to be there?"

"I'm there to open and shut gates. I also ensure the field does not trample crops. We respect the property, unlike some day-trippers who have no respect for the countryside, and ensure no damage is done. If say, a fence is broken, then, if possible, we repair it there and then. If we can't, we assess the damage and return to mend it later. Other than that, we try to keep out of the way of the hounds and the field while they work."

The phraseology and the way Lovell parroted his replies confirmed he had been coached, but Peter continued in the hope he might catch him out. "So why have the terriers with you?"

"I don't like leaving them alone at home for too long."

"Do you get along with the hunt monitors, or do you keep out of their way, as well?"

"Monitors. Is that what they like to call themselves, is it? If you mean the thugs in balaclavas who attack us, then yes. That lot are trouble. They taunt us and try to stop us from going about our peaceful business. Vandals and weirdos. The lot of them."

Peter flicked through his file. "And yet you were successfully prosecuted for assaulting a member of the public last year. What happened there?"

Crayston interrupted. "That case is closed, and my client is not obliged to answer any questions relating to it."

Peter raised his hands, accepting the point. "As a terrier boy, what are your duties in the summer months?"

"I'm a countryman, not a terrier boy, and there are no hunts then, so I'm not needed to open and close gates."

"You're not employed by the hunt to monitor or feed foxes in the area?"

Lovell looked to Crayston, who shook her head, before answering, "No."

Peter pulled a series of photographs from his file showing Lovell putting out raw meat on a stone wall. "How do you explain these? That's you, isn't it? In Hinnegar Woods, if I'm not mistaken. It's very close to where you were this morning, blocking up dens to discourage foxes." Peter frowned. "There seems to be a contradiction here."

"Ah, yes. I remember now. It was only the once. I saw a photograph of a fox being sold and thought I would try to get some snaps."

"Keen photographer, are we?"

"I thought there might be some money in it."

"And I think it was more than once," Peter said, placing another series of photographs taken in a different location.

Lovell shifted position in his chair. "Photography is a common hobby. Nothing wrong with that."

"What sort of camera do you use?"

"Just my phone camera."

"Do you have any snaps you could show us?"

"I do, as a matter of fact," Lovell said, pulling out his phone and turning the screen to face Peter. "There you are," he said triumphantly.

Peter leaned forward to peer at the picture of a vixen with her cubs. "May I?"

Before Crayston could react, the phone was in Peter's hand. His eyebrows raised as he flicked through several more images.

Realising his mistake, Lovell lurched across the table. "Give that back!"

"Please return the phone to my client," Crayston demanded.

Peter slipped the phone into his jacket pocket. "I have reason to believe there is evidence on this phone relevant to this enquiry, which is at risk of being deleted."

Crayston glared at Lovell and angrily shook her head while Lovell shrank back in his chair, muttering, "That's private stuff on there."

"We're only interested in the content relating to your hunt work," Peter replied. "Now, my colleague has some questions for you."

"Hello, Fred. Can I call you Fred?" Without waiting for a response, Fiona asked, "What can you tell me about Pat

Thomas?"

"That old witch. She's like him," Lovell replied, indicating Peter. "She uses fancy words to trick people. Twists things in her filthy mind. I know she's dead, but you can't pin it on me. I was nowhere near her place the day she was killed, but good riddance, if you ask me."

"Let's leave it there," Crayston growled. "Don't answer any more of their questions, Mr Lovell. You've said enough already."

"I believe you when you say you weren't there," Fiona said sweetly. "I understand banning the hunt from her land caused problems for lots of people."

"Too right it did. Stuck up cow."

"My client has nothing more to add," Crayston quickly said.

"Being at the centre of things, you must have a good idea about what really goes on in the area," Fiona said, ignoring the solicitor. "Were there any plans to persuade her to change her mind?"

Lovell opened his mouth to reply, saw Crayston glaring at him, and said, "No comment."

Starting to collect her things, Crayston said, "We were led to understand questions would be limited to this morning's events, and my client has given full and accurate replies. If you want to follow a new line of enquiry, I will need time to consult with my client first."

"Accurate isn't a word I would use," Peter said. "I will want to speak to your client again after I've viewed the images on his phone. It shouldn't take too long, and I'm sure you will have plenty to discuss to keep you busy."

"What! I've got to stay here and can't have my phone back?" Lovell asked. "Can he do that?"

"Unfortunately, yes," Crayston snapped. "You gave it to him."

"I'm pleased you witnessed that. I will send you copies of what we find so you have plenty of time to prepare your client before we meet again," Peter said. "Do you have any more questions, DI Williams?"

"I do," Fiona replied. "Were you aware of any plans to persuade

Pat Thomas to allow access to her land?"

Lovell looked again at Crayston before replying, "No comment."

"Who within the hunt is responsible for obtaining permission to cross people's land?"

"No comment."

"Oh, come on," Fiona said. "This is general information. I'll easily be able to find out from elsewhere."

"Then, I suggest you seek your answers elsewhere," Crayston said.

"The Hunt Master," Lovell said. "Brian Ford-Warren."

"Thank you, Fred," Fiona said. "I probably will have some more questions for you, but they can wait until you've consulted with your legal representative."

Peter scrolled through the images on the phone as he walked alongside Fiona. He stopped and turned to lean against the wall staring in disbelief at the phone.

"What is it?" Fiona asked.

"Disgusting is what it is. Fred Lovell's name will go down in hunt history for all the wrong reasons." Waving the phone, Peter said, "On here is a video of him pulling two foxes from the ground and releasing them directly in front of a pack of hounds. In the background are huntsmen shouting with glee before they set off after them. If this doesn't change things, I will leak it to the press myself. There will be no more hiding behind the smokescreen of trail hunting."

"That's great. Anything on there about Pat Thomas?"

"I've not seen anything yet. I've already asked my team to flag up any mention of her during surveillance. Once we've pulled the footage on here, we'll release it to you. It could give you leverage when you talk to him again."

"Now your surveillance has finished, I take it I can approach any member of the hunt if the evidence supports it?"

"I guess, but could you run it by me first? There will be some overlap as our investigation is ongoing, so it would be best if you were forewarned to avoid any slip-ups."

"That's fine as long as I have your assurance that it works both ways," Fiona said. "And can I add Eddie to my team? Your operation has left us rather short on numbers."

"Because your enquiry is more important," Peter snapped. "And the hours of work we've already put in on this are irrelevant."

"Whoa! I didn't say that."

"Whatever. You can have him later today."

CHAPTER FIFTEEN

Fiona wasn't used to Peter taking his bad mood out on her and was annoyed by his comments. It was good that he had agreed to release Eddie, but it had been begrudgingly. She hadn't said her murder enquiry was more important, although she did think it was. And why should it be one of her team that made a slip-up?

As she had rushed out of her house that morning without a flask of decent coffee, she decided to pop out to buy a decent takeaway coffee before returning to her desk. She walked briskly along to keep warm. She looked up to check the late winter sun was climbing in the sky as it wasn't providing any heat. It felt as cold as it had been when she left home in the dark. By the time she reached the coffee shop, she was starting to understand why her mother complained bitterly about winter weather as if it was a new phenomenon rather than an annual occurrence.

Fiona recalled her childhood memories of winter. They included surprise days off school, fun in the snow and sitting around the kitchen table with her brother drinking mugs of delicious hot chocolate. She didn't recall feeling a damp cold that chilled her to the bone. Which reminded her that she still hadn't called her brother to discuss their father's health. As children, they had been close and had easily shared secrets and dreams. It was sad to think that now he was a stranger who needed to be approached in a certain way. She walked up to the counter, trying to pinpoint when the change had happened. Was it as soon as he met Emma, the perfect wife, mother and daughter-in-law, after they married, or when they started a family?

"Usual, Fiona?"

"Yes, please. To take away," Fiona said, still thinking about her brother and how childhood relationships were so easy and uncomplicated. Children believe they will grow wiser with age, but maybe it's the opposite. What fuels the change in us? Do we become increasingly cowardly, creating complex facades to hide behind? How can we have authentic relationships when we hide everything we are away, to keep ourselves safe from harm? Do we even recognise ourselves half the time?

"Penny for them."

Startled, Fiona looked up to stare straight into Stefan's eyes. How did he always catch her so unaware? "I was going over an interview I've just sat in on."

"Of course. You would never be caught daydreaming," Stefan said with a half-smile.

It was the smile she used to find so endearing. Now, she thought it was mocking and creepy. She was saved from replying by the arrival of her coffee. She swiped it from the counter. "Must be going. Busy day."

Walking away, she heard Stefan shout after her, "See you Sunday night."

She pretended she hadn't heard and slipped through the door. She had plenty of time to cancel. She needed to forget about Stefan and concentrate on the murder investigation. Now she could approach the hunt members, they might make some progress. She nodded to Humphries, who was climbing out of his car as she crossed the station car park.

"Did you get me one?" Humphries said, referring to the coffee in Fiona's hand.

"Sorry, I wasn't expecting to see you this early," Fiona replied.

"I thought I would make an early start on the case," Humphries said. "I'll get a coffee and see you inside."

Back at her desk, Fiona was surprised to see Abbie was also in early. "Morning. If you're quick, Humphries is on his way to get a coffee."

"I'm good," Abbie replied, without looking up.

Fiona put thoughts of Stefan out of her head and read through the overnight reports until she was disturbed by Abbie. "What is it?"

Abbie tapped her computer screen, and said, "Cavanagh has been using his bank account. Or at least someone has."

"Locally?"

"Ish. It was last used in Birstall a week ago to withdraw a hefty amount of cash. Nothing more recent. I'll try the numbers I was given for his friends again."

"If you don't get any joy, I'll authorise a full media request for sightings of him and asking him to come forward."

Fiona perched on the edge of her desk to call the Hunt Master, Brian Ford-Warren and spoke to his wife, who pompously replied in clipped tones, "My husband is not prepared to comment at this stage."

Fiona assumed she was referring to the early morning raids, but asked, "Comment on what? I'm leading the investigation into the death of Pat Thomas and want to speak to people who knew her. Please ask him to come to the phone."

After a brief silence, his wife said, "He's busy."

"So am I. I am asking for a general, voluntary conversation, but if needs be, I can make a formal request for him to come into the station to give a statement."

"I'll go and speak to him."

Five minutes later, he appeared on the line sounding disgruntled. "Hello, what is this nonsense you've been telling my wife?"

"Am I now speaking to Brian Ford-Warren?" After confirmation, Fiona introduced herself and explained she wanted a brief chat about the history between the hunt and Pat Thomas.

"I'm not sure how much I can help with your enquiries, but as it happens, I have a meeting with my legal representative on routine matters this morning. You could meet me at their offices at ten o'clock?"

"That would work perfectly," Fiona said, amused by his reference to routine matters. If the video was as bad as Peter said, it would be panic stations.

◆ ◆ ◆

Fiona and Humphries walked the short distance to the legal firm for the interview. If anything, the temperature had dropped, and Fiona huddled into her coat, keen to avoid conversation.

Humphries had other ideas. "I've heard in graphic detail what's on the video that Peter found. They're depraved. And this guy we're going to see is the leader of it all?"

"The Hunt Master is his title," Fiona said, walking quicker.

"That says it all," Humphries said. "They make a mockery of the law. It's so obvious there's one rule for them and another for the rest of us. I wonder how they'll wriggle out of it this time. I'm sure their legal experts are already working on it."

"After the work Peter's put in, I hope they bring successful prosecutions and stop their illegal activities, but we're dealing with a murder, which in my opinion, should take precedence. Can you concentrate on our case, not Peter's," Fiona said, hoping that would be the end of the conversation.

"Yes," Humphries replied. "But I'm looking forward to telling him how barbaric I think his activities are."

"We need to stay professional whatever we think of his hobbies."

"Cruelty and torturing animals for entertainment is not a hobby," Humphries said angrily. "If it was a group of working-class people involved in dog fighting, rather than a bunch of toffs prancing around the countryside on horses in fancy clothes, they would all be in custody by now. We would be checking their details against all the unsolved violent crimes in the area, not handling them with kid gloves."

"Either way, I've promised Peter we won't stray onto his territory. During this interview, we keep our opinions to ourselves and limit our questions to his relationship with Pat Thomas," Fiona said firmly, which led to a sullen silence for the remainder of the walk.

Despite being on time, they were made to wait over ten

minutes before being escorted to a conference room on the second floor. They were greeted by Peggy Crayston and Brian Ford-Warren, who invited them to help themselves to the refreshments on a side table. Ford-Warren was a painfully thin, angular man in his late sixties with a weather-beaten face and a twinkle in his eye. On appearances alone, he appeared a kindly, grandfatherly figure. Fiona found it hard to connect him with the cruel scenes she had been told were on Lovell's video. But if criminals looked like criminals, their jobs wouldn't exist.

Once settled at the oval table, Crayston asked, "How can my client be of assistance?"

Smiling at Ford-Warren, Fiona said, "We would like to know about your relationship with Pat Thomas."

Ford-Warren gave a small chuckle. "I've known Pat since she was a wee thing trailing after her father, but I can assure you, we've never embarked on a relationship. Even if I had taken a fancy, I would have been too scared to try. She always had a mind of her own." Turning serious, he added, "I would like to add, at this point, how sorry I was to hear of her passing. We didn't see eye to eye on many things, but we shared a love of the countryside."

Fiona acknowledged the sentiment and said, "We don't need to go that far back. When was the last time you saw her?"

"A couple of weeks ago in the village shop. Not that we spoke, of course. She huffed at my presence, no doubt annoyed we were sharing the same air, paid for her items and left." Ford-Warren paused and gave a sad shake of his head. "As a country girl, I was surprised at her attitude. Growing up on a farm, you become a part of the cycle of life, and that includes fighting to survive and embracing death. That is nature's way. Hunt followers love the countryside as it is, not the sugar-coated version so many town people imagine it to be."

"Were there any other issues between you, or was it just hunting?" Fiona asked.

Ford-Warren offered a brief smile, and said, "We didn't know one another well enough to have personal disagreements."

"When was the last time you spoke to her?"

"That would have been shortly after her father's funeral when she told me the hunt could no longer cross her land."

"Have you spoken to her since? Tried to persuade her to change her mind?"

"I might have done shortly after, but it was all years ago. We have now accommodated her position."

"Have you ever visited Field Barn to discuss the subject of access?"

"My dear girl. That is not how it works," Ford-Warren said, looking offended by the suggestion. "I have told you we didn't share a friendship, and I wouldn't dream of going cap in hand to someone's home seeking permission for our legal sport to take place. The idea I would go knocking on doors is quite preposterous. Most landowners approach us and consider it a great honour to welcome us onto their land. We fund the annual Farmer's Ball and host an annual dinner dance to thank our landowners and other supporters. If land changes hands, we invite the new owner to those events and speak to them in a social setting."

"As opposed to a funeral," Humphries muttered under his breath.

"Just to be absolutely clear," Fiona said. "You've never visited Field Barn in any capacity and haven't spoken to Pat Thomas for years. Is that correct?"

"By Jove, you've got it," Ford-Warren said sarcastically, clapping his hands together.

"Please, just answer the question."

"I have not set foot in Field Barn since it was built, and I last spoke to Pat Thomas several years ago."

"Thank you. Who else from the hunt may have approached Pat Thomas about access?"

"There have not been any further official approaches."

"How about an unofficial approach?"

"It's possible, I suppose, but unlikely. As far as the hunt is concerned, we accepted her decision and have made alternative arrangements."

"Could you provide a list of the hunt staff and members?"

Crayston leaned forward in her chair. "My client would consider a properly presented, formal request."

"Could you tell me where you were on Thursday between four and seven o'clock?"

"Yes, of course. I had to travel to London to deal with some tedious investment matters that I couldn't put off any longer," Ford-Warren replied. "It turned out to be one of the rare days the trains were running normally, so I arrived on time. By three o'clock, I was settled in my club, where I had a late lunch before travelling home again. My wife met me at the station shortly after seven o'clock. I'm afraid I threw my train ticket away, but several prominent people can confirm my whereabouts. In fact, I had lunch with your boss. Well, one of them. The deputy assistant police commissioner. I also had a brief chat with Jim Black, our local magistrate in the bar, before leaving the club."

"Thank you very much for your time," Fiona said, gathering her things.

"It was an absolute pleasure."

Once outside on the pavement, Humphries asked, "Why didn't you push him harder?"

"He's given us an alibi we can check, and you heard who he was with."

"And that's why nothing will be done about fox hunting, no matter how hard Peter tries."

"He won't give up without a fight. He's got a real bee in his bonnet about it," Fiona said, pulling her phone out. "I'll telephone him now to warn him about the recent dinner dates, but it's another dead end for us if Ford-Warren was on the train and can prove there was a full acceptance of Pat's refusal to allow access."

CHAPTER SIXTEEN

"We can strike Ford-Warren off the suspect list," Fiona said, after ending her call. "His alibi has been confirmed."

"Was he ever on it?" Humphries looked up from the file he was reading. "People like him will always have a good alibi that can't be questioned."

"It still means he's out of the picture," Fiona said. "Let's look at where we are generally."

"I think your theory about a surprise visitor is good, and that it was someone Pat knew," Humphries said, closing the file. "I've been looking at the crime scene report. The wine bottles in the kitchen came from a supermarket, whereas the wine in the cellar came from specialist wine sellers. It makes logical sense to think she was heading to the cellar for a decent bottle to share with her guest."

"Which suggests there was no quarrel leading up to the attack. The unknown guest followed her through the kitchen, picking up the ornament on the way, intending to seriously injure, if not kill."

"So, pre-meditated?"

Fiona, who had read through the report on Pat's watch several times, said. "If the smartwatch data can be trusted, we know Pat had a raised heart rate a few minutes before her death."

"Someone who set her heart aflutter," Humphries said. "Like a forbidden lover."

"Ask Abbie if she's had any luck tracking down Cavanagh. His recent bank account records suggest he's in Birstall," Fiona said. "Searching for a decent bottle of wine suggests her visitor was someone she was pleased to see and wanted to impress, but not necessarily a lover. From everything we've heard about her, that rules out anyone connected to the hunt."

"If she had one lover, she may have had others."

"True. We know she was an active member of the local hunt saboteurs. What other groups was she involved in? If we're going to get anywhere with this, we need to focus our attention on Pat. How she spent her time, and who her friends, enemies and interests were."

"One of the witnesses said yesterday we should be looking at the hunt saboteurs." After reopening the file to check, Humphries confirmed, "It was her sister, Natalie."

"Natalie? What about her?" Abbie asked, walking over with Rachael. "Has something happened?"

"No, we're just kicking about ideas," Fiona said. "Have you tracked down Cavanagh?"

"Not yet."

"Go ahead and set up the media request," Fiona instructed.

"I have spoken to his ex-wife. According to her, he had a girl in every town and doing a disappearing act is his standard reaction to most things," Abbie said. "He has a bolthole in Spain, so he could be there." Pulling out a chair, she continued, "Our best chance of catching up with him if he's in the area is by visiting a nursing home in Keynal at three this afternoon. He's always been close to his mother and takes her out for afternoon tea most Saturdays."

"Okay, but still contact the media so something goes out this evening," Fiona said. "He could be unpredictable, so organise some backup support before you go."

"His ex-wife said he had many faults, but being violent wasn't one of them. She described him as totally irresponsible and immature but never nasty or cruel. She doubts he had anything to do with the murder."

"People can change, and it's best to be prepared. Take backup and let me know how it goes."

"As you wish," Abbie replied, her tone making it clear she disagreed. "What were you saying about Natalie earlier?"

"We need to concentrate our efforts on looking at all aspects of Pat's life if we're going to get anywhere," Fiona said. "Her sister is an obvious source of information, as are co-members of the anti-hunt group. She wasn't friendly with her neighbours, but that doesn't mean she didn't have a local network of friends."

"We were wondering that if she had one lover, maybe there were others," Humphries said.

"If she did, it hadn't attracted gossip and rumours," Abbie said.

"Neither did her affair with Cavanagh," Humphries countered.

"And the sisters were never close, so I don't know what you expect to achieve there."

Bristling at Abbie's antagonism, Fiona asked, "Can you concentrate on tracking down Cavanagh while we speak to Harding and Natalie again? And make sure you take backup."

CHAPTER SEVENTEEN

Humphries didn't receive any reply when he telephoned, so as the Hardings lived on the outskirts of the village, they decided to drive to their address on the off chance they would be at home, while on their way to see Natalie.

"I'm surprised there's no answer on the home phone," Humphries said. "Claire Harding described herself as a housewife."

"Shock. Horror. Housewives aren't tied to the kitchen sink even in rural communities." Shaking her head, Fiona added, "Maybe she's out the back milking the family cow or something."

"Whatever. She doesn't drive, so she can't have gone far." Expanding the map of the address on his phone, Humphries added with undisguised pleasure, "It looks like they live at the end of a farm track. Their home is on the property of Willow Farm. It's your turn to test your car's suspension for the good of the force."

Humphries scowled in disappointment a short while later when Fiona turned right onto a tree-lined, smooth tarmac track. "We should drive over to Field Barn to pay Duncan another visit."

"It's on the to-do list, but there are a couple of things I want to get straight first," Fiona replied.

"Like on the day I'm driving," Humphries mumbled to himself.

Once they rounded the corner, two fire engines came into view. Little more than a shell remained of what had once been a small bungalow, home to the Hardings for the past thirty years. The fire was out, but the fire hoses had waterlogged anything not destroyed by the fire.

Fiona showed her warrant card and asked the fire officer, "Did they get out, okay?"

"They've both been taken to hospital suffering from smoke inhalation, and the husband had some minor burns. They had a lucky escape."

"The benefit of living in a bungalow, I guess," Humphries said. "When was the fire reported?"

"Early hours of this morning. We're about finished here. Just dampening down."

"Any thoughts on the cause of the fire?" Fiona asked.

"It's too soon to confirm, but it's likely it was started on purpose."

Fiona handed over her card. "They are possible witnesses in a murder enquiry. Can you keep me informed?"

Back in the car, Humphries asked, "Connected?"

Fiona pulled a 'what-do-you-think' face in response and started the car. "Next stop, Natalie. We'll visit the Hardings in the hospital afterwards."

"Do you think Natalie could be responsible, or is she at risk?"

"Could be either. We know she was also near the house shortly before the murder," Fiona said. "Call the station and ask if we know where Duncan was last night."

There was no answer when they rang the bell, but there was the faint sound of someone working nearby. They followed an electric extension cable to a stable block behind the house. Inside, they found a woman in blue work overalls standing on a wooden box clipping the coat of a giant horse. The mound of discarded hair on the floor looked enough to stuff a small sofa.

"Natalie Godwin?"

"Yes," Natalie replied, switching off the clippers. "Who wants to know?" After squinting at Fiona's warrant card, she said, "I'll have this done in five minutes. Do you mind waiting while I finish? I can put the horse away then and make you both something to eat and drink?"

"We can talk here while you finish," Fiona said.

"I won't hear you over the sound of the clippers. The house is unlocked. You're welcome to go inside and make yourself at home."

Humphries nodded to a bench which looked to be in a sun trap by the back door. "We could wait over there."

"As you wish. I'll shout as soon as I'm done."

The bench was shielded from the wind, and the winter sun at last gave a faint hint of warmth and the promise that spring was around the corner. Stretching out his legs, Humphries said, "Well, we know she's alive and well."

Wrapping her jacket around her, Fiona replied, "For now. If she saw someone at Field Barn the evening of the murder, it's possible they saw her as well as Harding."

Keeping his voice low, Humphries asked, "Assuming Pat's killer was responsible for the fire, do you think the intention was to permanently silence the Hardings or just to scare them?"

"We won't know until we have the report on the fire and speak to the Hardings," Fiona said. "In a perfect world, Natalie will remember seeing someone, or the car belonging to someone in the area, with a lifelong grudge against Pat, and we'll have an arrest by teatime. Just a shame we don't live in a perfect world. Without a break, we might never discover who pushed Pat down those stairs."

"It's not like you to be so defeatist. It's not good for morale if you're already saying this will end up being an unsolved case."

"You're right. Ignore me. Something will turn up. A throw-away comment or a witness will come forward."

They were interrupted by a return call from the station. Putting his phone away, Humphries said, "The liaison officer was with Duncan last night."

"I've finished clipping," Natalie called from inside the stable. "I'll re-rug the old boy and turn him out. I won't be long."

Fiona watched Natalie lead the giant horse across the yard to a field gate in the corner of the yard. The horse dwarfed her slight build, but it politely waited while she opened and closed the gate. It was only when Natalie had removed the head collar and moved to the other side of the gate that the horse squealed, reared up and galloped away. It was amazing to think the horse had behaved impeccably, holding in all that pent energy to obey the commands of someone far smaller and weaker.

After watching the horse gallop away, Natalie hung the head collar on the gate and joined Fiona and Humphries on the bench. "Have there been any developments, or do you have more questions for me?"

"A bit of both," Fiona said. "Do you know Stewart Harding and his wife?"

"I know him from sight. He does all the stone walls around here. I sometimes think he makes sure they only stay up for ten years to keep himself in regular work." Smiling, Natalie added, "I'm joking. I'm sure he doesn't. I see Claire from time to time cycling to the village shop. I remember their children were well-behaved, but they've moved away now and rarely visit. I always think it's a shame when children consider themselves too busy to visit their parents when they get older. It makes you wonder if there was more going on than meets the eye behind closed doors. But you don't want to hear me idly rambling away. Why do you ask?"

"Have you heard about the fire at their place?"

"Fire! Good gracious, no. I've been doing chores around here all morning," Natalie said. "Not serious, I hope. Are they okay?"

"We're on our way to visit them in hospital, but they should be fine."

"That's good to know. What was it? A chimney fire?"

"We don't know for sure, but the fire may have been started deliberately."

"What's the world coming to? This used to be such a lovely little village. Outsiders come in with all their town attitudes and ideas. Instead of accepting our way of life that has gone on unchallenged for generations, they try to change everything with their new-fangled ideas. They bring the very things they say they're escaping from, and it infects everything. And now this. Murder and arson in the space of a few days. Will you be talking to the people in the new housing estate on the Sapperton road? Horrible little houses. A real blot on the landscape."

"Have they caused problems in the village before?"

"They're irritating and dangerous. They drive their clean, shiny cars through our lanes on their way to deposit their children at the school in the next village. I wouldn't mind so much if they would slow down or pull over occasionally to let other vehicles pass. They don't understand how to pass horses safely, and they certainly don't want to get their shiny cars dirty or scratched by the hedgerows. That's the problem."

"The lanes are public highways," Humphries said.

"But no vandalism or arson?" Fiona quickly asked.

"I have noticed more rubbish in the hedgerows since the houses were built. Thrown out of car windows, no doubt."

"Okay, so nothing specific," Fiona said. "It's the day of your sister's death we wanted to talk to you about. I understand you were walking nearby shortly before."

"I crossed the track some distance from the house. One of my dogs shot off after a deer, and I was trying to get him back. I wish I had known. I would have gone to the house and stopped it."

"Known what?"

"Whatever was going on up at the house. We don't think, do we? When we're with someone, we never consider it might be the last time we will ever see them alive. It's like that with lots of things. We record the firsts, but rarely the lasts, because despite all the evidence to the contrary, we refuse to accept they're coming." Natalie gave an exaggerated sigh. "I won't pretend we were close, but still, she was the only family I had. Now it's just me. The end of the line, so to speak. It's weird. I don't even know how I feel. I'm keeping myself busy and trying not to dwell on the what-might-have-been. There's the funeral to arrange, and I'm keeping an eye on Duncan and her horses."

"Did you see or hear anyone else that day? Even if it was just in the distance?" When Natalie shook her head, Fiona asked, "Not a vehicle or something else that seemed out of place?"

"Sorry, no. I wish I could help you. I was scanning the hedgerows looking for the damn dog, but I didn't see anything out of the ordinary."

"Did you see Stewart Harding in the area?"

"No. Nobody. Why do you ask?"

"He was working in the area. I wondered if you'd seen him."

"I thought he was working on the top road, but if you say he was there, then I suppose he must have been."

"Is there anyone you can think of who might have had a grudge against your sister?" Fiona asked.

"Like I told the other officer, she upset a lot of local people with her stance on hunting and some of her other wishy-washy hippy ideas. And I can understand why. As a country woman myself, born and bred, I find it all incredibly annoying drivel. If people want to hug trees and cows, that's all fine and dandy, so long as they go and do it in a way that doesn't interfere with the people who fully understand the countryside. If you are suggesting country folk would kill these idiots over their ridiculous ideas, every ditch in the countryside would be full of corpses. If you are looking for my sister's killer, take a closer look at her lifestyle and the type of people she associated with. I suggest you start with Tina Myles, as she shared my sister's *worldview.* She lives over on the other side of Tilbury, unmarried, with two children from different fathers. One looks a little foreign to me. I'm sure you can imagine what sort of mother she is."

"We'll add her to our list," Fiona said, biting her bottom lip to stop herself from attacking Natalie's opinions. She put a restraining hand on Humphries who she could sense was about to explode with indignation. "I know you weren't close, but do you know if anything had been troubling your sister recently?"

"Sorry, I really can't help you there."

"How about Duncan?" Humphries asked. "Are you on friendly terms with him?"

"I'm not sure what you are suggesting by friendly terms, but as he's my brother-in-law and I'm a great believer in family, we are on civil terms. On the rare occasions we bump into one another, we have a quick chat about the weather, the same as I did with Pat. Obviously, I'm doing everything I can to support him through this difficult time. In fact, I've invited him over for supper this evening."

"What do you make of him?" Fiona asked.

"I think he should have grown a backbone and stood up to my sister more and put his foot down as her behaviour had a detrimental effect on his business. Local people won't use him on principle."

"By local people, you mean pro-hunt people," Humphries said.

"I mean *real* locals. Ones that appreciate tradition."

Fearing Humphries was going to lurch into an argument about hunting, Fiona said, "Do you think he could have harmed your sister?"

"No, the opposite," Natalie said. "In my opinion, he was far too indulgent."

"Until we catch who attacked your sister, you should be vigilant about security and strangers in the area."

"Don't you worry, I've never trusted the incomers with their fancy colourful wellingtons and dietary needs. Vegans and the like. As for security, I have my dogs, a pitchfork and a shotgun."

"If you see something suspicious, it would be best if you contacted us before reaching for your shotgun," Humphries said.

"If you say so," Natalie said, in a way that implied she would do as she pleased.

"Thank you for your time," Fiona said, standing. "If you remember anything else or you have any concerns, please don't take matters into your own hands but contact us."

CHAPTER EIGHTEEN

Humphries called Tina Myles as Fiona drove towards the hospital. "She should be home from work in a little over an hour."

"Great. We'll see her after the Hardings. How did she sound?"

"Upset by Pat's death and keen to help in any way she could. A definite breath of fresh air after talking to Natalie. If that woman was my sister, I would give her a wide berth. What an ignorant snob! Why didn't you tell her to stop wasting police time with her false allegations against anyone she considers beneath her? Anyone would think she owned the roads. Didn't she make you want to scream?"

"I moved her quickly along from irrelevancies."

"You still let her get away with it," Humphries said. "I would have pointed out to her that her bigoted views were more than irrelevant."

"And that would have helped the investigation, how?"

"It would have made me feel better, and it might have made her stop and think about her outdated and selfish opinions."

"It wouldn't have caused her to re-evaluate her views, and I hate to break it to you, but our job isn't about us feeling good," Fiona said. While she often agreed with Humphries, she found listening to his righteous indignation wearisome at times. "We're supposed to be unbiased, so our personal views shouldn't come into it."

"We're also not robots," Humphries said as they pulled into the hospital car park. "Some of us still actually care."

Fiona shoved her hands deep into her pockets as they walked to the hospital entrance. Humphries had hit a nerve. She was as passionate about unearthing the truth and seeking justice as she had always been, but sometimes a scathing cynicism crept in and nibbled away at her enthusiasm for the job. Increasingly, she found herself feeling his comments were a personal attack on her waning commitment and she wished he would give it a rest for a while.

Inside, they followed the signs for the burns unit and finally found a harassed staff member with time to point them in the direction of Stewart Harding's room. Claire sat on the easy chair next to Stewart's bed. His hands were heavily bandaged, but otherwise, they appeared unharmed. They were talking to a man in worn jeans and a sweatshirt with a frayed collar. The unknown man turned with a startled expression as Fiona and Humphries approached. He dropped a bag of grapes onto the bed, and muttered, "Don't forget what I said," before scuttling from the room.

Watching him leave, Fiona asked, "Who's that?"

"Brendon Murphy. He's a friend," Claire said. "He kindly stopped by to see how we both are and whether we needed anything."

"Good of him," Fiona said. "And how are you, both?"

"Oh, we're fine. I've already been discharged," Claire said. "We're waiting for the doctor to discharge Stewart so we can go home. The daft idiot tried to put the fire out by himself."

"You know there's not much of a home to return to?" Fiona asked.

"So, we've heard. Brendon said we could stop with him, but my daughter is going to put us up for a few days while we sort ourselves out. Hopefully, the insurance will cover everything."

"What are you doing here?" Stewart asked in a gravelly voice. "Is it about Pat's murder or the fire?"

"A bit of both, to be honest," Fiona said, pulling out a hard-backed chair and sitting. "We think they may be connected."

"How so?" Claire asked, looking confused.

Dodging the question, Fiona asked Stewart if he could run through his visit to Field Barn on the afternoon of Pat's murder.

Stewart told the same story he'd told Humphries. He'd walked up there at Pat's request to examine a fallen wall, and on his way back, had seen her sister, Natalie.

"Did you see anyone else or spot anything out of place?" Fiona asked. "Even in the far distance?"

"No, nothing at all. The only vehicle parked outside was Pat's, and there was nothing to suggest she had a visitor. I left her fit and well and walked back to my van."

"And she seemed relaxed and happy when you talked? She wasn't anxious or nervous?"

"Everything was normal. She showed me the wall, and we agreed on a figure for the cost of rebuilding it."

"Was there anything suspicious about the wall's collapse?" Fiona asked. "Could it have been pulled over deliberately?"

Stewart scratched his head as he thought back. "I don't think so, but why would someone want to go to the trouble to do that? It's only a garden wall about so high," he said, indicating it was chest height.

"And Pat called you the day before?"

"Yes."

Claire, who had sat quietly while her husband spoke, asked, "What did you mean when you said there might be a connection?"

Unable to dodge the question a second time, Fiona said, "The full report won't be available for some time, but the fire *may* have been started deliberately. Can you think of any reason someone would set fire to your home?"

Claire and Stewart shared a worried look before Claire asked, "Are you serious? I mean, we're not the type of people … No. I can't think of any reason. That doesn't make sense. It was some sort of electrical fault, surely?"

"We don't know anything yet, but have you seen anyone acting suspiciously around your home in the last few days? Or had a falling out with someone recently?"

"No, nothing like that. We get on with all our neighbours."

"And you are absolutely sure you didn't see anyone else near

Pat's house when you were there, Stewart?"

Stewart looked at Claire before saying, "There was no one. The fire officer must be mistaken. No one would want to harm us."

A nurse appeared to say the doctor would be along to see Stewart shortly, so it was best if everyone left.

CHAPTER NINETEEN

Fiona and Humphries pulled up outside a modern detached house on a quiet, no-through road. Tina's home backed onto fields but was only a fifteen-minute walk into Tilbury town centre.

"We're earlier than we said. She may not be back from work yet," Humphries said, releasing his seatbelt.

"We may as well go in and wait. Didn't you say her mother was looking after the children? She might know something."

A grey-haired lady with a huge smile greeted them at the door. "Come in. Come in. I'm Maggie. My daughter won't be long. She rang a few minutes ago to say she's running slightly late but will get here as soon as she can."

After they were ushered into a cosy kitchen, two dark-haired children wandered in from a side room to stare at them. The sounds of a children's television programme wafted in after them.

Maggie handed the children a biscuit each and shooed them out. "Go on back and watch your programme. Mummy won't be long." Turning to Fiona and Humphries, she said, "Now, sit yourselves down, and I'll make a pot of tea."

"Please don't go to any trouble on our behalf," Fiona said.

"Away with you. There's nothing a cup of tea can't improve on."

"Did your daughter give an estimate of when she would be home?"

"Any minute now, I'm sure," Maggie replied, bustling around the kitchen. "What was it you wanted to ask her about Pat? Maybe I could help?"

"You knew Pat?" Fiona asked.

"From when she was a twinkle in her father's eye. I used to live in the village and taught in the local school. I moved out this way when I lost my husband to be closer to Tina," Maggie said, carrying the teapot to the table. "Help yourselves."

Pouring his tea, Humphries asked, "Did Pat and Natalie get along as children?"

"Oh, aye. Different as chalk and cheese, but they used to rub along okay. They were always off having adventures on their ponies. They both hunted back then, as I remember. While it's not something I support, it's a shame they fell out over it."

Maggie brought over a plate of homemade shortbread and sat at the kitchen table with Fiona and Humphries. "From day one, Pat was always more independent and a bit of a dreamer, whereas Natalie wanted to be popular and fit in. They started to drift apart in their late teens. Natalie slavishly followed fashion and was desperate to attend all the parties. You have a phrase for it now, I think. Fear of missing out, isn't it?"

"FOMO," Humphries replied with a smile.

"That's it. Tina always says it about the young girls she works with," Maggie said. "Now, where were we? Oh, yes. Natalie had lots of boys running after her when she was younger. She had them all twisted around her little finger and broke their hearts, one by one. Pat was more withdrawn and studious as a teenager. We rarely saw her around the village, but when we did, she had her head stuck in a book. Everyone was surprised when she returned from university with Duncan in tow. He was considered quite a catch back then. Good looking and intelligent. I think we all assumed his vagueness was an act. It certainly worked for him. Young girls fancied him, and older women wanted to mother him."

"Did you keep in direct contact with the sisters as they grew older?" Humphries asked.

"Not really. A quick chat here and there if we bumped into each other, but in an area like this, you tend to know what your neighbours are up to one way or another."

"Despite her popularity, Natalie never married?" Fiona asked, trying to connect the woman she'd met with an outgoing teenager excited about a local dance.

"No, and that was a shame. She fell in love with someone who couldn't love her back and withdrew into herself. It probably would have been a short-term thing, you know how girls are, but then events overtook her. Her father's health started to fail, and she took on more and more responsibilities around the farm, finally ending up as a carer to both parents. It's so sad that she has ended up alone. I was lucky enough to marry my soul mate. I advise anyone who'll listen, that if you find that special one, then never stop fighting for them. Maybe if …"

Maggie stopped at the sound of a car pulling up outside. The children burst through the kitchen, shouting, "Mummy!" The back door into the kitchen opened, and despite looking exhausted, Tina, still dressed in her nurse uniform, dropped her shopping bags and gathered up both children into an enthusiastic hug.

Maggie looked on proudly before standing. "Is that the time? I must be off. It was lovely talking to you. My daughter hopefully will be able to answer your questions." She waved to her daughter, and said, "See you at the usual time tomorrow," and slipped quietly out of the house.

CHAPTER TWENTY

Tina released her children and lifted the two shopping bags to the counter. Emptying the bags, she said, "It looks like mum has kept you going in tea and biscuits. How can I help you?"

"We're looking for background information on your friend Pat Thomas. We're trying to build a picture of her last few days and who her friends and enemies were."

"Let me put the frozen food away, and I'll try my best to answer all your questions," Tina replied, emptying the bags.

"Mummy, when's tea? We're starving."

"Soon. Now go along and play."

"But Mum."

"Go on with you."

After the children slinked back to the other room, Tina finished putting her groceries away and collapsed onto a kitchen chair. She stared at the floor before raising her head and saying, "I still can't quite believe it. She was such an active, alive person. I only spoke to her that day. She was fuming at your lot and intending to kick up a right stink about it."

"Sorry, you've lost me," Fiona said. "What was she so angry about?"

Tina gave a look of disbelief before crossing the room and grabbing a copy of the local, free newspaper. She folded it to the third page and slammed it down on the kitchen table. As Tina sat back down, Fiona picked up the newspaper and read the article before passing it to Humphries.

"I still don't understand why she was so angry. The article says a new rural affairs officer has been appointed, and all complaints about animal welfare, including hunting activity, should be passed to her. It even gives her direct line. I would have thought that would please Pat."

"Don't play stupid. You must know she's a hunt subscriber and follows them on horseback most Saturdays."

"I didn't know that. Can I take the article?" Fiona asked.

"Help yourself. I'll only be throwing it out."

"Do you know what Pat was planning to do about it?" Humphries asked, after eating the last of the shortbread.

"We were going to talk about it properly over the weekend. There's no point contacting our local MP as she's a hunt supporter. Pat had a journalist friend. He's freelance, but often has articles in the national press and has appeared in a few regional television programmes. She either had or was going to contact him."

"Do you know how to contact him?"

Tina pulled out her phone. "I don't have his number, but I have his email address somewhere." Continuing to look for the address, Tina said, "Corruption is what it is. The police, like everyone else these days, are riddled with it. Ah. Here it is. His name is Charlie Dando. He's based in London. I'll write down the email address for you."

"Thank you. How did you meet Pat?" Fiona asked.

"We're both members of the local anti-hunting group. When I joined, she took me under her wing, and we instantly hit it off and became friends."

"Was Pat well-liked within the group?"

"Absolutely. And very highly respected," Tina said. "Because of who she was, I understand some people were sceptical at first, but that changed over time. She suffered more than the rest of us at the hands of those bullies."

"Which bullies?"

"The hunt members. They all hated her. The toffs kept their hands clean by setting their minions on her, but they were just as bad."

"What type of bullying?"

"They made sure all their contacts socially excluded her, and then there was the usual abuse and anonymous threats if she didn't mind her own business. Being pushed around and spat at when we act as hunt monitors is grim, but just recently, they've become more desperate and violent. I think they know their time is nearly up. One of them rode his horse at speed into Pat a few weeks back. It turned out to be quite funny because the horse swerved at the last moment, and the rider fell off into the mud."

"Do you know who the rider was?" Humphries asked.

"Yes. James Cox. He's a whipper-in. I assume you know all about the assault?"

"The one by Fred Lovell? Yes," Fiona confirmed. "Had she received any specific threats recently?"

"Not as far as I know."

"Had she seemed worried or anxious the last few times you saw her?"

"No. Having recently met the journalist, she was optimistic about the future. She thought if we could show a wider audience what really went on in trail hunting, it would force politicians to ban it properly."

"Was this approach and optimism shared by everyone?" Fiona asked.

"Absolutely. Why wouldn't it be? She had the full support of the group."

"No jealousy or friction?"

"None."

"How was her marriage to Duncan?"

"Fine. They were devoted to one another."

"No affairs?"

Tina leaned back in her chair, studying Fiona. After a while, she said, "You know about Harry?" When Fiona nodded, she said, "It wasn't an affair. Not in the usual sense."

"What was it, then?"

"An experiment." After a long, audible sigh, Tina said, "Pat had only ever been with Duncan. Harry threw himself at her, and she wondered what it would be like with someone else for just one time. As she was growing older, she thought it might be her last chance to find out. Knowing what Harry was like, she was confident there wouldn't be any complications."

"I understood it carried on for several months rather than a one-off thing."

"Not on any regular basis, it didn't. Harry would call her from time to time. Sometimes Pat agreed to see him, but mostly she didn't. Often, they would just talk. They slept together only a handful of times at most."

"Are you saying Harry was far keener to pursue the relationship?" Fiona asked.

"He tended to call when he was in between other relationships. Neither of them wanted anything more, but he was the one who wanted to keep things going, yes."

"Presumably, that's the version Pat gave you?"

"I've no reason to doubt it. If you're thinking that way, I would say he wasn't involved in her death. Have you met him?"

"He's disappeared."

"That's nothing unusual. Pat said he often did for weeks at a time. It used to drive Duncan up the wall."

"How would Duncan have reacted if he discovered the relationship?" Fiona asked.

"They would have talked it out. He certainly wouldn't have killed her."

"How did you get along with him?"

"I only knew him as Pat's husband," Tina replied, folding her arms. "He seemed amiable enough, and Pat never complained. I had the impression they were more friends than lovers, but that suited them both."

"Did you like him?"

"I didn't dislike him," Tina said carefully. "I don't really have an opinion about him. He was just Pat's husband. Someone in the background when we were around there for meetings."

"Your group held meetings at Field Barn?"

"Once or twice if something urgent came up in between our

regular meetings."

"So, all the members would know the house's layout?"

"Not really, no. We only used the central hall," Tina said.

"How about you? Did you visit on other occasions?" Fiona asked.

"Again, once or twice. When we held meetings there, I helped Pat with the food and drink."

"Did that involve going to the cellar?"

"No. I didn't even know there was one," Tina replied. "Pat would have everything arranged on the side counter in the kitchen. I used to ferry bottles and glasses from there to the hall."

"Where were you on Thursday around six o'clock?" Humphries asked.

"You can't seriously … She was my best friend," Tina said, sitting up straight. "I would have been here. Work will confirm what time I left, and Mum will say when I arrived home. Shouldn't you be out there looking for the killer?"

"Who do you think killed Pat?" Humphries asked.

"If it wasn't your lot, I would say either a random stranger or a hunt supporter. Most likely a terrier boy or one of the other sad hangers-on. Not being able to cross her land was a massive pain for them. They lost several foxes by having to go around. Before Pat took over the land, they actively encouraged breeding foxes in the woods along the track."

"Did Pat have any other enemies you're aware of?" Fiona asked.

"No. Besides her work to ban hunting, she kept herself to herself." Tina's attention shot to the door at the sounds of an escalating argument between the children. "Are we nearly finished? I really should go and break that up before you have another murder to deal with."

"That's all for today, but we might want to speak to you again," Fiona said. "We'll find our own way out."

Walking to the car, Fiona asked, "Did you see anything about this new rural crime officer in the crime scene report? Draft letters of complaint, photographs of this woman following the hunt or anything like that?"

Humphries shook his head. "No, and the name doesn't ring a bell."

"Strange. The article is dated the day before her death. If Pat was as riled up as Tina suggested, I would have expected there to have been something at the house. We'll head back to the station and go through the file. I had better warn Peter about this rural officer, Rhianna Garland, especially if she was involved in his operation. It's worth talking to James Cox. Riding a horse at someone is pretty aggressive, and he must have felt a fool when he fell off."

CHAPTER TWENTY-ONE

At the station, Humphries looked for any possible reference to Rhianna Garland in the file and how she was appointed to the role of rural officer. Fiona asked Andrew to interview James Cox and went off in search of Peter. As she approached his door, a passing officer said, "Go careful. He's not in the best of moods."

"Case related?" Fiona asked.

He nodded, and Fiona knocked on the door, wondering if the new rural officer had somehow derailed his investigation. If she had, then the allegations of police corruption were valid. Maybe not on the scale of other recent national scandals, but it didn't look good.

"Come in."

Peter turned from the window as Fiona entered. Despite his welcoming smile, she had worked with Peter long enough to know he was tense and angry. She'd noticed before how tired he looked recently. "Hi, how's it going?"

"To pot. Shut the door, and I'll tell you," Peter said, perching on the edge of his desk. "It looks like most of the terrier boys will get off as farmers have popped up everywhere claiming they requested the blocking up of dens to protect their livestock, not the local hunts. The hunts are saying they had already decided to cancel their so-called trail hunt due to the forecast of heavy frosts. It's so frustrating. They know we know it's all lies, but there's nothing we can do. All I can say is their internal communications are slick. For their stories to all fit in so nicely, I think there was a last-minute leak, which is annoying when we managed to keep everything under wraps for so long. All those hours of work down the drain."

Taking a seat, Fiona said, "At least it sent the message we are taking the subject seriously. There's been a series of near misses of serious road accidents involving hounds recently. Maybe they'll resort to trail hunting and lay their trails away from roads, like they're supposed to, for the rest of the season."

"Not voluntarily, they won't," Peter said. "The whole debacle has merely shown how untouchable they are. With their combined wealth and connections, they know they're above the law."

"How about the videos on Lovell's phone? How are they wriggling out of that?"

"That did throw them into a panic to start with. Now, there's talk of whether I obtained the footage legally, and they're all looking a lot more smug."

"Ugh. So, it's all turned around to be a slapped wrist for you."

"I'm not letting them get away with it. I had reasonable grounds to seize the phone," Peter said. "And he handed it to me voluntarily."

Deciding it wasn't the time to mention, technically, Lovell had given access to one particular photograph, Fiona remained silent. If Garland was involved in the operation, news of her background would be explosive enough.

"Any progress on your murder investigation?" Peter asked.

"Some, and I think we've come across something that might be relevant to you," Fiona said hesitantly. "Have you met Rhianna Garland, the new rural affairs officer?"

"Only briefly. Why?"

"Was she aware of your planned raid?"

"She was advised late that evening so she could be prepared to answer any questions the following morning."

"I think she may have been your leak. According to Pat's friend, she's an active hunt member." Fiona handed over the newspaper. "Pat recognised her from this news article and was planning to expose her via a journalist friend."

"Have you found evidence of this at the house?"

"No, which begs the question, was evidence removed?"

"Before today, I would have said, go and put your tinfoil hat on," Peter said. "Now, I'm not so sure. Do you have the journalist's contact details? I'd like to speak to him."

"I do, but why do you want to speak to him? Pat's murder is my case. I told you about Garland as it has a bearing on your operation."

"I wasn't trying to step on any toes. I have my own reasons for wanting to speak to him. Which team was at the house?"

"I thought we just agreed that Pat's murder is my case," Fiona said.

"It is, but if there is any question of an officer being involved in a murder investigation and the tampering of evidence, you need to report that to me."

"Tracey Edwards was leading the team, but I wasn't questioning one of them removing evidence. I was suggesting the murderer may have before leaving."

"If you're correct, that suggests either the killer had a vested interest in hiding Garland's background, or she was the killer," Peter pointed out. "If something relating to an active special police officer was removed from the scene, I need to know everything about it. You're potentially wading into dangerous territory. Do you know who appointed Garland as a rural officer?"

"Humphries is currently looking into it. It's possible whoever appointed her to the role wasn't aware of the obvious conflict of interest."

"Whether she withheld information, or someone chose to ignore her link with the hunt, her appointment needs to be questioned, especially if she was responsible for undermining hours of work on the raids."

"I'll let you know what Humphries discovers, and I'll email the journalist's details when I return to my desk."

"Thanks. Do you want to meet up for a quick drink later to swap notes?"

"Could do," Fiona said, surprised by the offer. Although they had been close in the past, since Peter's new girlfriend had arrived on the scene, they had drifted apart and hadn't met up socially in ages. "Is Nicole out of town?"

"You could say that. She's in France, cooing over her first grandchild."

"When's she due back?"

"A For Sale sign appeared outside her house last week, so I guess never."

Not sure how to react, Fiona said, "I'll see you later and headed back to her desk. Peter had been much calmer and happier since he had met Nicole, and she hoped things weren't as final as he seemed to think they were for his sake.

Humphries was on the phone with his fiancé discussing the never-ending wedding plans when she arrived at her desk, but he had left her some information on Rhianna Garland. She worked full-time as a buyer for a large fashion chain, and in her free time, she had won some prestigious awards with her horses. As her privately educated background suggested, she had never been in trouble with the police.

"Everything I could find on Garland is there," Humphries said, ending his call. "Personnel applications are way above my pay grade, but Pat did ring the journalist about her appointment."

"You spoke to him?"

"Yes. He described Pat as incandescent with rage when she contacted him the morning before she was killed. He thought the appointment was interesting, but he was planning to sit on it and tag it onto another story for greater impact. He's now taking another look at it."

"Did Pat tell him if she planned to take any other action over the appointment?" Fiona asked.

"She said she was going to write to the local newspaper to complain about the article and contact Garland to give her a chance to stand down before exposing her."

"Time we paid Garland a visit."

"It will have to wait until tomorrow. She's currently in London for a work conference."

CHAPTER TWENTY-TWO

Peter and Fiona left their cars in the station car park and walked over to The Squire Inn, having agreed that if they went home first, they probably wouldn't venture out again. Fiona felt drained, but Peter looked positively exhausted. Once they were settled with their drinks, she asked him how he was.

"On a scale of one to ten, about minus five."

"That good?"

"Don't take any notice of me. I'm just fed up," Peter said, taking a drink. "I suppose I should take some positives from wasting the last couple of months of my life. A few minor hunts clearly weren't in the loop, and there should be some successful prosecutions. No doubt limited to the men they caught, rather than who instructed them." When Fiona asked him about the video, Peter merely rolled his eyes.

"Let's forget about work. How are the twins?" Fiona asked.

"They're doing just great. They call Jasper 'Dad' and are looking forward to having a new baby brother," Peter said, before taking a large gulp of his beer.

With both feet stuck in her mouth, Fiona looked around the bar for a distraction while pondering possible safe conversations to start. Early evening, there wasn't much to see. A group of men in work boots were sharing a laugh at the bar while watching another group huddled around a fruit machine. At least she knew why Peter had been looking so down recently. He was having to face the consequences of choosing his work over his marriage and his new girlfriend returning to France.

Wiping his mouth with the back of his hand, Peter said, "And just to make my life complete, despite the farce the operation has descended into, Dewhurst thinks I showed great leadership, and he wants me to head up another inter-force operation."

"Anything interesting?"

"Some specific similarities have shown up in recent disappearances in the southwest. He's put my name forward to oversee the task force being set up to see if there's a link."

"That doesn't seem so bad," Fiona said, sounding upbeat. "It'll get you out of the office and back in the field."

"You're kidding, right? I'll be bogged down with overtime sheets and reading other officers' reports."

"I'm sure you could make it more hands-on than that if that's what you want. You'll be the person in charge, after all."

"I doubt I'll have the time. What Dewhurst thinks I've excelled at, I've really struggled with. Previously, I've always worked in a small team. The last few months, I've found it a nightmare trying to keep up with so many moving parts and players. I won't even mention the realms of paperwork and reports I've had to wade through. I think it's time I got out."

"That's not the first time I've heard you say that," Fiona said. "Once you get stuck into the cases, do you think you'll feel differently?"

"Maybe, but how about you?" Peter asked in a way that made it clear he didn't want to talk about his troubles anymore. "How's the murder investigation going?"

"Slowly. Did Humphries pass on what he dug up on Garland?"

"He did, and I've passed it on. She made no mention of her hunt connections on her application. There's a good chance she'll be asked to quietly stand down from the role. Other than lying by omission on her application, she appears to be a model citizen. Do you think she could be involved with the murder?"

"I find it strange there wasn't any paperwork mentioning her appointment at the scene if Pat was so wound up about it," Fiona said. "I should have picked up on it sooner."

"How? Even I didn't know about her."

"I don't mean her appointment," Fiona said. "There was nothing at the scene to suggest what Pat had been doing immediately beforehand. I thought it was strange but didn't question whether evidence had been removed for a reason, and I should have."

"Possibly," Peter replied. "Put it down to experience and move on."

"Considering what we now know, there should have been something in the house, even if it was only the newspaper article."

"Hindsight is a wonderful thing," Peter said. "Any thoughts on who could have been responsible?"

"We have a few suspects but not enough evidence to narrow down our investigation," Fiona said. "I think the killer was someone Pat liked. Someone she was looking forward to meeting and wanted to impress with a decent bottle of wine, and that rules out anyone connected to the hunt, including Garland."

"Have you given any thought to who would benefit from Garland keeping her position?"

"I'll mull that over tonight, but only the hunt members come to mind."

"Which wouldn't fit your other criteria," Peter said. "Could it have been someone who hid their true opinions?"

"Like a mole in her anti-hunting group?" Fiona asked, thinking about Pat's friend, Tina Myles. "It's possible and they held a few meetings in Pat's house. I was told they stayed in the main hall but one of them could have slipped out to look around the rest of the house and seen the cellar. I have a meeting with the journalist she contacted tomorrow morning. Hopefully, he can tell us something more about Pat's intentions."

"Charlie Dando?" Peter spluttered. "Why are you going to see him? Humphries said he wasn't that interested in the story."

"After Pat's death, that may have changed," Fiona said, surprised by Peter's reaction. "He seems genuine enough on paper, but he ticks all the boxes for the unknown visitor. It might explain why we found nothing at the house relating to Garland or him."

"I see how your mind's working, but it seems unlikely that an up-and-coming journalist would kill his story source," Peter said. "That doesn't make any sense. The murderer is far more likely to be someone closer to home. Have you double and triple-checked the husband's alibi?"

"Yes, of course," Fiona said. She hadn't previously considered Dando as a suspect, but Peter's reaction irritated her. They had worked well together in the past, but she was an experienced officer with her own caseload. It felt like he was still checking her work.

Peter pulled a face. "Did I overstep the mark? I'm not telling you how to run your case."

"I know," Fiona said, softening. Peter's private life was obviously in a mess, and she should lighten up. The transition from his understudy had been hard, and she knew many people still thought of her as his prodigy. That didn't mean she should take out her frustrations on him, especially when he was down. "I'm a little tired and grumpy." Smiling, she added, "I wonder where I get that from?"

Peter raised an eyebrow and finished his drink. "Get an early night for your drive to London tomorrow."

CHAPTER TWENTY-THREE

Fiona set off to see Charlie Dando alone, leaving Humphries in charge during her absence. She settled back in her train seat to read some of Dando's past articles, concentrating on the ones that had made national publications. Most of his articles attacked the government's record on environmental issues, especially concerning waterways and the use of fertilisers. She found a few on pheasant shooting in Scotland and the damage caused to peat land and birds of prey, but only one on fox hunting. He had also written numerous articles in support of environmental protests around the country.

She ordered a coffee after she became sleepy, lulled by the train's swaying rhythm as it sped through the countryside. Sipping her coffee, she watched the fields whooshing by. It was surprising how much countryside there was, even on the approach to the capital, and she wondered if it was as much at risk as Dando claimed in his articles.

After her coffee, she felt more alert and called her brother to discuss their father. Her day improved when he brought up the subject of care homes. He was suggesting a short-term stay to give their mother a break while their father's needs could be assessed, rather than a permanent move, but it was a start. Rather than press for more, she readily agreed to his suggestion. She felt a mixture of guilt and relief when he said it would be better if he and his wife had the initial conversation.

Her argument that she should share the responsibility was rebuffed by her brother pointing out her work commitments made her unreliable. The criticism hurt, but she couldn't deny it on her track record. Her brother had an office job, and his wife hadn't returned to work after they had started a family, so it was easier for them to stick to plans. They had also received practical and financial help from their parents, so maybe it was fair they accepted a greater share of the burden, and she shouldn't feel so guilty. Even so, her exclusion hurt.

Despite the lingering guilt, Fiona ended the call feeling a weight had been lifted off her shoulders. She hadn't realised how much the worry about the situation had been lodged at the back of her brain, dragging her down. She had also seriously underestimated her brother's understanding of the problem. With everything going so well, she decided it was a good time to call Stefan to say she couldn't meet him as arranged. She called his number with high hopes, only to find his number was temporarily unavailable.

She returned her attention to the files but found herself thinking about Stefan. She daydreamed about them having a future together, somehow, somewhere. She pulled herself up short. In a parallel fantasy universe, they could make things work between them, but it could never be possible in the real world, so there was no point dwelling on the subject. He had proved himself to be an excellent liar, and she could never trust him again.

She had a last flick through her files and was putting them away when the announcement for Paddington station crackled through the train carriage. Despite the strong local accent, it was clear and audible. Taken with the train running perfectly to time and the cleanliness of the carriage, she questioned the doom and gloom reported daily in the newspapers about the failing transport network being indicative of a failing country.

Stepping down from the train, she was swept away with her fellow passengers swarming out of the station. Outside was sunny, but a cold breeze heavy with traffic fumes cut through her.

Fiona checked that her briefcase was securely fastened and set off on the five-minute walk to the café where they had agreed to meet. The streets were crowded with people rushing along with an urgent purpose, talking on their phones. The crowd flowed to a rhythm she couldn't hear as she was jostled along, always slightly out of time. She started to walk defensively, trying to anticipate other people's movements, but she still seemed to be in other people's way. She held on tight to her bag and quickened her step toward the café blackboard as soon as it came into sight. She dived inside, relieved to be off the busy street. Inside was warm and scented by the aroma of strong coffee.

Taking her place in the queue for the counter, she was wriggling out of her coat when she felt a tap on her shoulder. Startled, she turned to find herself nose-to-nose with Charlie Dando. He was instantly recognisable from the online photographs, only more haggard and older. She took a step back and offered her hand. "Charlie Dando?"

"The same. And you must be DI Williams," Dando said, shaking her hand. He released it with an amused look, and said, "Find a seat, and I'll order the coffee. What do you want?"

"A cappuccino will be great," Fiona replied, as she was shoved by a customer pushing past with a tray of drinks. She glanced around, and said, "I'll grab the table over there by the window."

From her chair, she watched Dando shuffle forward toward the counter. Years ago, she had considered applying to join the Met. Looking around at strangers bustling to be where they wanted to be, she was pleased she hadn't. The chaotic noise and number of people jumbled together made her feel insignificant. Back home, she genuinely felt her actions could make a difference. Here, she would feel whatever she achieved would be of no consequence, as her efforts would be smothered by so many people pulling in different directions. The tiniest of cogs in a massive machine. Perched on her chair, tucked away in the corner, she felt small and inadequate in the face of so much humanity.

Watching the teeming crowds speed along the pavement as one, made her feel dizzy. Feeling out of place, she questioned how and when she'd become such a country bumpkin. She was getting old and set in her ways before her time. Maybe she should push herself out of her comfort zone and apply for a position elsewhere. Not London, but a major city somewhere. Up north, perhaps.

"Here you go," Dando said, placing two coffees on the table.

"Thanks. Popular place," Fiona said, smiling at Dando as she removed the lid from her coffee to spoon in some sugar. He had an interesting face. Despite his grin and cheery disposition, she sensed a deep sadness and wondered about his past.

"Best coffee around at a decent price, so it's always busy," Dando said, sliding effortlessly into his chair. "I was shocked to hear about Pat. How can I help you?"

"How did you meet, for starters?"

"We didn't. Not in person, anyway. I was writing a report on the increasingly violent clashes involving environmentalists, and I heard about her assault. We corresponded via email." Shuddering, Dando added, "The only time we spoke was the morning before she was killed. She emailed me about the appointment of a special police constable and asked me to call her back, which I did. I told her I would investigate whether there had been any similar appointments before deciding whether to pursue the matter."

"Have there been similar appointments?"

"None that I've uncovered so far, but I'm still looking. If you give me your personal number, I'll make sure you're updated. We could meet up to discuss developments," Dando said, brushing Fiona's hand as he put down his coffee.

"That won't be necessary," Fiona replied, sitting back in her chair.

Dando raised his coffee, and looking over the rim of his cup, said, "If you think the appointment was connected to her death, you should come back to mine to go through my notes."

Dismissing the suggestion, Fiona asked, "How did Pat seem when you spoke to her?"

Dando leaned back in his chair and sighed. "She was livid. The appointment really riled her. She had convinced herself it was part of a bigger conspiracy."

"Did you agree with her?"

"I thought the idea a little far-fetched. You haven't answered my earlier question. Is there a connection to her death?"

"I've contacted you as you were one of the last people she spoke to, and I'm interested in establishing her state of mind."

"As I said, she was angry. Agitated. She was determined to kick up a stink about the appointment."

"Was she relying purely on the newspaper article?" Fiona asked.

"I understand there were social media posts as well. The constable was introducing herself and asking for people to contact her directly if they had any concerns about local animal welfare matters. It wasn't specifically mentioned, and I could be wrong, but I had the impression there was some personal history between them."

"Such as?"

"No idea," Dando replied. "It was just a feeling I had."

"Did you arrange to meet? If you discovered there were other appointments, it could be a big story for you."

"If it turns out the role of rural affairs is being stuffed with pro-hunt supporters countrywide, then I would run the story, but it wouldn't be my number one priority. I want to make people aware of how much of our natural habitat we're losing and what we can do to save it, rather than getting bogged down with the politics of rural police stations."

"Did you arrange to meet Pat?" Fiona repeated.

"We left it that I would do some digging around and get back to her," Dando said. "I'm contacted by lots of people with potential stories. It's a question of picking the right ones to pursue. One dodgy rural officer wouldn't make an impressive headline."

"Do you know where Pat lived?"

"In a village near Birstall, somewhere."

"Have you ever visited the area to report on the local hunt skirmishes or any other environmental issue?"

"No, I've never been out that way." Dando broke into a wide

grin. "Now I've met you, I may address that omission."

Fiona narrowed her eyes, and asked, "Where were you on Thursday?"

"Seriously?" Dando said with a shocked expression. "Why on earth would I …? Oh, never mind." He pulled up his diary on his mobile phone. "I was miles away in Devon investigating a river pollution incident. The locals reported the water turning green overnight. The water board and a local chemical company are denying responsibility. I can show you photographs but I would prefer not to hand over details of the residents I spoke with. I can give you the contact details of the waterworks manager and the chemical company's director. They both refused to talk to me, but they should confirm I was outside their offices badgering them for a statement."

"That should be sufficient. Can you email it all to me?"

"I'll do it now."

As Dando sent the information, Fiona asked, "Have you always been a journalist?"

"No, I was in the army," Dando replied. "I drifted for a while when I came out. That was when I fell in with a bunch protesting about the pollution of their local beach. They were so devoted to their cause that they couldn't see the bigger picture. It's no good viewing incidents in isolation and people can't demand change if they don't know what's going on all around them. I started to investigate the lack of government action and to publicise it. It's all grown from there." Putting his phone away, he asked, "Do you know a DCI Peter Hatherall?"

Suspiciously, Fiona replied, "Yes. Why?"

"Did he recently coordinate surveillance of the hunts?"

"He did, but you'll have to contact him for the details," Fiona replied, wondering why he was so interested.

"Fair enough," Dando said. "Would you be interested in lunch?"

"Sorry, I need to get back to the station."

"If I am down your way for a story, could we meet up?"

"I'm always very busy," Fiona said, packing her things ready to leave.

"I could walk you back to the station?"

"That's very kind of you, but I'm sure I can find my own way," Fiona said firmly. "Thank you again for your time."

Dando waved from his chair. "Until next time."

Fiona hurried out the door, hoping there wouldn't be a next time.

Walking back to Paddington station, Fiona switched on her phone to discover she had several missed calls from Humphries. Entering the station, she saw that the next train was about to leave, so she put her phone away and jogged to the platform, arriving just in time to jump aboard. Settled in her seat, she called Humphries.

"I've been trying to get hold of you all morning," Humphries complained by way of answering.

"What's happened?"

"Brendon Murphy committed suicide last night. We're treating it as suspicious. Abbie and Rachael have been trying to speak to him. He lives near Hinnegar Woods, and he's well known for poaching on Pat's land. He takes great pleasure hunting in the area she fenced off to let nature take its course. Someone they interviewed mentioned he would be worth talking to as they think he was there on Thursday."

"He was in the hospital visiting the Hardings, but he scurried out as soon as we arrived," Fiona said. "My train is just pulling out of Paddington. Find out everything you can, and I'll be back in the station within a couple of hours."

CHAPTER TWENTY-FOUR

It was gone lunchtime when Fiona caught up with Humphries. "What can you tell me about Brendon Murphy?"

"Fifty-six-year-old bachelor living in a rented cottage on the edge of Hinnegar Woods, worked for Sommer Fields Farms as a dairyman. The alarm was raised when he didn't turn up this morning for milking. He was discovered in his car in the garage with the engine still running. Carbon monoxide poisoning is the presumed cause of death, but there was recent bruising to his face and stomach. The autopsy will be in a day or two. No history of depression or anxiety. He was a regular at the Suffolk Arms, where he spent most of his lunchtimes and some evenings. He was his usual cheery self when he was in there yesterday, claiming he knew who had killed Pat Thomas."

"What! Why didn't we know about this before?"

Humphries shrugged. "You should bear in mind he has claimed to have seen Elvis, Lord Lucan and aliens in the past, so nobody believed him. And various governments have tried to silence him."

"What else do we know about him?"

"The people who had mentioned his poaching on Pat's land described him as a free spirit and a wily one. He liked to think he mostly lived off the grid and on his wits. He was also a bit of a conspiracy theorist and didn't own a television, computer, or mobile phone as he considered them all to be government-sponsored surveillance devices."

"Nobody had suggested Pat had any alternative views other

than being anti-hunt, so I doubt they were friends."

"I've spoken to the pub landlord and I'm due to see a couple of his friends in half an hour."

"Do you have a list of customers who might have overheard him saying he knew who killed Pat?"

"Not yet, but I will," Humphries said. "How did you get along with Dando?"

"Apart from the fact he's a total creep, he confirmed Pat was determined to kick up a stink over the appointment of Garland, so it's more surprising nothing was found at the house relating to her. He says he didn't arrange to meet her, but I'm going to check his alibi for the day."

"You think it could have been him?"

"I can't think of a motive, but he would be someone Pat would look forward to meeting and want to impress," Fiona replied. "He's also freelanced with complete freedom to move about, and he has military training."

"Wouldn't she have told someone if she was about to interviewed? If not her husband, the other hunt saboteurs."

"You're probably right, but I still need to check. He said something else interesting that I want to look into. He had the impression there was some history between Pat and Garland."

"I wonder what it was. There's quite an age difference," Humphries said. "I heard on the grapevine she is standing down as the local rural officer. I spoke to a couple of constables, and they thought she was okay for a special. Quick to learn with a good sense of humour."

"Were these male colleagues?"

"Yes."

"With no mention of how attractive she is."

"Yeah, that did come up," Humphries admitted sheepishly.

Deciding not to rib the perfectly politically correct Humphries about possible sexism, Fiona said, "Let me know how your interviews with Murphy's friends go."

"Do you want me to sit in on your interview of Garland tomorrow?"

"No need," Fiona said. "I'm meeting her in the morning on my way to work at her parents' farm. Although she has her own place, she keeps her two horses there and sees to them first thing every day."

Once Humphries had left, Fiona started on Dando's alibi. She quickly verified he was miles away on the day of Pat's murder pestering the managing director of the chemical company for a statement, so another dead end. She couldn't find anything to link Pat and Garland so if there was anything between them it was personal. She made a note to ask about it tomorrow.

She leaned back in her chair to think about how Murphy's suicide could fit into Pat's murder. It was possible they knew one another, even if only by sight as they lived only five miles apart, but she couldn't think what they might have had in common. It was more likely he was killed because his boasts had been overheard by the wrong person.

Fiona pulled up a map of the area to locate the wooded area where Murphy poached. It was some distance away from the house but ran alongside the track Harding had walked along to reach the house. If he had been there at the same time, Harding should have seen him. She couldn't tell whether it was possible to see Field Barn from there so someone would have to be sent out to check.

No one in the village had reported any strangers in the area or seen a vehicle on the track so it was possible the murderer had travelled by foot. The fields below Pat's land were farmed by her sister, but it wasn't clear who owned the land on the other side. As nothing had shown up on residents' security cameras it was possible the killer approached Field Barn from that direction.

She quickly discovered the land was part of the Earl of Ditchburn's estate. The estate office confirmed the parcel of land above Field Barn was leased to a sheep farmer called Bradley Sharpe who lived several miles away on the other side of Brierley. As he didn't live locally, he hadn't previously been contacted in connection to the murder. She asked for his mobile number and decided to ring him straight away.

Her call was quickly answered by Sharpe, but it was impossible to carry on a conversation over the sound of machinery. After several shouted, "What was that? I can't hear you," Fiona suggested she call him back in an hour once he finished the job he was working on.

She was about to call Abbie for an update when she was told there was a couple downstairs to see her. She arrived in the reception area to find Stewart and Claire Harding. They looked pale and drawn but Claire looked particularly anxious.

"Hello, I understand you were asking for me," Fiona said. "Come through and I'll find an interview room."

Stewart and Claire shuffled along behind Fiona in silence as she led the way. Finding an empty room, she ushered them inside. Once they were seated, they remained silent, staring at the floor.

Fiona was sure they had held back information about Pat's death and was tempted to let them squirm a little longer, but she didn't want to waste any more time, so prompted, "Do you have something to tell me about Pat's death and possibly Brendon Murphy's? Something you forgot to say in your previous statement, maybe?"

Stewart nodded but didn't speak, while Claire continued to stare at her feet.

"If you know something you have failed to tell us about, then it's best you get it over with. No point prolonging the agony and wasting more time," Fiona said. "I saw Brendon Murphy in your hospital room the day after the fire. Why was he there? Was it in connection to Pat's death?"

"No, no. Nothing like that," Stewart said. "It was like we said. We're old friends. He came to see if we were okay, and whether we wanted to stay with him while things were being sorted out."

"We're worried for our safety and don't want to put the grandchildren in danger," Claire blurted out. "We were wondering, like, if we could stay in one of your places. A safe house. That's what they call them on television."

"Why do you think you're in danger?"

After the couple exchanged a look, Stewart shrugged an

acceptance of the situation, and admitted, "On the day Pat was murdered, it wasn't just Natalie I saw. On my way back I saw Brendon coming out of the woods. I didn't mention it because he was walking away from the house."

"And he was your friend."

"Well, yes, that as well. But I didn't want to get him into trouble for trespassing."

"Or poaching."

"Okay, yes, poaching," Stewart said. "And like I said, he was walking away from Field Barn."

Fiona considered making more of a point of them withholding information in a murder enquiry but decided against it. They were obviously distressed and had just lost a friend. "Go on."

"Well, the thing is," Claire said. "We were thinking it doesn't make sense. Brendon wouldn't kill himself, so we figured he must have been murdered. By the same person who murdered Pat and tried to kill us by setting fire to the cottage. God knows where we would be if I wasn't such an insomniac. That's why we need protection. From him. The killer. If he saw Brendon, then he could have seen my Stewart."

"Now, we don't know that, for sure," Stewart said, patting his wife's knee. "I didn't see anyone, so I don't see how anyone could have seen me."

"Please think carefully about that evening. Are you positive you didn't see or hear anyone else?" Fiona asked.

"No. There was no one else on Pat's land."

"How about in the fields above? The ones farmed by Bradley Sharpe?"

"I can't say for sure there wasn't someone up there, but if there was, I didn't see them."

"Would it be easy for someone to walk across from there to Field Barn?"

"They would have to climb over a few gates and cross the river," Stewart said. "It gets muddy along there this time of the year, but possible, I guess, if they came prepared."

"And Brendon. Did he see anyone else that day?"

After looking back at Claire, Stewart said, "I don't know. Possibly."

"This is important. Did he see somebody else? Who?"

"I don't know," Stewart repeated. "If he did, he didn't say."

"But he did say something strange the day he came into the hospital," Claire said, reaching for Stewart's hand. "Tell her what he said."

"We were talking about Pat's murder. With us both being nearby at the same time. Shortly before you came in, he said something along the lines of some things are best kept under wraps for a rainy day."

"What do you think he meant by that?"

"At the time nothing," Stewart said. "It was just his way. He liked to pretend he had secrets and to dramatize things."

"But with hindsight," Claire interrupted. "I think he saw someone but chose not to mention it, thinking it was something he could use later. Which brings me back to why we're here. We need protection."

"It does sound like he might have seen somebody he recognised. Somebody you both know possibly as I understand you both drink in the Suffolk Arms." Fiona said. "Any idea who that could be?"

"We've no idea," Claire said. "Like Stew said he might not have seen anyone. He liked to make things up and pretend he knew more than he was saying. He was like that."

"Could Brendon see Field Barn from where he was?" Fiona asked.

"No, because of the way the land curves around," Stewart said. "From there he could possibly catch glimpses of a car lower down on the track, and he had excellent hearing. He could tell the make and model of a vehicle from the sound of the engine."

Claire leaned forward anxiously with her hands between her knees. "What about protecting us? We could be next."

"Have you friends or relatives living outside the area you could stay with for a few days?"

"Not really, no, and we don't want to put anybody else at risk."

"How about I arrange for officers to stay with you at your daughter's house for the next couple of days," Fiona said, thinking she should also arrange protection for Natalie.

"I guess, that would be better than nothing, but there's not a lot of room there," Claire said. "We were thinking we should go somewhere some distance away, where no one would know us."

"Wait here, and I'll see if there's anything more we can do for you."

Fiona returned to her desk at the same time as Abbie and Rachel entered the room. "How is tracing Cavanagh going?"

"We're getting nowhere fast and have pretty much hit a dead end. He didn't visit his mother, and so far, the media request has brought out the usual nutters but nothing useful."

"The Hardings are downstairs in interview room 3 and are asking for protection. In the circumstances, I think it's a good idea. Could you contact the Protected Persons Service and arrange protection for the next couple of days? Can you mention we are likely to have another person in need of protection? I'm going to call Natalie now, although I have the feeling that may take some persuading."

CHAPTER TWENTY-FIVE

Fiona was about to call Natalie when she was interrupted by a call from the sheep farmer, Bradley Sharpe.

"I've been waiting for you to call me back," he said gruffly. "What is it you want?"

"Yes, sorry, something came up. I'm investigating the death of Pat Thomas. It's possible someone may have been on the land you lease from the Earl, watching Field Barn. Have you seen any suspicious activity up there?"

After a long silence, Sharpe said, "I haven't visited recently. I reckon the last time I did was mid-November when I moved the sheep back down here. I take an early cut of hay off those fields around May, but there's not much for me to check this time of the year. It's an exposed spot, and even regular dog walkers aren't keen because of how the wind cuts across the ridge. There's not much up there except an old stone barn that's falling down."

"Does it have a good view of Field Barn?"

"Yes. On a clear day, you can see right across to Wales."

"So, somebody up there could watch all the goings on at Field Barn and the rest of the village?"

"For sure, with binoculars."

"And could they access Field Barn from there?"

"With a pair of waders, they could, but it's not an easy trek."

"Could you check whether someone has been up there recently?" Fiona asked.

"I wouldn't know what I was looking for. Shouldn't one of your officers come out and do that?"

Fiona looked around the empty room. Everyone was out following up on other enquiries. As Pat's neighbour, he should have been interviewed earlier. A derelict building overlooking the murder scene needed to be checked, especially as they hadn't received any sightings of Cavanagh, but she didn't want to send out forensics for such a longshot. Reluctantly, she asked, "Could you meet me there, in say, an hour?"

"I don't see why not, but I suggest you meet me at the bottom of the track, and we go up in my Landy. It gets muddy in places this time of the year, and the off-roaders make it worse. I had a good tidy-up of the barn in November, so I might be able to tell if someone has been using it."

With arrangements agreed with Sharpe, Fiona called Natalie to explain the situation and advise she accepted some additional protection for the next couple of days. After listening without comment, Natalie said, "What utter rot. I've told you already. I have my dogs, a pitchfork and a rifle. What more could I possibly need?"

Not doubting Natalie's willingness to defend herself, Fiona said, "As I'm sure you know, there are rules about levels of reasonable force when defending ourselves and ..."

"That explains everything that's wrong with the country, right there. An intruder can enter my house intending to steal or kill, and I'm not allowed to do anything about it. What am I supposed to do? Sit them down with a pot of tea to talk about their difficult childhood? People would think twice about breaking into other people's property if they thought there would be some personal risk. This country is full of criminals because they know they will receive no more than a slapped wrist. If they do eventually end up being detained, they use their time to obtain degrees and write best-selling memoirs. There again, I suppose properly dealing with the problem would put you out of a job."

Fiona had heard the argument too many times before to try to disagree with such an entrenched viewpoint. "Unless you want to be arrested and charged with assault or murder, your safety would be best left to us."

"I have animals depending on me. I can't go running away and hiding at the drop of a hat, so if you don't mind, I'll take my chances."

"How about we arrange for a couple of officers to stay with you?"

"I really don't like the sound of that. I enjoy my own company and want to relax on an evening, not entertain strangers."

"It's a large house, and they will keep out of your way."

"How about in the daytime? Are they going to trail around behind me when I see to my livestock?"

"They are trained professionals and will keep a discreet distance if that's your preference," Fiona said. "I strongly advise you to accept some protection until we catch your sister's murderer."

"I think it's totally unnecessary, but if you insist, would it be the two young ladies that visited the morning after my sister's murder? They were the least annoying officers I've had to entertain this week."

"They're not trained protection officers."

"Well, they're the only ones I'll accept."

"I will speak to them," Fiona replied, expecting Abbie and Rachel to refuse. It would be near impossible for Rachael because of her young children, even if Abbie could be persuaded. "Meanwhile, I will arrange for a patrol car to drive past regularly. If you see or hear anything that concerns you, can you call us before reaching for your pitchfork?"

"If I must," Natalie replied grumpily before ending the call.

Although it was cutting it fine to leave on time to meet Sharpe, Fiona called Abbie. Abbie agreed reluctantly to call in on Natalie and stay for one night. Along with a patrol car making regular checks, Fiona hoped it would be enough to keep Natalie safe. From herself as much as anyone else.

Unfortunately, by the time arrangements were made for Natalie's partial protection, it slipped Fiona's mind to call Stefan to cancel their meeting. Already running late to meet Sharpe, she hurried out of the station and dashed across the car park to her car. When she arrived at the start of the track, Sharpe was there, waiting for her.

Fiona estimated him to be in his seventies, far older than she imagined from his voice. Wrapped up in a frayed thick tweed coat and mud-splattered waterproof trousers, he leaned across to open his passenger door. Fiona grabbed her wellingtons from the boot of her car and hurried over. "Sorry. I hope you haven't been waiting too long."

"Time is never wasted. I've been watching a family of pig deer over there," Sharpe said, pointing to the brow of the hill.

Fiona looked but couldn't see anything. Sharpe's weather-beaten, lined skin broke into a toothless grin, and Fiona couldn't help noticing the alarming amount of hair sprouting from his ears. Climbing up into the cab, she mentioned his car registration couldn't be read and warned he could be pulled over and charged by traffic officers.

Sharpe patted the steering wheel. "Old Betty is only used around the farm, but thanks for your concern."

Fiona smiled weakly, knowing that probably meant the vehicle wasn't insured to be on the road. The truck's interior was covered in a thick layer of dust, and an overpowering smell of wet dog and manure hit her. As well as the awful smell, she felt hot breath on her neck from the assortment of dogs on the back seat. If she thought there was any chance of her car making the trip, she would have jumped out of the truck as quickly as she had jumped in.

Sharpe steered the truck erratically left to right to avoid deep tractor ruts as they slithered up the track. "I normally come up in the tractor during the winter months, but you being a lady and all, I thought this would be best."

"Thank you," Fiona said, as the truck nosedived into a water-filled rut with a thud, throwing her forwards and causing a spray of brown water to cover the windscreen. The wheels span before gaining traction and shooting them forward. "Is this the only access?"

"Aye, but that's the worst of the track done."

"Would it be easier to walk over the fields?"

"Aye, if you're happy to wade through mud or swim the river. Tis but a pretty trickle in the summer months, but this time of the year, it can get wild," Sharpe said. "A bridge would make sense, but Pat wouldn't hear of it. She didn't want the area disturbed. I'll wait a respectful time and ask that husband of hers."

"You had a dispute with Pat over access?" Fiona asked, wondering why Duncan hadn't mentioned it.

"Dispute? Nah. I asked and she said no. End of," Sharpe said. "I assume you want to see the old barn that overlooks Pat's place."

It was obvious there was no easy access, and Fiona was annoyed with herself for not checking first. "Sorry, no. I hadn't realised how inaccessible it was."

"Aye, I did wonder. I can't turn around until we reach the top. Nothing I can do to change that," Sharpe said, shaking his head. "It's a rum old business. She could be blunt, but she wasn't a bad lass, and nobody deserves that."

"How did you get along as neighbours?"

"Well enough. She didn't bother me, and I didn't bother her."

"Other than by refusing to put in a bridge," Fiona said.

"Like I said, it wasn't a big thing. If our paths crossed, we always had a chat, but I'm only up here in the summer months." Nodding out the window, Sharpe added, "You can see why I don't make it a regular trip for no good reason."

Fiona had to agree, but as she was stuck in the truck until they could turn around, she resigned herself to making the most of it. As a neighbour, he might have some other useful information. "What did you think of the way she managed her land? And the banning of the hunt?"

"It's her land, and she could do whatever she wanted with it. There's plenty who envied her being able to stick two fingers up to the hunt. Most of the land around here is rented out by the Estate with the express condition that the hunt is given access. They apply indirect pressure to the rest. Given the choice, a lot wouldn't have them churning up their fields. Whether they agree with it or not, the damage done to the land far outweighs any benefit."

"So, you agreed with Pat? We thought her views weren't popular locally. Her sister thought so."

"I wouldn't go that far, but even I can feel the tide's turning. With the cost of living and everything else, people are fed up with being taken for mugs by the rich. Problem is, lots around here are tied one way or another by the estate and the other toffs, so they can't speak their mind." The truck slid to a stop, and Sharpe cranked the hand brake. "Mind you, it's a lifeline for people like Natalie."

"How do you mean?"

"It's okay for the young 'uns. They'll always find a way to entertain themselves, but it's harder for older people. In towns, you get events and activities laid on. Around here, there's nothing, unless you can afford the inflated price of a pint in the fancy pubs. The hunt serves as a sort of social club for some on isolated farms. It's the only time they meet up with people, and keeping the horses fit gives them something to do the rest of the time." Pointing, Sharpe added, "That's the barn. As we're here, we may as well check it over. I should know if anyone has been in there since my last visit."

Fiona's wellingtons sank in the soft mud as the gusty wind whipped her hair across her face as she followed Sharpe to the back of the stone barn. As they neared, there was a short respite from the cold wind that stung her face before they made their way, head down into the wind along the side of the barn. When they reached the open front, they took a few steps inside. Pushing her hair from her face, Fiona took in the view. Beneath them, Field Barn and the surrounding fields looked like a child's playset in the bright winter sun as the blustery wind sent shadows skittering across the scene. The track that linked Field Barn to the village ran like a deep scar across the landscape. With binoculars, it would be possible to record the movements of everyone in the area.

Fiona sensed Sharpe moving around behind her. "Anything to suggest anyone has been up here?"

Examining the old bed of straw, Sharpe shook his head. Returning to Fiona's side, he looked down at the ground at the barn's entrance. "No footprints other than ours." He pulled a bunch of keys from his pocket, and added, "As we're here, I'll just check the storeroom."

Fiona watched as he moved to the rear of the barn, where a small section had been partitioned off with plyboard and unlocked the door. He shook his head as he returned. "I don't think anyone has been up here. Not even kids for a sneaky smoke, which makes a change."

Fiona held her hair back and stepped forwards to where the ground sloped relentlessly down to Pat's land. It was steep, but anyone relatively fit could walk the climb. She turned her head so the wind wouldn't carry her words away. "How about lower down?" She jumped at Sharpe's closeness to her.

Sharpe pointed and shouted back, "Some of the sheep prefer to shelter there, behind that rock. Shall we go down, and see?" Without waiting for a reply, he skipped nimbly down, his speed and agility defying his age.

Fiona carefully followed him down, stumbled as she approached the outcrop of rocks and fell into Sharpe's arms. Apologising, she quickly found her balance and stood back.

Sharpe gave a toothless grin. "Long time since I had an attractive woman in my arms."

Fiona put his lewd looks down to a generational thing. She was quite safe, alone, in the middle of nowhere, with a man of his age, even though she had just discovered he had an ongoing dispute with a recent murder victim. She pushed to the back of her mind how easily he had made the climb, jumping from level to level like a mountain goat. It was a by-product of the job viewing everyone as a possible murder suspect, but would he have killed to gain better access to his land? Wrinkling her nose at the aroma of body odour and manure, she couldn't imagine him cleaning up a murder scene, and she was quite sure some of his unique smell would have lingered. "Has anyone been down here recently?"

Sharpe shook his head, looking at the ground before taking in the view. "Reckon not."

Fiona pulled out her phone, and said, "Could I make a call before we head back?"

"You won't get a signal here."

Despite running several days a week, only Fiona was puffing when they reached Sharpe's truck at the top. Driving down the track, Fiona asked Sharpe more about the sisters.

"Pat seemed happy enough with her lot. I've never been too sure about Natalie. One thing I'll say for her, is she looked after her parents well. They were both as mad as a box of frogs by the end, but Natalie soldiered on. Wouldn't have them going into no care home."

"How recently did they pass?" Fiona asked, realising she didn't know.

"Her father went first, and that was when the farm was split up. The mother lingered a while." Sharpe scratched at his hairy ear. "She went about a year ago, give or take."

"Oh, I didn't realise it was so recent."

"Like I said, I reckon it was the hunt that kept Natalie sane through all those years, so you can see why she felt so betrayed when Pat turned all anti. But there's families for you. If you had asked me when they were girls, I would have said it would be the other way around. That Pat would have made sacrifices to care for their parents, not Natalie. Just goes to show you can never tell what people are made of until their backs are against the wall."

When Sharpe dropped Fiona back at her car, he said how much he had enjoyed their chat and asked if she was single. Fiona rolled her eyes as she waved him off without answering him. First, she called Humphries for an update. Next, she took a deep breath and called Stefan's number to tell him she was working late so couldn't meet him. Ignoring the butterflies in her stomach, she waited for a response only to be told the number was no longer available.

CHAPTER TWENTY-SIX

Fiona checked the number she had written down in her address book for Stefan as soon as she arrived home. Despite it being the same as the number she had already called, she tried it again. Predictably she received the same message. She leaned against the kitchen counter, looking at the ceiling. She was tired and hungry and didn't want to go out at all, let alone to meet Stefan, but a little voice in the back of her head reminded her of her manners. The scolding voice was that of her mother.

She pushed herself off the counter and crossed to the fridge. A quick peek inside told her there was nothing there she fancied. The overhead cupboards told her the same. She had done her last proper food shop in a must-eat-healthy mood and had failed to make any allowance for an emergency need for an unhealthy, sugary snack. Preferably chocolate based. Crunching on a celery stick wouldn't improve her mood in the same way.

She headed up to the shower with a sigh. Maybe telling Stefan face-to-face in a relaxed setting, once and for all, that they were definitely over wasn't such a bad thing. It might be uncomfortable, but in years to come, she would look back and see it as a turning point. The moment she moved on and made only good decisions for the rest of her life. As it was going to be such a momentous occasion, she would make sure she looked fantastic.

When she came out of the shower, it was blowing a gale outside, and hailstones rattled against the windowpane. It would be so much easier to be glamorous in a hot country.

Rather than look ridiculous, she opted for practicality and pulled on a pair of jeans and a chunky knit jumper. Applying the final touches to her makeup, she had the answers to all the questions except one. Why did she have butterflies at the thought of meeting Stefan?

Driving to the pub, she thought of all her disastrous relationships. There had only ever been two men who had proved themselves to be trustworthy and reliable. The first was her father, whose mind was rapidly fading. The second was Peter Hatherall. It was ironic that her friendship with Peter was one of the things she and Stefan had argued about when they were together.

She arrived early at the pub and headed for the bar, choosing a stool with a clear view of the entrance. Waiting for her drink, she took in the busy surroundings, while listening to the raucous laughter coming from a hen party. The bride was already two sheets to the wind in her mock wedding dress and pair of wings. A group of men at the corner of the bar found them entertaining and were egging them on. Most of the remaining tables were couples out for a quiet meal. In typical English fashion, they chose to tut occasionally or pretend they couldn't hear the shrill shrieks from the bride-to-be's table, rather than complain.

Her heart somersaulted and completed several backflips when Stefan walked through the door, looking impossibly handsome. Looking away, she spotted several girls watching him with interest to see who his lucky date would be. For fear her voice would give her emotions away, Fiona merely nodded to acknowledge his arrival. She used the time he took to order his drink to give herself a stern talking to and remember all the lies he had told her.

She was proud of how she held it together as they chatted at the table. They stayed on the safe ground of light topics, and she felt herself relax. She had forgotten what good company he was, with the power to turn hours into minutes. He could draw her into any conversation and make everything sound interesting, including her. More and more, she felt herself looking into his eyes as she fell under his spell despite all her intentions.

Slowly he edged the conversation to where he wanted it to be. "I understand why you felt betrayed by me. I promise you that it tore me apart as well, which is why I'm considering a new role. There's talk of a new task force being set up to look at overall patterns of crime, especially unexplained disappearances. I'm considering putting my name forward. If I did, would it make a difference? To us?"

Fiona felt her resolve to shout, 'There is no us,' disappearing in her confusion. She settled for, "I'm sorry. I'm not sure what you're suggesting," while her brain fought her rapidly beating heart.

"I'm saying we had something special, and I don't want to lose you. If I wasn't working undercover, could we try again?"

"I'm not sure," Fiona said, playing for time, trying to sort through her jumbled emotions as she was completely blindsided by Stefan's suggestion. She had never felt the way she felt about Stefan with anyone else. From the moment they met, she had felt drawn to him, like they were supposed to be. Was it cowardice that held her back? Wasn't this everything she had wished for?

Then the doubts started to crowd in. He turned all her thoughts upside down and inside out, making it impossible for her to think straight. That was dangerous enough. In a man able to live a lie, it was treacherous. Could he ever be trusted? What if he changed his career for her, and months down the line, his feelings changed? Would she be caught up in his web of deception with no escape?

Then another thought came crashing in. Was this the new task force Peter was talking about? Stefan would never work for Peter. She was sure of it. With relief and some disappointment, she realised the whole thing was academic.

"Well?" Stefan asked.

Fiona's heart melted. Stefan's face was full of hope. She couldn't deny her feelings for him, and here he was, prepared to put everything on the line for her, and yet... Finally, she said, "I ... Can I think about it?"

Stefan sat back in his chair; his disappointment was obvious. "Of course. Take your time."

"It's just you've taken me by surprise."

"You know how I feel about you."

Instead of answering, Fiona couldn't stop herself from asking, "Who was the brunette in your car? The other day outside the convenience store."

Stefan ran his hand through his shock of unruly black curls. "Iskra. My sister."

The name came like a kick to the stomach as it opened old wounds, bringing Fiona's hopes crashing back down to earth. "The one you said had been trafficked here as part of your cover story. You know, when you nearly had me in tears telling me how your family were devastated and that you would never stop searching for her."

Stefan threw up his hands and looked up to the ceiling. "You're never going to forgive me, are you? I had no choice. For your own safety, you had to believe that story. What else was I supposed to do?"

"I don't know," Fiona replied. Maybe if he hadn't gone into so much detail and been so convincing, it wouldn't be such an issue. The depth of his deception was his decision.

"So that's it? You can't see past that one thing," Stefan said.

"It's not that one thing as you call it. It's a question of trust. How could I ever trust you again."

"In a new role, I wouldn't be forced to lie to you."

"You were so convincing. I believed every word of it," Fiona said.

"Is that a no?"

"I need time to think about it."

"I guess that's something. Do you want another drink?"

"No. I should be going. I have a lot on tomorrow, but I'll think about it and call you." Rising from the table, Fiona added, "There's something you might want to bear in mind. I think

Peter Hatherall's name has been put forward to head up the task force you mentioned."

Also rising from his seat, Stefan muttered, "There are other positions I could apply for," before saying, "I'll see you to your car."

CHAPTER TWENTY-SEVEN

After a restless night's sleep, Fiona slumped at her kitchen table with a mug of coffee. Tired of dissecting the previous night's conversation and how she could have reacted differently, she scrolled through the news headlines on her phone. She stopped at a headline, spilling her coffee as her heart missed a beat. Reading it a second time in disbelief, she exclaimed, "Peter. What have you done?"

Video footage of hunt releasing foxes to a pack of bloodthirsty hounds.

She took a deep breath and slowly read the article, trying to convince herself it might not have been Peter who released a copy of Fred Lovell's video. It could have been any of the officers who worked on the case. Her denial became harder to maintain when she read the journalist's name at the bottom of the article. It was that creep, Charlie Dando. Was that why he asked her about Peter? He was looking for an endorsement, and she was the one who gave it.

It was early, but she wasn't too concerned about waking Peter. She drummed her fingers on her kitchen table, scrolling backwards and forwards through the article while she waited for him to answer his phone. His croaky voice confirmed he had been asleep, but she made no allowance as she blurted out, "What the hell have you done?"

"The article's live, I take it," Peter replied after a brief pause, sounding pleased with himself.

Still not believing he would throw his career away in such a cavalier way, Fiona asked, "Was it you? Did you give a copy of the video to Dando?"

"I did," Peter replied, sounding even more pleased with himself.

"Are you crazy? Once they find out it was you, that will be it. You'll be suspended and out of the door with nothing."

"I know."

"What do you mean, you know? Have you taken leave of your senses? What do you think will happen when you walk in this morning? There'll be a full investigation, and they'll discover it was you, and …."

"Calm down," Peter said, sounding infuriatingly calm. "There won't be an investigation. I left my letter of resignation on Dewhurst's desk last night."

"You what? Why? I get it's a horrid, cruel practice that should have been stopped years ago, but to throw everything away over it."

"I told you the other night about how fed up I am. My future with the force is being stuck behind a desk which would destroy me. Blame it on my age or Covid. I don't know. I want something more for the rest of my life."

"You could have simply resigned if you felt that way, and held on to all your benefits," Fiona said, struggling to understand what she was hearing.

"I would still have to live with myself. My entire career, I've watched these people getting away with all sorts of things. Think of it as me having the last laugh."

"Is it one you can afford?"

"I'm not sure I could afford not to do it," Peter said. "For my peace of mind, it was worth it."

Accepting she had no option other than to accept the situation, regardless of how stupid she thought Peter had been, Fiona asked, "What will you do?"

"Firstly, I'm taking a holiday. Then, who knows? I'm open to suggestions."

Seeing the time, and as she still had a job to go to, Fiona said, "If you're not doing anything tonight, do you want to meet up for a drink this evening?"

"On one condition. You don't sit there looking all concerned for my welfare. It was the right decision for me." There was the sound of a ping in the background, before Peter said, "Yes!"

"What?"

"The National Trust is stopping all hunt activities on their land, pending a full investigation."

Not knowing what else to say, Fiona said, "That's great. I'm pleased for you. See you tonight."

"Come to mine at about eight."

Fiona felt deflated after the call. It was so unexpected. Peter was a man of principle, but to throw his career away in such a flippant way was out of character. She took a sip of her rapidly cooling coffee. As the shock wore off, she realised her initial reaction had been selfish. While she wanted to forge an independent identity in the force, Peter was someone she'd always expected to be there. Even when they argued, she knew he would always have her back. The station would be a strange place without him, but it was his decision to make. Whether or not she thought it a stupid move, as a friend she should be there to support him.

It possibly went deeper than the initial shock and selfish reaction. Peter's action highlighted her cowardice. Her fears of rejection and change. It was stupid as things would change whether she wanted them to or not. It was fear of being hurt again that prevented her from admitting to the feelings she had for Stefan. He said last night that he was prepared to resign from a role he loved to be with her. And how did she react? By throwing his cover story about tracing his sister in his face, because she was too scared to risk her cold, little heart again. She had to make a clear decision like Peter had.

She thought she had her answer worked out when her phone pinged. It was Eddie confirming he had finally been assigned to her team and asking where he should start. She agreed to meet him at the station after her interview with Garland to brief him on the case.

Ending the call and going to get dressed, Fiona ran through in her head where they were with the investigation, realising there were still more questions than answers. They had no evidence to link Pat's murder, the arson attack on the Harding's home and Murphy's death, but she was sure they were. The only obvious connection was their proximity to Field Barn the evening Pat was killed. What did Harding and Murphy see that Pat's killer was so concerned about? It was too late to quiz Murphy, and Harding was adamant he hadn't seen anything of note when asked numerous times. And what about Natalie?

If it wasn't something they saw that day, what else connected them? Harding and Murphy were friends, and both drank in the Suffolk Arms. It was unlikely the connection was the appointment of Garland as the local rural officer. Harding knew nothing about it, and it was unlikely Murphy had either. A local rural officer was hardly a position of any great status or power. And where the hell was Harry Cavanagh?

Accepting she was going around in circles, getting nowhere, she called Abbie to check on Natalie. "Morning. Everything okay overnight?"

"All quiet. We've already seen to the horses, and we will be walking the dogs shortly. How much longer do you want me here?"

"She's made it clear she won't accept anyone else in her house, so a couple more nights at least."

"Really? She isn't the easiest person to babysit. She's sure she didn't see anything, and I've lost count of the times she's said she can protect herself. Having spent an evening with her, I don't doubt it," Abbie said. "She is meeting friends for lunch later today. Am I supposed to shadow them in the restaurant? Surely, she'll be safe somewhere like that. And what about my caseload? I still haven't found Cavanagh, and who's handling Murphy's death?"

Fiona was torn. While they had their differences, she was a good officer. Eddie was a useful addition, but he lacked Abbie's experience. Natalie was causing the problem by refusing to have fully trained protection, but if she pulled Abbie and something happened to her, it would be on her head. Her conversation with Sharpe had also strengthened the possibility of Natalie being a suspect. "Go home and take a break when Natalie meets up with her friends. Can you stay with her tonight, and then we'll reassess the situation tomorrow morning?"

"If I must."

"We've not considered Natalie as a serious suspect. After a conversation I had with a neighbouring farmer yesterday, that may have been a mistake. Could you have a general nose about?"

"Could do. Am I looking for anything in particular?"

"Not really. Has she said anything that has given you pause to think?"

"Everything's in my report, and I can't think of anything she's said or done that's made me even slightly suspicious," Abbie said. "She may be a little socially awkward, but she takes the idea of family commitments seriously. Did you see that Duncan came to the farm yesterday? He was returning Natalie's dishes, but he stayed and chatted a while."

"Interesting. Keep me updated on that," Fiona said. "The first time I spoke to Duncan, he referred to Natalie as the pretty one. There could be something there."

Fiona called Harding while she finished her coffee. He confirmed all was well, although his wife's nerves were getting the better of her. He again said when he saw Natalie on the track, she looked distracted and wasn't heading towards the house. Fiona wondered if she could have been playacting because she had known she had been spotted.

CHAPTER TWENTY-EIGHT

Humphries called as Fiona set off for Valley Farm to interview Rhianna Garland.

"Morning. Have I caught you before your meeting with Garland?"

"I'm on my way now."

"Good. You're going to want to hear this," Humphries said, sounding relieved. "We've finally received Pat's phone records. On the morning of her death, she tried to call Garland three times."

"The calls were never answered?" Fiona asked for clarification.

"It seems that way. One assumption being that Garland knew what she was calling about, so she didn't pick up."

"Or something as simple as her phone was switched off, but thanks Humphries. That's useful to know."

Fiona mulled over Pat's calls as she drove. If they weren't answered, they couldn't have arranged a meeting. Dando had hinted at some history between the women. It was possibly connected to fox hunting, or it could have been something completely different. Either way, she came back to the same problem. It was unlikely Pat would have rolled out the red carpet and gone searching for a quality bottle of wine if Garland was her unknown visitor. She doubted she would have been any keener if her sister had paid a surprise visit.

Fiona pulled off the narrow lane onto a long driveway leading up to Valley Farm. The property was more rugged and functional than Fiona expected. She was anticipating something far more twee with manicured lawns and perfectly arranged horse paddocks. The house was a perfect rectangle of grey stone perched on the ridge of a deep valley. A chalk dust drive led through a tumbled-down stone wall to a row of stone outbuildings, where Fiona spotted someone pushing a wheelbarrow. She parked her car and dodged puddles to retrieve her wellingtons from the boot, before walking to where the wheelbarrow had disappeared.

"Rhianna Garland?"

"Hi, you must be DI Williams?"

Muscular and hearty, Garland looked more Scandinavian than British, and the image of a Viking warrior sprang into Fiona's mind. Wearing no makeup and being wrapped in a baggy tweed overcoat and woollen hat, couldn't dampen her beauty or her healthy glow of vitality. She had a wide, open smile revealing perfect white teeth, and Fiona could see why she was popular. "Yes. Thank you for agreeing to see me."

"I'm done here," Garland said, propping the wheelbarrow up against the wall. "Would you prefer to come up to the house to talk?"

"That would be more comfortable," Fiona said. "Will we have somewhere private to talk?"

"Yes," Garland replied, leading the way back along the track to the farmhouse. "My parents have never thrown me out of the annexe. It's handy to have somewhere to shower and change, and it means I can leave all my smelly horse gear here." She waved to her mother at the kitchen window before ducking around the side of the house.

The annexe was a one-story, grey extension in keeping with the rest of the building. Inside, it was warm and brightly decorated, but tiny. Fiona made them both an instant coffee in the galley kitchen while Garland disappeared to change into clean clothes. There wasn't room for a table and chairs in the kitchen, so Fiona carried the cups to the living room to wait. It was small and cosy with practical, probably second-hand, mismatched furniture. Garland's love of horses was evident from the wall photographs, although Fiona noted none were of hunting scenes.

Garland reappeared with her hair up in a towel, wearing smart trousers and a pale blue blouse. She took a grateful sip of coffee before casting it to one side. "I assume you're here to talk about my dismissal as a rural officer and my decision to resign. I guess the correct procedure must be followed. I don't really know what the problem was. I only wanted to help and thought my knowledge would be beneficial." She picked up her coffee again, and added, "I expect I'll find something else worthwhile to do."

"You must have realised there would be a conflict of interest if you took up the rural affairs position."

"Not really, no. The position covers a range of local issues, not just trail hunting. While I sometimes follow the trails, I'm as concerned as the next person about obeying the law. I wouldn't have become a special constable if I thought otherwise."

The statements sounded rehearsed and wooden, and Fiona doubted they contained the whole truth. Knowing how easily Garland could lie with her big round eyes making her look a picture of innocence, was useful. "How well did you know Pat Thomas?" Fiona wasn't expecting the fleeting look of panic that crossed Garland's face. She'd clearly touched a nerve.

"It's absolutely dreadful about her death, but I didn't know her well," Garland said, her look of wide-eyed innocence returning.

"Did you speak to her after your appointment as the rural officer?"

"No," Garland replied, emphatically shaking her head.

"Her phone records show she called you three times on the morning of her death. Did you arrange to meet her?"

Garland jumped up, knocking her coffee mug. "No! What is this? I thought you were here to discuss the debacle of the rural officer position."

"No, I don't know where you got that idea. I'm investigating the murders of Pat Thomas and Brendon Murphy."

"Who? I don't know who you're talking about. I should call Daddy," Garland said, looking panic-stricken. "I would like you to leave now. I've work to do."

Fiona rose from her chair, and asked, "Before I go, can you tell me where you were on Thursday evening?"

"I don't know. When was that?"

"The evening Pat died."

"Seriously? This is harassment. I had nothing to do with that. Do I look like the type of person who goes around killing people I disagree with?"

"You disagreed with her?"

"I did, but so did lots of people. Why am I being singled out?"

"It's a simple question. Where were you?" Fiona asked, moving between Garland and the door into the kitchen to block her exit. "You can answer it here or down the station. The choice is yours."

"Not that it's any business of yours, I was in the office that day and then went to the theatre with a friend. We saw *My Fair Lady*." Garland pulled out her phone and pushed the screen up close to Fiona's face. "See. Here's my work diary, and here's the ticket confirmation."

Fiona studied the electronic ticket. "I'll need your friend's contact details."

"This is an invasion of privacy. You do know Daddy owns a law firm, don't you?"

"I still need the name and contact details for your friend."

"Sara Eirens," Garland said, scrolling through her phone. "Here's her number. Now please leave. If you want to speak to me again about this, I want legal representation."

"Thank you," Fiona said, closing her notebook once she had the number. "And where were you on Friday and Saturday night?"

"Why?"

"Just answer the question. Where were you?"

"On Friday, I had dinner with my parents, and I'm pretty sure I was having a night in on Saturday. I'll have to check."

"You do that and let me know. I'll see myself out, but we will need to speak again."

"Next time with proper warning, so I can talk to Daddy and

arrange legal representation."

'And what to say,' Fiona thought to herself.

CHAPTER TWENTY-NINE

Before starting her car, Fiona called the station and spoke to Eddie. "I'm on my way to the station now. While you're waiting, could you look up everything you can find on Rhianna Garland for me?"

"Is that the special constable people are gossiping about."

"Probably. I've just interviewed her about phone calls Pat made to her the day she was killed. I was expecting it to be routine, but to say she became very defensive would be an understatement," Fiona said. "While you're at it, could you take a quick look at her father and find out what law firm he works for?"

"Will do," Eddie said. "I think Andrew wants a word."

"Put him on."

"The huntsman who rode his horse at Pat has his leg in plaster following another riding accident and has been recuperating at his father's house in Essex for the last few weeks."

"Thanks, I'll be in soon," Fiona said. "Can you help Eddie look at the Garland family?"

While driving into the station, Fiona called her brother to see how the chat with their parents had gone.

"Better than expected, to be honest. They've agreed to look at a couple of places."

"That's brilliant, Richard. Do they need someone to drive them?"

"Emma offered, and they seemed happy to take her up on it. So, fingers crossed."

Fiona felt a mixture of relief she wouldn't be the one jollying them along as they visited residential care homes and guilt that her sister-in-law had made the offer. She had been a real daddy's girl when she was younger, and she would have a better idea of the type of places he would like, but as it seemed everything was agreed, she wasn't going to argue. She called Emma to thank her. Receiving no reply, she left a message saying she appreciated her help, and that she would be around to assist if needed.

Fiona then toyed with the idea of calling Stefan. Her excuse would be to tell him Peter was now unlikely to be involved in the new task force. But he probably already knew about Peter. Everyone probably did. She was pretty sure she had an answer for him, but she wanted one more night to sleep on it.

She put her phone away and concentrated on the drive back to the station. Rain was forecast for later, but currently, a bright blue sky masked the chill of the season and the cold winds that buffeted her car.

On her desk, she found the completed fire officer's report on the Harding's cottage. It confirmed what she had already been told. The fire had been started deliberately with traces of petrol found just inside the front door.

Eddie interrupted Fiona's reading, "Rhianna Garland is as clean as a whistle. She's never even received a speeding ticket, and her alibi for the evening Pat was killed checks out."

Fiona wasn't surprised by the clean record, but it didn't mean she was the perfect upstanding citizen. Chances are, if she had any run-ins with the law, Daddy would have sorted everything out for her. He probably coached her on how to reply to questions about the rural officer role, and she was now consulting him on what she should say about Pat. "Did you find anything on her father?"

"Nothing controversial there, either. He's a senior partner in a local firm that specialises in family law. He handles divorces and wills mostly," Eddie said. "And before you ask, the firm wasn't used by Pat's parents."

"Okay, thanks for that," Fiona said. "Andrew, did you find anything on the neighbouring farmer, Bradley Sharpe?"

"No, nothing," Andrew replied. "There's no record of a request for access, so he must have only asked Pat unofficially. I also reviewed previous statements, and no one mentioned a dispute or any ill feeling between him and Pat."

When Humphries walked in, Fiona asked him for the names of the constables he spoke to about Garland. "I think she knows something about Pat's death. I want to know more about her before I decide whether to bring her in for questioning."

"You don't think she killed her over something so petty as the rural officer role, do you? It's not even a paid role. It's purely voluntary," Humphries replied. "Doesn't she have a high-flying job in the city?"

"Me asking questions about Pat seriously rattled her. I want to know why," Fiona said. "What are you doing this morning?"

"I've arranged to see Murphy's neighbours. They weren't available yesterday, but it seems they might have seen something in the early hours of Sunday morning."

"Garland doesn't have an alibi for that night," Fiona said. "Take Eddie with you."

CHAPTER THIRTY

The constables Humphries mentioned, confirmed Garland was good fun and competent. They didn't know much else about her but told Fiona that the officer she was regularly partnered with was about to finish her shift. Fiona caught up with her as she was hurrying towards the staff exit. "Louise Woods? Can I have a word?"

Louise turned in surprise. She was a plain-looking girl with mousy hair and spectacles. "Is it important? My car is stuck in the garage, and I'm relying on buses. If I miss the one that leaves in ten minutes, I'll have to wait an hour for the next one."

"Where are you heading?"

"Just outside Sapperton. Who wants to know, anyway?"

"I'm DI Williams, and I need to ask you some questions about Rhianna Garland. I can give you a lift if you like, and we can talk in the car."

"Aren't you investigating that woman's murder? What on earth has it to do with Rhi? I know she's been suspended, but I thought it was over her not disclosing her hunt interests. Are you saying she was involved in the murder?" Louise's eyes, already magnified by her glasses, were the size of saucers.

Fiona sidestepped the question by replying, "She was at the theatre the night of the murder, but we understand the two were known to one another. I'm after background information. Do you think you could help me?"

"Sure, if you can drop me home," Louise replied. "Although I doubt, I can tell you much."

Crossing the car park, Fiona made small talk about why Louise chose to become a special and whether she enjoyed it.

"Yes, I do. More than I expected, to be honest," Louise enthused. "I'm thinking of applying for the police, proper."

"Excellent," Fiona said, unlocking the car. "We need good people." She started the engine, and asked, "Did you know Garland before she joined? I understand you were usually paired up."

"No," Louise said, chuckling. "I went to the local comprehensive and have never mixed in fancy circles. I only knew her through the station, but she was okay, really. She wasn't anywhere near as snobby as I feared. In fact, we used to laugh about how she was more careful with money than I am. If we were invited to an after-shift drink or were having a collection for some celebration or other, she always claimed to have forgotten her purse. I guess that's how rich people hold onto their money. Me, I'm a financial disaster. There's always too much month for my salary."

"I know the feeling," Fiona empathised as she turned the car onto the Sapperton road. Some people had moths in their wallets by nature, but she wondered if it was possible Garland had money worries. "What's your day job?"

"I'm a teaching assistant. The pay is rubbish. I enjoy helping the children, but it doesn't pay the bills. I could earn more working in a supermarket. Nothing exciting like Rhi. She's a buyer for a fashion chain in London, although post-Covid she mostly works from home."

"That sounds like a lucrative position."

"It sounds very glamorous, but it's a graduate position, so maybe it doesn't pay that well. I guess they don't give staff discounts as her clothes were from the same stores as I use. I noticed her handbag was a fake, which surprised me. I've seen them for sale in Birstall market."

"Was there anything else that suggested she might be short of money?"

"No, not really. I mean, she had all the important things. A fancy car and a couple of horses. I've never been to her home, but I bet it's somewhere fancy."

Fiona nodded, knowing Garland lived in a small hamlet a few miles from Tortworth, where the smallest of cottages sold for just shy of a million. That, along with the car and horses, could be a gift from *Daddy*. Cashflow being a possible problem was interesting. "Did she have hobbies other than horses?"

"No, it was horses this and horses that all the time. She was proud of her horses and their achievements, but she also knew a lot about racehorses. She understood all the terms and betting odds. It's all a mystery to me. I don't really agree with it. Well, not the Grand National, anyway. It's horrible when the horses fall over and they shoot them, don't you think?"

"I'm not a fan," Fiona said. "Presumably, if she talked about odds, she had a flutter every now and again?"

"She had an app on her phone. She was always checking it for the results."

Putting that snippet of information to one side, Fiona asked, "Did she talk about other aspects of her life? Her full-time work, friends, boyfriends?"

"Not really, no. She told me there was no one special in her life. I expect her social life was a whirlwind of posh cocktails and the like, and she didn't want to show off. She was always very down to earth."

"How was she generally? Was she ever moody or stressed?"

"No, not at all. She was always cheery and relaxed."

"One last question. Did she ever mention hunting or Pat Thomas?"

"No, never. I didn't even know she was involved in any of that. It's cruel and should be totally banned." Louise chewed her nails. "If I apply for the force, do you think I could end up with you? Solving murders?"

"Maybe. There are lots of different roles that might interest you. Thanks for your help, and good luck if you decide to apply."

"Oh, I will. Definitely."

"Where do you want dropping off?"

"Just over there will be fine."

Fiona smiled until her jaw ached as Louise enthusiastically

waved her off. Once she had turned the corner, she pulled over to make some calls. First, she rang Rachel. "Hi, I've just had a very interesting chat about Garland. She might have a gambling problem. Serious debts could have made her vulnerable and easy to manipulate. Could you take her photograph around the local bookies? See if anyone recognises her."

"I can't see her sipping out of a plastic cup in any of them for social reasons, and most bets are made online these days, but I'm not following you. Are you saying she was somehow coerced into killing Pat to clear her gambling debts?"

"Possibly, maybe. Her reasons for becoming a special didn't ring true to me, and her reaction to me asking a few routine questions was excessive. Something is off about her, but we don't have reasonable grounds to access her accounts, so we need to be more creative with our digging around. Someone might recognise her from race meets."

"Okay, I'll give it a go. Anything else?"

"Yes. See if you can talk to a few of her friends."

Next, Fiona rang Natalie to ask if she knew of any history between her sister and Garland. When she answered the phone, it was clear she was in a public place from the background chatter.

"Oh, what now? I've just gotten rid of one of you lot." Natalie snapped, before turning the phone to her friends chatting in the background. "Can you hear that? I'm in a public place surrounded by friends and quite safe."

A slurred voice asked, "Is that a police detective, Natalie?" When Natalie confirmed it was, her lunch companion said, "Shame on you, sending doctored video evidence to the press. That's what it is. Those evil antis with their clever tricks hounding law-abiding people. The truth will come out in the end."

Fiona hoped there was no truth in that, for Peter's sake. Natalie's voice returned on the phone. "Did you want something in particular, or are you calling just to interrupt my lunch?"

"Did your sister know Rhianna Garland?"

"How should I know? I thought I had already explained we didn't move in the same circles."

"Does the name mean anything to you?"

"I remember her as a child. Now, if you've no more questions, I would like to return to my meal."

Finally, Fiona called Tina, Pat's friend. "Do you know if Pat had any previous history with Rhianna Garland?"

"The so-called rural officer? I'm not sure. She didn't say anything but ... I do remember Pat saying she was always a sneaky little madam. I suppose that means they must have known each other previously. Sorry, I can't help you any more than that, but it might be worth calling my mum."

"Your mum?"

"She keeps up on all the gossip much more than I do. She meets up with several women in the village for a dog walk every Monday."

"By village, do you mean Willbury?"

"Yes. She lived there all her married life and has kept in contact with some of her old neighbours. Only she won't be at home today. She's on a day out to Bletchley Park with her book club. She'll be back later this evening."

CHAPTER THIRTY-ONE

Fiona chewed on a pen as she looked out the window. It was a grey, miserable day, and cars and shops were turning their lights on early. Nothing was more depressing and drearier than a damp, cold February afternoon, and she hoped they would have an early spring. Everyone needed a lift. On days like this, she thought about packing it all in and disappearing somewhere warm to live, and she doubted she was the only one.

Her head hurt trying to work out who killed Pat and why. She was convinced the same person killed Murphy and targeted the Hardings' house because they thought they had been seen. So why not Natalie, who was also nearby? Was their presence at the farm keeping them away? Neither the patrol car nor Abbie had seen anything suspicious. And where did Garland fit into it all?

She turned back to the empty office. This would be a good time to call Stefan. Until she made the call, she was never going to fully concentrate.

"Sorry, I didn't get anywhere with the local bookies," Rachel said, walking in and throwing her coat on a desk. "That wind's freezing. It cuts right through you. It feels more like December than the end of February."

"Anything from Garland's friends?"

"They hadn't seen much of her recently. Whenever they've arranged to meet up, she has dropped out at the last minute with an excuse. Everything from work commitments or illness to the deaths of family members they'd never heard of. They're starting to think she's become a recluse or doesn't like them anymore."

"Or she can't afford to socialise with them," Fiona said, moving away from the window. "We need to see Garland again to ask her about her finances. She's unlikely to admit to any problems with her father present, but seeing how she reacts will be interesting."

"Why doesn't she ask her parents for help?"

"Maybe she has in the past, and their patience has run out? Or possibly pride? If she hides her money problems because she finds the situation embarrassing, it makes her more vulnerable to manipulation. Two people have said Pat was incandescent with rage about Garland's appointment the morning of her murder, yet we found nothing at her house to verify it. Somebody has removed any reference to Garland's appointment from the house to protect her. Garland has an alibi, so that leaves the person who was manipulating her. I can't think who else would benefit from her taking that role other than a hunt member."

"Are you going to re-question her?"

"Eventually," Fiona said. "I'll give her a little time to chew over this morning's conversation. Do you want to come with me to see Duncan first?"

Fiona was surprised to see Natalie leaving Duncan's business as they approached. "Hello. I thought you were having lunch with friends?"

"I was passing on my way home, so I popped in to see if Duncan needed anything."

"And did he?"

"Apparently not," Natalie replied. "Don't let me hold you up."

When Fiona and Rachael entered, Duncan looked up from his desk in surprise, "Have you some news for me? Do you know who killed my wife?"

"Not yet, but we are getting closer," Fiona replied. "We would like to go over a couple of things with you."

"I'm very busy, as you can see," Duncan said, waving his hand over the files on his desk. "I've already had several interruptions today, and I'm not sure I can add anything to what I've already said."

"Would that be by Natalie?" When Duncan grimaced, Fiona said, "We won't take up too much of your time. What were the other interruptions?"

"The neighbouring farmer dropped by to ask about some bridge. I told him to go away as I was busy."

"Have you heard from Harry Cavanagh since we last spoke?"

"No, why should I have done?" Duncan asked sharply. "I don't expect to ever hear from him again."

"I wondered if he would get in contact to pass on his condolences if he heard about Pat," Fiona asked, concerned by Duncan's certainty.

"Well, he hasn't."

"When you drove to your house the evening of the murder, you said the only unusual thing you noticed was that the dogs were outside. Now you've had time to think about it, are you sure there wasn't anything else?"

"No, everything was as I expected to find it. Apart from Pat being at the foot of the steps," Duncan replied.

"Do you remember how many vehicles you passed on your drive home, and did you recognise any of them?"

"No, the road was quiet as usual. I passed a few cars travelling in the opposite direction, but it was dark, and I only saw headlights."

"Did Pat ever talk to you about Rhianna Garland?"

Duncan shook his head. "The name doesn't ring any bells."

"She didn't express anger the evening before or that morning about her appointment as a rural officer."

"Oh, now you mention it, she was complaining about something like that. I'm afraid I tended to zone out whenever she had one of her rants. Once she had the bit between her teeth there was no stopping her."

"When was this? The evening before or that morning?"

"In the morning, over breakfast. As I said, I wasn't really listening. I was more focused on the day ahead than her little issues."

Fiona bristled at the little issues. Maybe their marriage was nowhere near as contented as he had claimed if that was how he regarded her concerns.

As if reading her mind, Duncan said, "I know it was important to her, but to me, it was an irrelevancy. There are far more important things to worry about."

"Had you heard the name before?" Rachael asked.

"Sorry, what name?"

"Rhianna Garland," Rachael repeated.

"No, I don't think so."

"You don't think so," Fiona said. "Did you know the woman or not?"

"Or not," Duncan replied. "I have no idea who the woman is. Pat would throw out all sorts of names when ranting. If she had mentioned the name before, it hadn't registered with me."

"I noticed Pat had a small writing desk in one of the rooms. Did she always leave it neat and tidy and clear of paperwork?" Fiona asked.

"Yes, she was very particular about things like that. She hated it if I spread paperwork over the table. She said it made the place look untidy and ruined the ambience."

"What else did you argue about?" Fiona asked, registering Duncan's sarcasm.

"Nothing. We were happily married and didn't argue," Duncan said.

"Not about her affairs?"

"She didn't have affairs."

"What did she have with Harry Cavanagh, then?" Fiona asked.

"A mere dalliance," Duncan said, batting the subject away like an annoying fly, and became suddenly engrossed with the paperwork on his desk.

"How were you when you found out about the affair?" Fiona asked. "Jealous? Angry?"

"It wasn't an affair and certainly not anything to get upset about. I asked her to stop seeing him, and she did," Duncan said.

"Are we finished here? I have work to do."

Fiona was about to say something more, but settled for, "For now."

In the car, she asked Rachael what she thought of Duncan.

"He seems to have gotten over the death of his wife quickly," Rachael said. "It was only four days ago, and he was more concerned with keeping on top of his work."

"It could be his way of coping," Fiona said.

"He's the first man I've met who thought an affair was nothing to get excited about. That didn't ring true."

"How about his vague recollection of Garland's name?"

"That I could believe. My husband doesn't hear half of what I say in the mornings. I generally ring him later in the day to check he has remembered what we agreed," Rachael said. "Although I admit, with the three girls now at school, it's a bit manic at breakfast time, and sometimes I have to shout to be heard."

CHAPTER THIRTY-TWO

Garland wasn't answering her phone, but as her employers confirmed she was working from home, they drove to the address they had for her. Fiona and Rachael pulled up outside a pretty, terraced cottage on the outskirts of the picture postcard village of Tortworth, noting Garland's car wasn't there.

"Could be in the garage," Rachael said, climbing out of the car and looking up at the honey-coloured stonework. "Funny how these old farmworkers' cottages are so desirable now. Often, no major work was carried out on them when they were tenanted, so they have all their old features. It's a crying shame that only Londoners can afford them, and the first thing they do is rip everything out to put in a modern kitchen. If I got my hands on one of them, I would keep it as it should be."

"Not you as well," Fiona said. "Humphries has taken to viewing every house we visit as a potential new home."

"Sorry, with the girls growing by the hour, we're bursting at the seams and are looking for somewhere bigger."

Fiona walked past Rachael to knock on the front door. Receiving no reply, she stepped across to peer into the front bay window while pulling out her phone to call Garland's parents.

Rachael gave a last longing look at the front of the cottage before opening the side gate and wandering to the back garden. She returned to the front. "No sign that she's in, but it has a lovely garden."

Ending her call, Fiona said, "Her parents haven't seen her since this morning. They assumed she was here working, but she occasionally takes her laptop to a local cafe to work."

"Do we know which one?"

Fiona's phone rang before she could reply, and Rachael took the opportunity to have a good look through the front window.

"Come on. She's not here. We're heading back to the station," Fiona said, returning to the car.

Fastening her seatbelt, Rachael asked, "What's happening?"

As she pulled out, Fiona said, "Two things. That was Humphries. A neighbour saw someone jogging away from Murphy's house the night he was killed. They thought the person who slipped out from behind the garage dressed in black was acting suspiciously. They nearly went over to check on him but thought better of it."

"I bet they wish they had, now."

Fiona nodded. "Anyway, they watched the stranger until they disappeared into the night. They couldn't identify any features, but they think it was either a teenager or a slight woman."

"Are you thinking it was Garland?"

"She has no alibi for that night. She says she was home alone," Fiona said. "But she has a confirmed alibi for the time of Pat's death, and her parents swear she was with them the night of the fire."

"Are you now saying there were two murderers?" Rachael asked.

"I'm wondering if Pat's killer used what they took from the house to manipulate Garland into killing Murphy. If so, she's possibly on the run and petrified. We need to find her and bring her in," Fiona said.

"Okay, but that doesn't explain why we are rushing back to the station?"

"Because Harry Cavanagh has walked into the station wanting to know what all the fuss is about. He's waiting in an interview room. When we return to the station, can you write up our conversation with Duncan and our aborted visit to Garland's home?"

CHAPTER THIRTY-THREE

Fiona and Humphries found Cavanagh waiting patiently in an interview room. His shirt sleeves were rolled up, giving the impression he was ready to do business while showing off his muscular arms. His dark eyes, broken nose and slightly overlapping front teeth somehow combined with his strong jaw to make him look appealing, especially when he smiled. He jumped out of his chair and offered his hand to shake as soon as they walked in.

Ignoring the outstretched hand, Fiona said, "Please take a seat."

Over the scratching of chair legs across the floor, Cavanagh said, "I've only just heard about Pat. It's come as quite a shock. Do you know if Duncan has finalised the funeral arrangements yet? Obviously, I want to pay my respects."

"Can we start with where you've been the last few days," Fiona said. "Didn't you see the requests we've made for you to come forward?"

"Duh. I came in as soon as I saw them," Cavanagh said, pulling a face. Reading Fiona's unimpressed expression, he bowed his head like a naughty schoolboy, and said, "Sorry. I've been off the grid the last couple of days. I visited a friend of mine in Birstall. His wife has just left him, and he's gutted. Getting blind drunk wasn't fixing it, so we headed off fishing for a few days. He has a small fishing hut in a tucked-away spot. We stayed there by the river and checked out of everything else."

"And your friend will confirm this?"

"Sure, he will. He's waiting outside to drive me home."

Fiona nodded to Humphries to go and talk to the friend, before asking Cavanagh, "Fan of the great outdoors?"

"Not really, to be honest. But Bob is a good friend. It's what you do, isn't it? Be there when someone needs you."

"Could anyone else verify where you've been? I'm especially interested in last Thursday, Friday and Saturday."

"That's three dates? When was Pat killed?"

"Thursday evening. Let's start there, shall we?"

Cavanagh creased his brow in thought, smiled and said, "Yes. That was the evening we were thrown out of the Duke on King Street. I'm sure the landlord will remember us. Bob got into a fight with a guy wearing a wedding dress. He had a beard."

"Thanks for that image," Fiona said dryly. "And earlier in the evening?"

"We started drinking in town at lunchtime. I'll give you a list of the pubs I remember we visited earlier on. Later, it all becomes a bit blurred, but some of the landlords should recognise us."

"Thank you, that would be helpful," Fiona said, knowing that central Birstall was heavily covered with cameras, so they should be able to track his movements during the relevant times. "What did you do afterwards?"

"I don't remember how we got home, but we did," Cavanagh said. "Once we sobered up in the morning, well, the afternoon if I'm honest, we decided to go fishing. From then on until this morning, we were in the middle of nowhere."

"Can anyone apart from your friend confirm that?"

"There was an old guy who walked his dog along the river every morning and evening. He might remember us as I waved to him a few times."

"Okay, when was the last time you saw Pat?"

"Now you're asking," Cavanagh said, stroking his chin. "I reckon that would be getting on for four weeks ago."

"And you were having an affair?"

"We hooked up occasionally, but it was nothing serious."

"Have you ever been out to Field Barn?"

"No, never. I wouldn't go to their house. What sort of man do you take me for?"

"Someone who had an affair with his boss's wife," Fiona replied.

"Okay, not my finest moment, but it really wasn't anything like that. We got along, and once or twice, one thing led to another, like it does," Cavanagh said. "She was a passionate woman, and probably more than Duncan could handle."

"Were you angry Duncan found out and sacked you? Did you ever think Pat must have said something?"

"What? No. Nothing like that happened," Cavanagh said, laughing at the suggestion. "I'm a very take-it-or-leave-it guy. The work with Duncan was steady, but I didn't rely on it, and I was getting itchy feet, anyway. Me and Bob are talking about getting a pub together. Somewhere out of the way. Nice little village pub by a fishing stream, maybe."

"Are you saying Duncan didn't sack you?"

"Over this so-called affair?" Cavanagh asked, laughing. "He probably knew about it from the start. No, we argued, but it was more of a mutual decision to go our separate ways."

"What did you argue about?"

"With Duncan?" Cavanagh asked.

"Yes," Fiona said. "Stop trying to waste time while you make something up."

"I'm not. I'm just amused by your assumption and wondering whether the real reason could be relevant."

They were interrupted by Humphries returning to the room. "Bob confirms they've been together. They were involved in a skirmish in town the night of Pat's murder. I've called the landlord, and he remembers it. He's sending over security footage of the event. He said that it's rather humorous."

"Okay, we can check that later, along with footage of earlier in the evening," Fiona said. Returning her focus to Cavanagh, she said, "We'll decide whether it's relevant."

"Okay. I happened to mention I saw him with a certain lady who lives out Brierley way. When I mentioned it, more in jest if I'm honest, it seriously rattled him. He aggressively denied it, and thinking back, he looked relieved when I said I was getting out and not coming back."

"The name of this woman, and where we can find her?"

"Angela Olive. She's the manager of the Kendleshire Golf Club," Cavanagh said. "She's not bad looking. I think she'll prove too feisty for him."

"And you saw them together, how?"

"I was playing a round of golf with a potential client. I don't usually play, and I was being hammered. I was off in the rough looking for yet another lost ball, and that's when I saw them *getting friendly* in her car."

Making a note of the name, Fiona asked. "Can you think of anyone who would want to harm Pat?"

"Some of the toffs who like their hunting. I've never thought of it as an issue. Live and let live is my motto, but Pat had a serious beef about it. She probably wasn't keen on fishing either, but there you go."

"Anyone in particular?"

Cavanagh shrugged in reply. "I'm not sure any of those chinless wonders would really have it in them. Galloping around the countryside on horses isn't the same as murder, is it."

"Some would say it is," Humphries said.

"Nobody springs to mind. Will that do?"

"Have you ever heard the name Rhianna Garland?" Fiona asked.

"Garland. Garland. That does ring a bell. Something to do with horses. We were out having a drink, and we bumped into her. A very attractive girl. I remember it was a frosty encounter, and it was caused by something to do with a horse," Cavanagh said. "Wait a minute. Yes, her horses. What was it? Ah, that's it. One of her horses died, and she blamed Pat and her sister. I think that was what it was."

"How long ago was this?"

Cavanagh gave another little smile and a shrug. "I don't know. Not recent. I think it happened a while back, but there was still a grudge there."

"How about the farmer who keeps sheep on the land above Field Barn? Did Pat ever mention him and access to her land?"

Cavanagh shook his head. "Don't think so."

"And Brendon Murphy?"

"Never heard of him."

"Thanks for coming in, Mr Cavanagh. You're free to go, but can you leave your contact details and let us know if you're likely to be leaving the area."

"Of course. I'm happy to help."

After seeing Cavanagh out, Fiona returned upstairs to update everyone on the new development. Duncan possibly having an affair was unexpected. She was going to visit Angela Olive as soon as the meeting finished. The family dispute with Garland was interesting. She couldn't recall explicitly asking Natalie if she knew the name, but she could have mentioned there had been a past incident when she asked if Pat knew her. She asked Rachael to find out what she could about Olive, leaving Andrew and Eddie to focus on finding Garland.

Before the meeting ended, the city centre footage of the night of Pat's murder arrived, and they gathered around Humphries as he scrolled through it. He quickly found the pub brawl, which showed a portly, dark-haired man rolling around on the floor with another man in a wedding dress with wings. Cavanagh looking worse for wear, was staggering around in the background holding two beer glasses. Humphries sped back through the tape and found a date-stamped grainy picture of Cavanagh drinking beer on a pub bench at the time of Pat's murder.

CHAPTER THIRTY-FOUR

The long driveway off a narrow country lane was the only vehicular access to the Kendleshire Golf Club, but there were numerous access points for someone on foot, including a public footpath. Fiona planned to wait a short while in a convenient layby to see if Olive sped off somewhere after the interview. In the car park, she spotted a small electric car parked in the spot reserved for the manager and parked her car a distance away in the corner.

After some initial reluctance, Fiona was told Miss Olive would see her in half an hour, so she wandered into the bar to wait. Floor-to-ceiling glass windows along the back wall overlooked the patio and the course beyond. Other than the light spilling from the smoking hut on the patio, outside was all in darkness. Fiona sat at the bar, keeping an eye on the reception area. A bored-looking teenager poured her a drink before returning to a stool to examine her phone.

"Is it always this quiet?" Fiona asked.

"It can be at this time of the year, yeah," the girl said without looking up.

"Different in the summer, though?"

"Yeah. Or on member's birthdays," the girl said, finally looking up to consider Fiona. "There are lots of other functions which can get quite lively. Are you thinking of joining?"

"Possibly. I'm here to see Angela Olive. Is she an okay boss?"

"I guess. She lets us get on with things and doesn't involve herself much." Finally putting her phone away, she added,

"Rumour has it she's off to pastures anew, though. Not that it makes any difference to me. I'm hoping to go to university in the summer."

"Any idea where she's going?"

"No. All I heard was that she had some rich fella, and they're going to take off together."

"Did you catch a name?"

"Nah. It's probably not true, anyway. Someone made it up to alleviate the boredom."

They were disturbed by the clacking of the receptionist's heels. "Jenny, can you wipe the tables down? Miss Olive said you may as well close the bar as it's so quiet."

"Will I still get paid for the shift?"

"Sort it out with her tomorrow." Turning to Fiona, she said, "Miss Olive will see you now."

Olive was a petite brunette in a smart, fitted black skirt and crisp white open-necked blouse with a silk scarf around her neck to hide any tell-tale signs of ageing. She looked at least a decade younger than the fifty-five years old Fiona knew her to be. Although slight, she looked toned and well-muscled.

Once the introductions were out of the way and they were seated, Fiona came straight out and asked, "How well do you know Duncan Thomas?"

Olive poured herself a glass of water before replying, "Sorry, who?"

"Duncan Thomas."

Olive shook her head. "Sorry. I don't know him. Is he a member here? I can't be expected to know everyone personally."

"No, he's an architect living in Willbury. His wife was murdered recently. You may have read about it."

"Do you know, I'm so busy I rarely catch up on the local news," Olive said, her expression guarded, giving nothing away. "I'm afraid I'm still none the wiser as to why you're here."

Looking at Olive's wrists, Fiona said, "You've some nasty scratches there."

Dismissively, Olive said, "I went into battle with my rose

bushes last weekend."

"Does the club have security cameras?"

"Of course," Olive said, putting down her glass. "Why?"

"We may have to ask to see them."

Olive's jaw briefly twitched, before she said, "Surely you would need a warrant."

"That won't be a problem in a murder enquiry," Fiona said with more confidence than she had. "So, how do you know Duncan Thomas?"

"I'm not sure I do."

"That's strange because we have a witness who saw you together in your car here, out on the course."

Recovering some of her earlier confidence, Olive said, "Your witness must be mistaken. I don't even recognise the name. Do you have a photograph?" After being shown a picture of Duncan, she shook her head. "Sorry. I don't know him."

"Where were you last Thursday evening?"

"I would need to check my diary, but probably here."

"And Friday and Saturday night?"

"Same answer. We had several functions last weekend and were busy. Sorry, I can't help you."

"Can you come to the station to make a statement to confirm that, once you've checked your diary to be sure?"

"Now? Have you seen the time?" Olive asked. "I have tickets to a dinner dance at The Grange Hotel, and I can't add anything more to what I've already told you."

"First thing tomorrow morning. If you don't arrive, we'll issue a warrant for your arrest."

Olive stood and said, "That seems rather excessive, but as you wish. I've some work to finish off before I leave. Do you think you could find your own way out?"

Fiona nodded her agreement. "I look forward to seeing you tomorrow."

Outside, the temperature had dropped dramatically, and a frost was forming on car windscreens. Huddled in her coat, Fiona returned to her car and adjusted the seat and wing mirrors before slowly driving out along the drive. She pulled over into the layby on the lane and settled down to watch the golf club entrance, cursing how long the car heater was taking to get up to speed. Ten minutes later, just as the car was warming up, Olive pulled out and sped away through the lanes. Disappointingly, she drove straight to her flat and disappeared inside. While Fiona waited for her to reappear, she called the station for an update. It worried her that Garland still hadn't been found and no one had heard from her. A short while later, a taxi turned up. Fiona followed it to The Grange Hotel before setting off to meet Peter.

She didn't have time to go home first, so she stopped on her way to buy a bottle of wine. Clutching the bottle of red and a torch, Fiona carefully made her way along Peter's front path. She'd been caught out before by the lack of any lighting in the area. Peter answered the door in jeans and a faded sweatshirt, spilling light onto the frosty grass.

Handing over the bottle, Fiona asked, "Any thoughts on where you want to go?"

Peter opened the door wider. "Come in. I've cooked for us. I promise not to poison you." He read the bottle label, and said, "This will do perfectly."

Peter had gone to the trouble of laying up a table in his dining room. An open hearth with original bread ovens dominated the cosy, quirky room. The vegetable chilli Peter brought out was surprisingly good, and she wondered if Nicole had given him lessons in the kitchen.

Peter's mood was erratic over dinner. At times, he was animated with eyes a little too bright, but at others, he was reserved and reflective. Every so often, he became distant and lost in his own thoughts, leaving Fiona to babble away to herself. Fiona restricted herself to neutral topics of conversation, interspersed by long silences while she thought up the next safe subject. It felt alien to the light banter they had exchanged in the past.

When they finished eating and moved to the front room, Fiona decided to stop avoiding the subject of Peter's resignation. "How did Dewhurst take things?"

"I have the pleasure of his company to look forward to tomorrow. He's *pencilled me in* for mid-morning," Peter said, rolling his eyes, before taking a seat. "I can't wait."

Fiona sat in the armchair by the window with her feet tucked under her. "Oh? I'm surprised he wasn't waiting at the entrance for you this morning."

"Luckily for me, he had to be elsewhere today. A last-minute emergency, apparently. I was able to quietly clean out my desk without any fanfare."

"No regrets?"

"None whatsoever," Peter replied too quickly, before standing. "I'll grab another bottle of wine."

"Not for me," Fiona said, placing a hand over her glass. "I'm driving."

Looking disappointed, Peter said, "You can stay over. The spare room is made up. I've something for you."

"Another time, I'll take you up on the offer, but I have a busy day tomorrow. I need to be in early," Fiona said, feeling awkward about raising the subject of going to work. "You know how it is. No rest for the wicked," she said, trying to make light of it but digging a deeper hole. "I'm not stopping you from drinking more," she added lamely.

"As if you could. I'll go and grab the bottle." Returning, Peter asked, "Are you sure?" before filling his glass.

"Sure, I'm sure."

Fiona took a deep breath before lurching into the unspoken subject that had hung between them all evening. "I didn't realise you cared so much about fox hunting."

Peter swilled the wine around his glass before replying, "I'm not sure I do. It's the principle. I've dedicated my whole life to enforcing the law. I've been a fool. It's all a sham. The law only exists to protect the wealthy and their interests, and I've been used to enforce it."

"That's not entirely true," Fiona started to argue.

Peter raised a hand for her to stop. "You're wasting your time. I'm too disillusioned to continue. At least this way, I might take some of them down with me. But let's talk about something else." After taking a sip of wine, Peter put his glass to one side and fumbled in his back pocket. "I've something for you," he said hesitantly, before holding aloft a small jewellery box.

Fiona nearly choked. A long time ago, they had flirted with one another and in the past, she had felt attracted to him. But that was years ago. There had been so much water under the bridge from the few times they had come close to taking their friendship further. What was he thinking? Was he having some sort of breakdown? That would explain his rash decision to leak the video footage and some of his earlier comments.

"It's just a little something to express how much I've appreciated working with you. We've always worked well together, but you've become more than a work colleague to me over the years." Blushing, Peter leaned forward, holding out the box. "Anyway, I bought you this."

Fiona took the box and stared at it in her hand, still shocked and confused.

"Well? Aren't you going to open it?"

"Umm … Yes, of course," Fiona said, nodding like a crazed dog. On top of everything else, she wasn't ready to deal with this. She wondered if she should call someone, but who and what would she say?

"Go on, then," Peter urged.

Trying to disguise her shaky hands, Fiona lifted the lid. She hoped the relief on her face wasn't too obvious. Inside was a beautifully carved Saint Christopher on a chain. She turned it over to see her name engraved on the reverse side. A lump formed in her throat, as she said, "Thank you. It's gorgeous. But I don't understand."

"Put it on, and it'll protect you on your drive home. Your driving has never been the best," Peter joked.

Fixing it around her neck, Fiona again said, "Thank you, but I don't know what I've done to deserve this."

Leaning back in his chair and picking up his wine glass, Peter said, "I wanted to mark our time working together. Give you something to remember me by. Now I'm done with the soppy stuff, are you sure you don't want to change your mind and have another drink?"

"It's tempting, but I really do need to get home. A rain check for another day? When I'm not in the middle of a murder investigation."

"You're on," Peter said, toasting it with his glass. "How's it going? I heard the ex-boyfriend turned up at the station."

Wondering where Peter got his information from, Fiona nodded. "He did."

"What did you make of him?"

Finishing the last of the glass of wine that she had been nursing all evening, Fiona said, "Sorry. I can't talk about an active case."

"I get it. Not with a civilian."

"I didn't mean … It's all up in the air, busily going nowhere. Every day I seem further from discovering what happened. I can't seem to get a handle on it. It's like walking through treacle."

"Do you remember our first case together? You said you couldn't understand Tim Potter's attitude to the death of a young girl, and I said I hope you never do?"

Fiona thought back to the evening spent in a pub garden with Peter and his family and how much younger and happier he was then. "Yes. Why do you ask?"

"And do you understand, now?"

"Not really, no."

"Good. Never lose your humanity, Fiona." After an audible sigh, Peter said, "Jealousy! That's what will be at the centre of it."

"Sorry?" Fiona noticed Peter slurred his words, and his eyes weren't entirely focused. She hadn't seen him drinking that much during the meal, but he might have started drinking before she arrived.

"Envy is the driver," Peter continued. "It's the heartbeat of evil. Wanting what someone else has. Oh, it can be dressed up as revenge or financial gain, or even love. But it all stems from the cancer of jealousy."

Fiona had never heard Peter sound so bitter, and she wondered whether he was thinking about his ex-wife Sally, Nicole or Pat's murder. Firmly putting her glass on the small side table, she said, "Thank you for a lovely evening, but I think we both need a decent night's sleep. But we'll meet up together soon."

"I get the hint. Do you want me to show you to your car?"

Fiona pulled out the torch from her back pocket. "This time, I've come prepared. You stay here in the warm." Fingering the Saint Christopher as she stood, she said, "Thank you again for this. It's lovely."

"No, thank you."

Unclear what she was being thanked for, Fiona made her final goodbyes and slipped out of the room. A brutally cold wind sent shivers through her as she stepped outside the house. Wrapping her coat around herself, she hurried to the car. Reversing out of Peter's driveway, she noticed him watching her from the living room window. She waved before concentrating on cranking up the car's heating.

CHAPTER THIRTY-FIVE

Fiona arrived late at the station, still trying to fathom Peter's strange behaviour from the night before. He wasn't prone to making grand gestures, and she worried something serious was going on under the surface. She made a mental note to call him after his meeting with Dewhurst as she opened the door to the incident room.

Inside she was met with a flurry of activity. Humphries seemed to be the only person not on a call. She hurried over to him while taking off her coat. "What's going on? Was Garland brought in overnight, and if so, why wasn't I contacted?"

"We still haven't found her," Humphries replied, shaking his head. "She's not at home or with her parents. Her employers are expecting her in today, but we're not holding our breath."

"Have you checked with friends?"

"We're doing that now."

"Car registration checks?"

"So far, it hasn't been picked up anywhere."

"Okay," Fiona said. "Could you check whether, as a special, she would know the camera locations?"

"Will do."

"What, if anything, do we know about her dead horse and her dispute with Pat?" Fiona asked. "And why didn't we know anything about it before?"

Overhearing them, Rachael said, "It happened several years ago when Pat's father was still alive. Garland was a teenager, and her parents decided to move her two horses to the farm while work was being carried out on their home. Pat's father abandoned a tractor with a roller attached in the horses' paddock. Being inquisitive, one of them caught its leg somehow and had to be euthanized. Pat and Natalie were very apologetic about it. They helped her to find a new horse, and their father was banned from using any farm machinery. The matter was resolved amicably and forgotten about."

"By the adults maybe, but possibly not by Garland. It was her horse, after all," Fiona said. "Have you heard from Abbie this morning?"

"Yes," Rachael said. "That's how I found out about the horse. Natalie had totally forgotten about the incident until it was mentioned."

"I'll speak to Abbie and try to persuade Natalie to accept additional protection. We could really do with her here."

"Should finding Garland be such a priority?" Humphries asked. "Although we now know she had a reason to hold a grudge against Pat, she has an alibi for the murder, which has been checked."

"Only if we rely on the smartwatch data," Fiona said. "Gibson gave a wider time frame. She could have gone to Field Barn between leaving work and meeting her friend for a pre-theatre drink."

"Even if we ignore the hard evidence from the smartwatch, it's unlikely Pat would have welcomed her with open arms," Humphries said. "I doubt she was the mystery visitor."

"Her alibi for the night of the fire is weak, she doesn't have any alibi for the night of Murphy's murder, and she does fit the vague description of the person seen running from the scene," Fiona said. "Rachael, have you found anything to connect Garland to Murphy?"

"They likely knew of one another, but there's nothing to connect them directly," Rachael said. "But, along the way, I found some historical complaints about Murphy from local schoolgirls."

"How long ago and what sort of complaints?"

"Twenty-plus years ago, he taunted the girls getting off the school bus. One of the parents complained, and it snowballed from there as other girls mentioned incidents."

"Any convictions?" Fiona asked.

"No. He was given an official warning to stop harassing them and hasn't come to our attention since."

"Garland was sent to private boarding schools and is still in her twenties, so she can't have been involved," Fiona said. "Although Pat and Natalie would have been young women, then."

"Already checked," Rachael said, picking up on Fiona's train of thought. "There's no mention of either of them in the reports."

"Okay. Humphries, can you ask the Hardings if they know anything more about the complaints? I will try to arrange extra security for Natalie and pay Garland's parents another visit. Even if she's not our murderer, she's mixed up in this somehow. Maybe her parents can shed some light," Fiona said. "Did we access her bank accounts?"

"Yes," Andrew said. "As you thought, she's up to her ears in debt."

"Any unusual payments in or out?"

"Nothing stands out, but I'm still working through it."

CHAPTER THIRTY-SIX

Fiona tried everything she could think of to persuade Natalie to agree to better protection, but she refused to budge. Her animals depended on her, and she was perfectly capable of protecting herself. It was all Fiona could do to persuade her to allow Abbie to stay for at least another day.

An angry call from Abbie quickly followed the one with Natalie. Fiona appreciated Abbie's frustration, but despite all her protests, she had no option but to insist she stayed with Natalie. With her head starting to pound, Fiona called Garland's parents. She was told Garland's father was with clients all day, but her mother was at home.

Following a lengthy conversation with Garland's mother in the farmhouse, Fiona was none the wiser about where Garland might have bolted or why, as Garland's mother didn't seem to know her adult daughter at all. She thought of her as a child obsessed with horses and couldn't name a single current friend or work colleague.

Garland had confided in her mother about her financial problems but not the full extent of them, and together they had decided to keep it from her father. Her mother had been giving her money here and there out of her housekeeping allowance, but it was barely enough to cover half of the monthly repayments. Her mother insisted relations with Pat and Natalie were good, and nobody blamed the sisters for what had happened years ago. It was an unfortunate accident, and she had a lot of sympathy as her own mother had suffered from dementia. She was resolute that her precious daughter wouldn't harm a fly, let alone a neighbour.

With a full-blown headache, Fiona stopped for a decent coffee on her way back to the station. History repeated itself as Stefan appeared behind her in the queue at the counter.

"Hi, I thought I saw you ducking in here. You said you would call me with your decision, but …"

This wasn't how Fiona wanted to convey her decision, but at least she had an answer for him. She opened her mouth to speak when her phone rang. Looking at the screen, she said, "Sorry, I need to take this." Stefan nodded and stepped back when Fiona asked irritably, "What is it, Humphries?"

"Sorry to disturb you," Humphries replied. "It's not case related, but have you heard from Peter this morning?"

"Peter? No, why?" Fiona asked, her mind returning to his strange behaviour the night before.

"He was supposed to come into the station this morning to see Dewhurst, but he hasn't turned up, and he's not answering his home phone or mobile. We were just wondering if you had any idea where he is?"

"Damn," Fiona muttered, reaching for the Saint Christopher she wore around her neck. The gift she was supposed to remember him by. She had known something was terribly wrong. Why hadn't she paid closer attention to the signs? She should have stayed with him last night. It wasn't as if she had managed a proper night's sleep at home, worrying about the train wreck of her investigation into Pat's murder. She took a deep breath. Despite the dull weight in her stomach telling her she was correct she didn't want to call in the cavalry in case she was wrong. "Leave it with me. I'll see if I can find him."

Turning to rush out the door, she ran straight into Stefan's chest. The smell of his aftershave embraced her and momentarily confused her senses. She pushed back, "Sorry, I've got to go."

Not moving, Stefan looked at her quizzically. "You seem to be sorry a lot recently. What is it?"

"It's Peter. I'm worried about him. I need to get to his home."

"I'll come with you."

187

"There's no need. It could be nothing."

"You clearly don't think so," Stefan said. "You've gone as white as a ghost. What is it?"

"I'm worried he's done something stupid."

After studying Fiona's face, Stefan said, "We're wasting time. I'll follow you in my car."

"Okay, thanks," Fiona said, slipping past Stefan and jogging to the door. "I'll see you there."

Fiona skidded her car to a halt outside Peter's cottage, with Stefan pulling up behind her. He had stuck rigidly to the rear of her car despite her erratic driving. He was out of his car quicker than her, and at her side as she clambered out and looked along the lane.

"His car isn't where he usually parks it," Fiona said, trying to keep the rising panic from her voice. "I'm sure it was there last night." She rushed up the front path, knocked on the door and called Peter's name, before moving to the front window to peer in.

"Shh," Stefan said from behind her. Does he have a garage?"

"He doesn't use it. It's around the back." Fiona gulped back bile when she realised what Stefan was listening to before he sped off around the side of the cottage.

Stefan forced open the side gate, breaking the catch with a crack of splintering wood. Knowing where she was heading, Fiona overtook him, running across the neat lawn to the back of an old wooden garage that faced the lane running behind the cottage. Fiona yanked the catch on the small garden gate to the lane before she felt Stefan roughly pull her back.

"Call emergency services, now!" Stefan demanded. "He'll need proper treatment."

Fiona didn't waste time arguing as Stefan sprinted past her to the garage. She couldn't get Peter out any quicker. As her call was answered, she watched Stefan wrench open the garage doors and disappear inside, holding his jacket over his nose and mouth. The sound of the car engine drowned out the emergency operator's voice. Fiona stepped back, fighting to remain calm, shouting out the address and Peter's details, praying they were in time. She stayed on the line as requested but stuffed her phone in her back pocket, freeing her hands to help Stefan.

When she reached the front of the garage, Stefan was already dragging Peter out. "Is he …. Is he alive?"

"Yes," Stefan said, laying Peter out in the recovery position on the grass verge of the narrow lane.

"Will he …?"

"I've no idea how long he's been in there," Stefan said, straightening up. "Looks like he polished off a bottle of whisky in the car while he was waiting. Is the ambulance on its way? He needs oxygen and professional treatment."

"Yes," Fiona replied, stifling a sob. "Can we move him into his garden? Behind the hedge? I don't like the thought of him being out here where people can see."

Wordlessly, Stefan started to lift Peter and carry him through the narrow gate with Fiona helping.

"Thank you," Fiona said, angrily wiping away a tear once they had Peter inside his garden, hidden from sight. "Is there something we should be doing?"

Stefan shook his head. "He's out in the fresh air. That's all we can do for him unless you happen to have a canister of oxygen."

"I should have realised he was planning something like this last night," Fiona said. "It's my fault."

Still breathing heavily from his exertions, Stefan said, "No, it isn't. The bloody idiot is only alive because of your quick thinking."

Fiona furiously shook her head. "I could have prevented this."

"How?" Stefan asked. "You can't save people from themselves."

"I should have …"

"What? Stayed with him and held his hand indefinitely as he wrecked his career and life," Stefan said, moving forward to comfort Fiona. "This isn't your fault."

Angry with herself and everything else, Fiona spun away. "I'll wait for the ambulance out front." She was pleased Stefan didn't follow her. She needed time to get her feelings under control. Seeing Peter, someone she thought invincible, looking so vulnerable twisted her insides. She'd dealt with numerous suicides, but Peter was the last person she thought would attempt it. Attempt it. She had to hold onto that thought. He couldn't succeed. He just couldn't. Answering the paramedics' questions as she led them to the rear garden gave her some sense of self-control. Shivering, she hung back as they crouched next to Peter.

After speaking to the paramedics, Stefan joined Fiona. "They'll be moving him soon. Do you want to go to the hospital?"

"I feel I should, but I'm in the middle of a murder investigation that is going nowhere," Fiona said. Feeling a sudden chill, she wrapped her jacket around herself. "Did they say when he's likely to regain consciousness?"

"Not for a few hours, at least." Tentatively putting an arm around Fiona's shoulders, Stefan added, "They probably won't let you see him until he's been fully assessed. Physically and mentally. You'll only be hanging around the waiting room, but I'll drive you if you want to go."

Fiona nodded her thanks, not trusting herself to speak, fearing it might set off the tears that were threatening to spill. Her throat was so constricted she wasn't sure she could form recognisable words anyway. Whatever Stefan said, she knew she had let Peter down. Last night he was asking for her help, and she had failed him. If she could go back in time, she would have drunk the bottle of wine and stayed overnight. Talked out his feelings and been there for him, as he had been there for her in the past.

"You're shivering," Stefan said. "Come and sit in my car to warm up. I'll ask one of the paramedics to check you over before they leave. You've had a nasty shock."

"I'm fine. They've got more important things to do," Fiona said, but she allowed Stefan to lead her back through the garden to his car. "A quick sit down is all I need, and I'll get back to work. I must call the station and let them know what's happened."

"I'll do that," Stefan said, holding the broken side gate for Fiona to pass through. "I'll call Dewhurst, and he can decide what to announce."

After listening to Stefan's call while sitting in Stefan's car, Fiona said, "Thanks for being here. It's appreciated."

Stefan reached across and squeezed her hand. "I'm just pleased we arrived in time. I know he means a lot to you."

"So do you," Fiona whispered.

"Pardon, what did you say?"

Fiona jumped and pulled her hand away when her phone rang. Checking the screen, she said, "Talk of the devil," before getting out of the car to answer it. She returned five minutes later, full of resolve, her earlier vulnerability gone. "I'm needed back at the station. They've got Garland in custody."

"I don't think ..." Stefan started to say, but Fiona was gone.

CHAPTER THIRTY-SEVEN

Fiona arrived at the station with no recollection of the car journey. Working hard to block out her jumbled thoughts of Peter and Stefan, she hurried across the car park, trying to plan her interview with Garland. She had no idea what to expect from Garland. Humphries said she'd walked into the station offering to give a statement without a legal advisor present. The lack of legal representation concerned her, but Humphries confirmed it had been offered and refused twice, and she was insisting that she wanted to cooperate and help with the enquiry as much as she could.

Fiona was grateful Humphries had called her before carrying out the interview himself. She wondered if she would have been willing to wait when she worked with Peter. She blocked out that train of thought. She knew she wouldn't have waited, and she didn't want to think about Peter right now. That was something she had to come to terms with later.

After grabbing a lukewarm coffee from the station machine, Fiona headed to the interview room with Humphries in tow. Despite the sterile surroundings, Garland somehow looked relaxed and elegant in white chinos and a blazer. Even her complexion appeared rosy in the lighting that usually drained faces of any colour and highlighted every blemish.

A battle between adrenaline and exhaustion raged inside Fiona as she took her seat. She forced a smile and said, "Thank you for coming in. I understand you have come here voluntarily to make a statement, and legal representation has been offered and declined. Is that correct?"

"Yes. Can we get the preliminaries over with and get on with it?" Garland asked.

"In time for cocktails?" Humphries muttered.

Fiona gave him a stern look while Garland casually smiled. Calmly, she said. "I thought you'd be in a hurry to hear my statement considering the efforts you've made to disturb my little break."

"Okay. Let's get started," Fiona said, switching on the tape and running through the necessary phrases they all knew. Settling back in her chair, she asked, "Where have you been?"

"I have been concentrating on my well-being and being kind to myself. The last few days have been most trying," Garland said.

"Oh, good. So, your chakras are all aligned now," Humphries said, receiving a sharp kick from Fiona.

"Believe it or not, I liked my role with the police. I genuinely wanted to contribute something to my local community." Making a point of staring at Humphries, she added, "I thought I could bring an alternative viewpoint."

"You say that you joined the specials to help your community," Fiona said. "How about the application to become the local rural officer? Was that always your aim?"

"I wasn't previously aware the role existed."

"But when you discovered it did, are you trying to say that you applied for altruistic reasons? You didn't see it as an opportunity to silence local opposition to a sport you enjoy?" Fiona asked. "Only to find that your position was threatened when Pat Thomas recognised you."

"When did you decide she needed to be silenced as well?" Humphries asked.

"I didn't. I swear I had nothing to do with her death."

"She called you numerous times the morning of her murder," Fiona said. "Did you agree to meet her at her home?"

"No. I didn't respond to any of her calls."

"Because you knew what she was calling about? That she recognised you, and there was a clear conflict of interest with you taking on the role?"

"No!" Garland said, slamming the desk, her cool exterior at last ruffled. "I had nothing to do with her death. I didn't even want the damn role."

"What do you mean?" Fiona asked. "You didn't want the role? Then why did you apply?"

Garland closed her eyes and took a deep, audible breath. Opening her eyes, she asked, "Do you want to hear what I have to say in my own words or not?"

"Go ahead," Fiona said. "I will only interrupt if I need clarification of something."

"I saw the role advertised, and I thought about it. I discussed it with a few friends and decided against it. But then, I received a call from Natalie. She said I should apply for it. When I said I wasn't keen, she said she would make it worth my while."

"This is Natalie? Pat's sister?" Fiona asked, any lingering brain fog disappearing.

"Yes," Garland replied, nodding her head. "It was her idea."

"What did she mean by making it worth your while?" Fiona asked.

"I've been a little enthusiastic with my support for some horses recently."

"You have gambling debts," Humphries said.

"Nothing too excessive, but yes."

"So, if you silenced any complaints about the hunt, by let's say, accidentally losing them, Natalie would financially reward you? Is that how it was going to work?" Fiona asked.

"No," Garland said, shaking her head. "I would never agree to do something like that. I'm sure you know about the leaking of last summer's hunt seminar."

"The one where people were instructed how to create a smokescreen and carry on hunting illegally."

"It was taken out of context," Garland replied. "But Natalie was convinced there was a mole within the hunting community passing on information. She only wanted me to give her the names of people making a fuss. That was all. Nothing else."

"That's bad enough," Fiona said.

"You hatched a plan to clear your gambling debts, and Pat was going to expose you," Humphries said. "So, you went around there to discuss it. Maybe things got out of hand, and you hit out in frustration."

"No! Absolutely not. I never even answered her calls. I was deciding what to do when I heard about her death. I would never do something like that."

"It's surprising what people will do when their backs are against the wall," Fiona said. "Your father is the sort of person who cares about his reputation and that of his family. You didn't want him to know about your addiction and debts. It might have all come out if you didn't receive the promised money from Natalie to clear them. Pat was going to ruin everything."

"It's not an addiction. The horses didn't run as well as they should have. I'll make it up."

"If you can get hold of some money to place some more bets." After a brief silence, Fiona asked, "How do you know Brendon Murphy?"

"Brendon?" Garland said, looking surprised. "I know he's always propping up the bar in the Suffolk Arms, but that's about it. Why? He committed suicide, didn't he? What's that got to do with me? I don't think I've ever spoken to him. Not recently, anyway."

"He liked a flutter on the horses as well," Fiona said.

"Was it him who gave you the bad tips?" Humphries asked. "Got you into this mess in the first place?"

"What? No! I don't make a habit of talking to people like him," Garland said indignantly, colour rising to her cheeks. "And if I did, I wouldn't take any notice of any rubbish he tried to dish out. Why are you asking me about someone like him?"

Fiona noted again how Garland changed whenever a subject she hadn't prepared for arose. It occurred to her that she may have been coached again, but who by? Had she confessed everything to her father? It was clear she shared the same snobby attitude as Natalie. All people were not equal in their eyes. But Natalie wouldn't want them to know anything at all about her involvement.

"We're treating his suicide as murder," Humphries said. "The day before, he was overheard saying he knew who killed Pat Thomas. And someone matching your description was seen running from his house the night he died. The evening you were apparently alone at home watching television."

"What, no! I was. His death was nothing to do with me." Garland resolutely folded her arms. "I came here voluntarily to discuss my brief role as a rural officer, not to be badgered about things I know nothing about. I have nothing more to say, and I would like to leave now."

CHAPTER THIRTY-EIGHT

Rather than face people's constant questions about Peter, Fiona slipped into Peter's office to watch Garland drive away. Even stripped of his things, it still felt like his room. As Garland's small city car disappeared, she stepped away from the window and started randomly opening empty drawers, strangely nervous that Peter would walk in any minute and catch her nosing about. She ran her hands over his desk, refusing to let the tears that bubbled beneath the surface spill. She jumped, feeling instantly guilty, at the sound of a knock on the door.

The door creaked open, and Humphries poked his head in. "I thought I might find you here. How are you feeling?" he asked, stepping into the room, and closing the door behind him.

Humphries seemed to crowd the small room in a way Peter never had, and Fiona felt breathless from the dull ache in her heart. "I'm mostly fine," she said. "I feel guilty. I should have known and been able to stop it. People constantly asking me about him doesn't help."

"You shouldn't feel that way. From what I've heard, you and Stefan saved his life."

Fiona turned away to look out of the window. Stefan was another question preying on her mind. Turning back to face Humphries, she asked, "What sort of car did the neighbour see leaving Murphy's place?"

"It wasn't seen. It was heard. The neighbour said it was something small and quiet, so probably a new model."

"Garland drives a two-year-old Renault Clio."

"That would qualify," Humphries said. "Look, it's just the two of us. If you ever want to talk about things, you know I'll always have time to listen."

"Thanks," Fiona said, trying to push away snippets of her last conversation with Peter that ran through her mind on a relentless loop. The switch from annoying Humphries to compassionate Humphries had caught her off guard, breaking down the wall to her emotions. She was back in Peter's cottage, reliving their last conversation. She couldn't do this. Not now. Pulling herself away from the memory, she stopped at the word, 'Jealousy.'

"Are you okay to be working?" Humphries asked. "If you wanted to take a few days out, everyone would understand."

"I told you, I'm fine," Fiona snapped. "Who would be envious of Pat?"

"Anyone on a police salary," Humphries replied. "I wouldn't mind that house. The land must be worth a fortune."

"It was owned jointly with Duncan. Why kill her and not him?" Fiona asked. "Have we checked what happens to it all?"

"Yes. The farm goes to Duncan with an agreement that it be passed to Natalie if he dies first. A plan the sisters hatched because despite their differences, they didn't want the farm to be split while either of them were alive."

"So, what would happen if Natalie died first?"

"Her half would have gone to Pat. Now, I don't know. It would go to Duncan, I guess."

"A guess isn't enough. Check," Fiona said.

"Will do," Humphries said. "I didn't come in here to talk about the case."

"It's all I can focus on, right now," Fiona said. "How did you think the interview with Garland went? Is it possible that Natalie visited her sister to ask her not to oust Garland, and they argued? We overlooked her because we had more likely suspects to consider. Even if it wasn't offered, she's the sort to insist on a quality bottle of wine. It would explain why only Harding and Murphy were targeted when she was in the area as well, but …"

"But what?"

"Nothing. It's not important. My mind is all over the place at the moment and I'm thinking out loud," Fiona said. "Duncan has the greatest motive, especially if he was having an affair, but he has water-tight alibis. Never mind, we'd best go and see Natalie."

"Are you sure you're …"

"Up to it? Yes," Fiona said firmly.

"Okay, well, I suppose it's a good job Abbie is already there, babysitting her," Humphries said. "Should I call her to let her know what's happening?"

"No. We'll call Abbie when we're on our way. That will give her time to keep herself out of danger but not enough to accidentally say something that might put Natalie on warning."

"You don't have much faith in Abbie, do you?"

"It's not that, at all. Natalie has been astute enough to keep herself off the suspect list, and I don't see the need to pile unnecessary pressure on Abbie," Fiona replied, thinking Humphries was probably correct. "Can you check to see if Angela Olive has turned up to make a statement? Even if Duncan is not our killer, it annoys me that he's been lying to us from day one."

"Will do. Anything else?"

"While you're doing that, there's another call I want to make before we leave," Fiona said, pulling out her phone, Peter's comments still circling the periphery of her brain.

"Hi, Maggie. It's DI Fiona Williams here. When we spoke to you at your daughter's house, you said Natalie fell in love with someone who couldn't love her back. Who was that?" Fiona looked at Humphries as she received the answer, she had half-anticipated, and mouthed the name, "Duncan Thomas."

Watching Humphries walk away to check whether Olive had come in, Fiona said to Maggie, "You've known Natalie all her life. Would she resort to violence to get her own way?"

"Why would she do that after all these years?" After thinking for a while, Maggie said, "Many people would disagree, but I think all of Natalie's bluster is to hide the fact she's far more vulnerable than people realise. And lonely too. She gave up her youth to care for her parents. Whatever jealousy she felt towards her sister, I don't think she's selfish enough to have harmed her. This is only my opinion, but I don't think she is the sort of person to take what doesn't belong to her."

Fiona ended the call and found Humphries. "Well? Has Olive turned up?" When Humphries shook his head, she said, "Arrange for her to be brought in while we bring in Natalie. Both fit the description of a small adult as much as Garland did. As Natalie has already mentioned her dogs, guns and pitchforks, we had better grab vests and organise some backup before we head out."

CHAPTER THIRTY-NINE

Abbie pulled up her horse alongside Natalie's after their long gallop. Both horses were blowing from their exertions, so they dropped their reins to let the horses relax, as they cooled down on the walk back to the farmhouse. Some elements of babysitting Natalie were more enjoyable than others, but overall, Abbie was fed up with her assignment. It all seemed so pointless. Natalie was more than capable of looking after herself, and Abbie doubted she was at any risk. She had questioned her in every conceivable way, and it was clear she hadn't seen anything the evening of her sister's murder. If there was going to be an attempt on her life, surely it would have happened by now.

The idea she could be a potential suspect was equally ludicrous. While Natalie was abrasive at times, there was a basic honesty to her. She didn't pretend to be anything she wasn't and said what she thought. There was almost a refreshing morality to her bluntness.

She sighed as the farmhouse came into sight. Much as she would like to slink off home for the evening, she knew her conscience would never allow it. She was stuck with Natalie in the draughty house until Fiona said otherwise.

As they rode the horses into the yard, Natalie said, "You know my system by now, and it's time you made yourself useful. I'll leave you to untack and settle the horses down for the night." She jumped off the bay she was riding and threw the reins to Abbie. "I've an important dinner engagement this evening, so I need to shower and get ready. It's an exclusive event, so you won't be joining me."

"That won't be possible," Abbie said, annoyed at being treated like a minimum-wage groom. "Anyway, why the sudden change? We were late riding out because you were fussing over the casserole. The one that's in the oven, now."

"There's no change," Natalie said. "I'm taking it with me, silly."

"Duncan, again?"

"Where I go is none of your business."

"I'm afraid it is," Abbie replied. "I'm here to protect you, so wherever you go tonight, I'm coming with you."

"Sorry, but this evening is invite-only," Natalie said, striding towards the house.

"If I don't go, then neither are you," Abbie shouted after her, receiving a dismissive wave in response. She silently dismounted and led both horses into the barn. She had the depressing thought that the likely compromise was that she would end up chauffeuring Natalie to Field Barn and sitting outside in the cold all night. If she was really lucky, they might bring her out some leftovers. That wasn't much consolation as she was fed up with eating Natalie's pheasant casseroles, which seemed to be all she could cook.

In a bad mood, she pulled the tack off the horses and gave them a quick wash down before leading them into their stables. She noted the bay had some nasty sores caused by his ill-fitting saddle, but there was no point saying anything. Natalie had sneered at her when she had pointed out that one of the other horses was slightly lame. She had curtly replied that if it wasn't fit for hunting, it would be shot.

Walking to the house, Abbie telephoned the woman she was paying an exorbitant amount to care for her two horses while she was stuck with Natalie. It was money well spent as far as she was concerned. Nothing was too good for them, and it was her well-earned money, so nobody else's business. Her horse's care included regular checks by her veterinarian, farrier and saddler.

Abbie could hear Natalie in the shower when she entered the house. She would like a shower herself, but accustomed to the ancient plumbing of the farmhouse, she knew she would have to wait another hour for the boiler to heat sufficient water for a second shower. A fault in the system Natalie had never noticed as she lived alone. Not that it mattered, as she couldn't risk Natalie sneaking out while she was in the shower.

While making herself a coffee, Abbie decided to have a poke around the kitchen drawers. She doubted she would find anything interesting, but it was the one room she hadn't searched because Natalie rarely left the room if she was home.

The kitchen drawers held nothing but piles of ancient junk, unsystematically jumbled together. Most of the lower cupboards were jammed with dust-covered, ancient pots and pans. One was full of mismatched crockery, covered with an unhealthy amount of grime and dust. The upper cabinets contained an eclectic array of rusted cans and unlabelled plastic containers of basic food ingredients. Abbie dreaded to think how much of it was years out of date, and how by some miracle, she had managed to avoid food poisoning.

She moved to the centre of the room and wondered where someone would quickly stuff things they wanted to hide. She noticed the corner of a brown envelope sticking out of the small gap between the top of the overhead cabinets and the ceiling. She carefully carried a kitchen chair over the stone floor and climbed up to look. Balancing the chair as best she could on the uneven floor, she listened out for signs of movement from upstairs. Hearing nothing, she pulled out the envelope and slipped her hand inside. It contained three hand-written letters dated the day of Pat's death. Abbie held the top of the cabinet for support as she quickly read them. They were complaints about the appointment of Garland and addressed to the police, the local newspaper editor and the council, signed by Pat.

"What the hell are you doing up there?" Natalie demanded. "You nasty little snoop. How dare you go through my private things!"

Abbie spun around looking guilty, which caused the chair to rock violently. Natalie's face was contorted in anger as water dripped from her wet hair onto the shotgun she casually carried by her side. After re-balancing herself, Abbie started to stuff the letters back into the envelope, although it was a pointless exercise. She had been caught red-handed, precariously balanced on a chair holding evidence of a murderer's identity. What could she say?

"Have you found what you were looking for?" Natalie asked. "You've got guilt written all over your face."

"I... No. I wasn't looking for anything," Abbie spluttered.

"Then, what are you doing up there?" Natalie laughed, walking in a small circle before lurching towards Abbie, shouting, "Boo!" Natalie laughed louder as Abbie struggled to maintain her balance by grabbing hold of the overhead cabinet. "Why so petrified of me, dear?" she asked in an over-sweet voice.

"You made me jump."

"I hate deceit. Let's be honest here," Natalie said, sitting at the kitchen table while aiming the shotgun at Abbie. "No! Don't try to step down. Stay there where I can see you while I think. Maybe, this is all for the best, as I've every intention of going out tonight without you." Tapping the gun on the floor, she added, "As you can see, I'm very capable of looking after myself, and I have good instincts. I had a feeling you were up to something down here while my back was turned. That's why I came down to check."

"Why don't you put the gun down, and we can talk?"

Natalie laughed. "I don't think you're in any position to tell me what to do. Do you?"

"No," Abbie admitted.

"I never planned any of this, but now that it has happened, I may as well take advantage of the situation. That was my downfall, you see. I let events dictate to me. Now, I'm grabbing events by the scruff of the neck and reclaiming what is rightfully mine. Do you understand?"

"Not really. Perhaps you could explain it all to me," Abbie said, keen to keep Natalie talking while she thought of a way out of the situation.

"I was the pretty one, you see. Everyone said so. We all think we have more time than we do. I thought it would be fine if I sat out one dance. One lousy dance. But then the music stopped, and I was stuck here, stranded with two batty parents to take care of. I didn't even realise we were playing musical chairs, but *she* did. She used my sense of duty to take everything that should have been mine, and I couldn't do anything about it at the time."

"Sorry, who are you talking about?" Abbie asked, desperately looking around the room for an exit strategy before focusing back on the gun barrel. "Why don't I come down from here, and we can have a good chat about what happened?"

"Sadly, I don't have the time. I'm going now to meet my destiny. The one that was stolen from me." Natalie slowly stood, keeping the gun trained on Abbie. "Sorry, but I can't let a minor inconvenience like you stand in my way. Not this time." She walked over and snatched the envelope from Abbie, and after briefly smiling at the handwriting, she stuffed it in a drawer.

Abbie desperately tried to steady herself by grabbing at the cupboard doors as the chair was violently jerked from under her.

CHAPTER FORTY

Fiona decided they would approach the farmhouse without warning, and she briefed the small team accordingly. She would knock on the front door with Humphries and one team behind her, ready to burst in and carry out the arrest. The second team would skirt around the farmhouse to guard the rear entrance. Humphries was going to call Abbie to prewarn her once they were on their way. Satisfied everyone was fully prepared, they set off.

"I still can't believe we overlooked her as a serious suspect," Humphries said, as soon as they were alone in the car.

"Well, we did, and you should bear in mind it's not a foregone conclusion."

"What do you mean by that?" Humphries asked.

"We've discovered that Natalie had a couple of reasons for wanting her sister out of the way," Fiona said. "That doesn't necessarily mean she was responsible. Don't forget Duncan is having an affair, and he's the only person to benefit financially from Pat's death."

"He also has a confirmed alibi and would have no reason to hide anything relating to Garland's appointment," Humphries said. "Quite the opposite, in fact. Until Garland told us that her appointment was Natalie's idea, there was nothing to suggest she might have been involved."

"Abbie is a good judge of character, and she hasn't noticed anything untoward about her behaviour." Fiona sighed, thinking over the implications if Natalie had killed her sister. She would have to come up with something better when Dewhurst questioned her about the oversight. She was leading the investigation and had interviewed Natalie, and she wouldn't stoop so low as to blame Abbie. It didn't help that she couldn't stop thinking that Peter wouldn't have made the same mistake.

Although Natalie was the obvious suspect, she still had a nagging doubt about Duncan. A secret affair and the land's value gave him plenty of motive, and he hadn't been honest with them from the start. But why would he remove everything relating to Garland's appointment from the house? "Have you called Abbie?"

"Doing it now," Humphries replied, punching in the number. He tried the number a second time. "She's not answering."

"The last update I saw said she was exercising the horses with Natalie. Maybe they're not back yet."

"It's dark," Humphries said. "Do horses have headlights?"

"I've seen horses on the road in semi-darkness in these rural areas, and Natalie is a law unto herself. Or it could be they're riding off-road. Check the log to see if she's been in contact since. That update was several hours ago," Fiona said, becoming worried. Maybe they should have delayed leaving the station until they were sure Natalie was relaxing at home.

"Nothing has been heard from her since," Humphries said, scrolling through pages on his laptop. "She usually gives an update around this time to confirm Natalie's plans for the evening."

"Contact the teams behind. There's a truck stop just before we turn off for the village. We may as well wait for the update if it's likely to be imminent."

Fiona bought coffee for everyone, and they returned to the warmth of their cars to wait. The temperature dropped rapidly, and it started to rain as they huddled in their cars.

"Peter called me the day before he... Well, you know what," Humphries said without preamble.

Fiona glanced across at Humphries, fiddling anxiously with the cuff of his rain jacket. He could be a right pain sometimes, but he was one of the good guys. Because of all his bluster and regular political rants, it was easy to forget other aspects of his personality. He was a generous and loyal colleague who could always be relied upon. He had known Peter for longer than her, albeit in a junior role. He had also been very close to the young detective who was killed in the line of duty not long after Fiona had joined the station, and she recalled how hard that had hit him. "What did you talk about?"

"This and that. My wedding, mostly. With hindsight, he did say some things that should have alerted me to his state of mind."

"Such as?"

Humphries shrugged. "Out of context, it doesn't seem anything much. He praised me and said I should continue to seek promotion opportunities. And I should look out for you. He also asked me a strange question. He asked how I kept the darkness at bay. I thought he was referring to politics and the state of the country generally, as that was what we were talking about, and I gave a flippant reply. Now, I'm not so sure."

Fiona reached over and squeezed his arm. "Hindsight is a wonderful thing. If you had picked up on it, he would have only backed away and made light of it. Don't blame yourself. And anyway, he's going to be fine. We'll be there to support him as he recovers. Right?"

"That goes without saying."

"Just for the record. How *do* you keep the darkness at bay?" Fiona asked.

"I go on long bike rides sometimes, but mostly it's Tina. I'm so glad I met her, and I can't believe she wants to marry someone like me. Meeting her has changed everything. You need someone special, Fiona. A couple of Tina's cousins are coming down for the wedding. I'll introduce you."

Fiona smiled and shook her head. Adjusting her position in the seat, she said, "We're not back on that subject, are we?" She took the tablet Humphries had left on the dashboard and scrolled through the entries. "Abbie has normally checked in by now. Try calling her again, as I'm starting to worry that something has happened."

"She didn't answer five minutes ago when I tried," Humphries replied, shifting his own position. "Could she have fallen off a horse?"

"Possibly, but I was thinking she might have stumbled across something." Fiona peered out at the rain that was becoming heavier and driven by a strengthening wind. "I don't like this. We'll give it another five minutes. If you can't get hold of her then, we're going in. Let the others know."

Despite the rain, Humphries climbed out of the car to speak to the others. Fiona started the car and switched on the heater and windscreen wipers, wondering if she had been too sharp in ending their conversation. Later, she would suggest they pop into a pub to see if he still wanted to talk. She could listen to him even if she wasn't ready to share her feelings. Everything was so raw and mixed up in her mind, it would take hours to unravel everything she wanted to say, and she didn't have the luxury of time. For now, she needed to push her thoughts away and concentrate on the case.

Fiona looked again at the times of Abbie's updates. She could think up a million and one reasons to explain why her update was late today, but she couldn't ignore the sinking feeling in her stomach that told her something was dreadfully wrong. Seeing Humphries sharing a joke with the driver of the car behind, she opened her car door to call him over.

When Humphries saw Fiona open the car door, he ended his conversation and returned to the car. "Okay? I was just checking we're all sure what we're doing."

"Yes. We should get going." Fiona refastened her seatbelt and started the engine. "The lack of contact is making me uneasy. Maybe, we should have called and got her out of there as soon as we knew about Natalie's involvement in Garland's appointment. If anything has happened …"

"It'll be okay," Humphries soothed. "We'll be there in a few minutes. It could be something as simple as she forgot to charge her phone."

CHAPTER FORTY-ONE

Satisfied Abbie was going nowhere, Natalie quickly dried and styled her hair. She was a private person and hated the idea of Abbie nosing around her kitchen. Her finding Pat's letters had seriously rattled her, so she kept the shotgun by her side, and her eyes regularly darted to the window as she applied her makeup.

She didn't understand why she wanted to keep Pat's letters. Could she be becoming sentimental in her old age and wanted something tangible to remember her sister by? She hadn't felt the same way about her parents' possessions. She had handled them with brutal indifference. Some of them had been dumped in black plastic bags and deposited at the back door of the local charity shop, a few days after they had died. The rest had been piled up in one of the unused bedrooms. When she had time, she really should go through it all. Just thinking about the task made her feel weary.

Either way, she wasn't going to worry about it now. Abbie finding the letter was just another little quirk of fate. The universe, at last had had a change of heart and decided to help her to find her true destiny, and she couldn't let the stupid woman put a spanner in the works. Not this time.

She locked the front door and tutted when she saw Abbie's car parked out front. Moving it would delay her, but she couldn't leave it there. She returned inside and grabbed Abbie's car keys from the counter. With the time ticking by, she decided to park it inside the old milking shed and deal with the matter properly when she returned.

She walked around the back to the garage that housed the little run-around car she had bought for her father. She had taken the keys of the truck and other machinery away from him but had relented over his need for some independence. The little Kia was the perfect solution. She'd forgotten it was there until recently but had discovered she enjoyed its nippiness for short trips. It purred along quietly and gave her the anonymity, her noisy Land Rover didn't.

The bottle of red wine and her homemade pheasant pie, nestled in the wicker basket on the front passenger seat, bounced around so much on the drive to Field Barn that Natalie had to hold onto it. She had been looking forward to this evening all day. They were going to pick up where they left it, all those wasted years ago.

Field Barn was in darkness when she arrived, but she spotted Duncan's gleaming car parked next to Pat's rusty, old truck. A little act of defiance, as Pat always insisted that he parked it in the garage. It had never made any logical sense when her truck was always left on the drive.

Duncan was probably in his little snug. The perfect spot for the romantic encounter she imagined. There would be time later for grand gestures in the main hall. She'd already planned a fantastic breakfast spread for the first time the hunt returned to where it belonged. She would amaze everyone with her slick change from elegant hostess to huntswoman in the blink of an eye. She grabbed the basket along with her shotgun and hurried through the rain to the front door.

After ringing the bell, an outside light came on, blinding her. She looked away, willing her eyes to quickly adjust. A squint was never attractive at her age.

"Who is it?"

"It's only me. I've brought supplies," Natalie said brightly, resting the shotgun against the wall to adjust the basket's weight, as she eagerly waited for the chunking of the locks to end and the door to swing back. Her heartbeat quickened as the heavy door slowly creaked open.

Duncan poked his head out to look at the torrential rain blowing across the driveway before ushering Natalie inside.

"Come in, come in. I think a nasty storm might be brewing, and I wasn't sure if you would come."

"Oh, dear, what will I do about driving home? I've come in Daddy's little car so I may be stranded here awhile." Natalie laughed and offered up her basket. "I've brought us plenty to eat so we won't starve if we're cut off from the rest of the world. I even thought to bring candles in case of a power cut."

"We'll eat later," Duncan said. "I've something to show you first, so I'll need to pop my coat on."

Natalie picked up her shotgun and walked past Duncan into the entrance hall. Positive that his eyes were drawn to her swaying hips in the tight-fitting dress, she said, "Close the door, dear. You're letting all the heat out." She was so sure Duncan was right behind her, she didn't realise he wasn't until she reached the kitchen door. She put the basket down on the counter in the central hall, flicked the safety check on the shotgun and turned to go and find him.

CHAPTER FORTY-TWO

Through the sheets of rain, they could see from the lane that the farmhouse was in darkness. When they turned onto the driveway, Fiona's relief at seeing Natalie's Land Rover parked up outside was short-lived. "Where's Abbie's car?"

"Maybe they have gone out in it somewhere," Humphries said.

"Or it could be parked around the back. Ask the team covering the back to check," Fiona said, shielding her eyes from the rain as she stepped out of the car. Pulling her coat hood up, she jogged to the shelter of the front porch, sidestepping the deepest puddles. When the others joined her in the confined space, she knocked on the door. The only sound from inside was the incessant barking of Natalie's dogs.

They shifted uncomfortably when Fiona knocked a second time. All eyes turned to Humphries when his phone buzzed.

"There's no sign of her car, and everything is in darkness around the back," Humphries told the others. "Do you want them to check the outbuildings?"

"Yes," Fiona recalled the layout from when they waited for Natalie to finish clipping the horse. "As well as the old stables facing the yard, there's a large barn off to the side. Ask them to check that as well."

"Too soon to break in?" Humphries asked, squaring up to the solid oak door.

"Hang fire on that," Fiona said. "I'm going to look through the windows to see if I can see or hear anything. Try Abbie's number again."

"Still no answer."

"Keep it ringing. I'll see if I can hear it inside," Fiona said,

walking off to peer through the downstairs windows. She
shortly returned to the porch, shaking her head. "Nothing. As far
as I can tell, the house is empty."

Humphries jogged over from the window on the other side of
the house. "They've found Abbie's car. It's in one of the barns.
There's no sign of her or anyone else."

Standing back from the house and looking up, Fiona said,
"Okay. Get us in there."

An officer appeared from the side of the house. "The back door
would be the easiest option."

"Well, what are you waiting for?" Fiona asked. "I want two
officers to stay here in case someone is waiting behind the
front door. Everyone else, around the back. Remember, the
householder has a shotgun and has threatened to use it to
protect herself on several occasions, so take care everyone."

"And the dogs?"

"To date, they've been non-aggressive, so don't harm them
unless they attack. We can think about calling in dog handlers
when we know what we're dealing with."

The back door gave way easily with more of a soft whimper
than a resounding crack, and they moved forward in formation,
taking care to cover each other as they moved through the
house, searching the rooms systematically. The dogs had been
locked in a second living room. They stopped scratching and
bounded out as soon as the door was opened, wagging tails
and looking for attention. As Fiona calmed them, the room was
searched and confirmed empty.

"Over here!" Humphries shouted.

Fiona shot along the corridor and poked her head into the
kitchen. A chair was upturned, and there was a small pool of
blood on the stone floor.

"Keep the dogs out! This room needs to be secured," Humphries
shouted from his crouched position.

Fiona pushed the dogs behind her and quickly scanned the rest
of the orderly room before closing the door. The only thing out
of place was a solitary mug on one of the counters. She heard the

other officers climbing the stairs as she locked the dogs back in the living room. Ignoring their whines, she hurried back to the kitchen, trying not to jump to conclusions.

Humphries stood from a crouched position by the fallen chair, and said, "It's obvious someone fell from this chair, but there's no other signs of a struggle. It could have been accidental, and they're on their way to the hospital."

"Except both cars are here."

"Maybe they called for an ambulance," Humphries said. "Has anything else been found?"

"Downstairs is clear. They're searching upstairs. We may as well leave this room as it is until we know what happened," Fiona said, walking backwards to the door. As Humphries was wearing gloves and she wasn't, she added, "Feel the kettle first."

"It's lukewarm at the base, so whatever happened in here, it was within the last hour."

Fiona waited in the hall for Humphries to come out. "I'll ring the emergency services to see if they've been called out to this address. Can you check on the others?"

There was no record of an ambulance call out, and neither woman had been admitted to the main hospital, so Fiona started to ring the smaller emergency walk-in centres in the area, hoping the blood came from a minor injury and Natalie had asked a friend to drive them. She was interrupted by the sound of boots hammering down the stairs.

"All clear upstairs."

"Anything from the team outside?" Fiona asked.

On cue, a phone rang. Humphries pulled his phone in his fleece pocket. He shook his head to indicate that nothing else had been found so far.

"So, where are they?" Fiona asked.

CHAPTER FORTY-THREE

Gathered in the hallway, Fiona confirmed she had called all the local surgeries without any luck. "I'm going to have one last look around in here, and I suggest we then start searching outside."

"All the barns have already been thoroughly searched."

"Search them again, and the gardens and the horse paddocks. They can't be far away if both cars are here," Fiona said.

"Someone could have picked them up?" Humphries suggested. "Natalie didn't strike me as the type to be too concerned by a minor accident and a spot of blood. They could be relaxing over a meal while we're getting drenched out there."

"If they were going somewhere, Abbie would have called and let us know," Fiona replied, before turning to climb the staircase. As she walked along the corridor that ran the length of upstairs, she heard Humphries following behind her over the sound of the wind and rain rattling against the windows. The upstairs rooms were furnished with heavy, dated furniture and bedspreads rather than duvets covered the beds. They all felt drab and damp, especially the ones only used for storage. Abbie's haversack was neatly stored in one room. Humphries checked in the bag and the bedside drawers for her phone but couldn't find it. In another room, a damp bath towel was draped over a chair. The wardrobe was full of the type of jeans and sweatshirts that Fiona thought Natalie would wear.

Fiona returned downstairs and entered the main living room. An ancient carriage clock on the mantelpiece over an open fire loudly clunked through the seconds, reminding her of the passage of time. The only thing out of place was a newspaper on a side cabinet, neatly folded to show the horse racing results. Like the other rooms, the décor was functional and comfortable if a little cold and damp, but it had a slightly cosier feel and was the only carpeted room in the house. The carpet was stained and threadbare in places, but a pattern of faded red flowers on a beige background could still be seen. The seating area was separated from a reading area by three uneven steps. Fiona stepped up to examine the bookcases. The books were mostly heavy hardbacks on farming and horse management, but there were a few battered romance novels with yellowed pages.

"I wonder if they've moved onto dessert yet?" Humphries asked.

Fiona wished she could share his optimism, but her stomach told her that something was very wrong. She didn't see eye to eye with Abbie, but she was an efficient and often excessively pedantic officer. She wouldn't let her phone battery die. Something had prevented her from calling in to tell them that they were going out for the evening. As she carefully negotiated the steps to return to the living area, she had a flashback to a similarly decorated home she had visited with Peter years before. The home of Andi, a local gamekeeper.

She crouched down, examining how the carpet had been cut to cover the steps. "Humphries, help me to look for the join."

"Sorry? What am I looking for?" Humphries asked, looking confused as Fiona tugged at the carpet.

"Here! Look!" Fiona said triumphantly, and she started to pull away the heavy fabric. "Grab that end and pull."

Once they had a firm grip on the edge of the carpet, it pulled away easily to reveal wooden, not stone steps.

"Now what?" Humphries asked.

Fiona felt about for a catch of some kind but found nothing. She remained crouched, staring at the steps as if they would magically give her the answer she sought. She noticed the middle step had a slight lip. Standing, she placed her fingers under it and pulled. On well-oiled hinges, the steps lifted easily to reveal a steep staircase into a cellar.

"How did you know?" Humphries asked.

"I didn't. It was a guess," Fiona admitted. "I saw something like this in a cottage, ages ago."

Humphries shone the light on his mobile phone into the hole. "Are we going down or just going to stand around talking about it?"

The stone steps were uneven, and there was no handrail to hold onto as they descended into the cavernous dark. When they reached the bottom, Humphries shone his phone's torch around while Fiona looked for a light switch. When she found it, the dark shapes surrounding them turned into old packing cases and boxes. She had the feeling it had been the family's dumping ground for decades, and there were probably valuable antiques hidden amongst the dust-covered junk.

"Listen!" Humphries said.

A small, muffled sound came from a heavy bookcase, followed by several bangs. Behind it, they found Abbie, gagged and attached to metal pipework with handcuffs that belonged in a museum. Fiona released the gag while Humphries examined the handcuffs.

"Thank God it's you. I think Natalie's the killer," Abbie said, as soon as the gag was removed. "Have you got her?"

Examining the gash and dried blood on Abbie's head, Fiona said, "Unfortunately not. What happened?"

"I found the letters Pat had written about Garland's appointment. They were stuffed on top of the kitchen cabinets. Natalie caught me with them, and here I am."

"These handcuffs were made by Tower Handcuffs and are over a hundred years old," Humphries said. "Fascinating."

Abbie looked at Humphries over her shoulder. "Can you get them off?"

"Not easily without a key, and these are too interesting to damage."

"Humphries!" Fiona rebuked. "Let the others know we've found Abbie. Maybe they can use the bolt cutters on the pipe to free her."

Abbie rolled her eyes and said, "I would hate to see such an important piece of police history be destroyed."

Humphries looked at his phone. "There's no signal down here." He stood and said, "I'll go and let them know."

Fiona looked back at Abbie. "Natalie isn't in the house. Have you any idea where she's gone?"

"I think I was out cold for a while, and my memory of what happened this evening is hazy, but I think she's gone to Field Barn to see Duncan."

"Did she say why?"

"After she pushed me from the chair, there's a blank. When I came around, she was handcuffing me here and talking nonsense. I vaguely recall her mumbling something about it being her destiny to collect what was rightfully hers. She seemed to think she was the pretty one. I've no idea what she meant by that."

"I think I do," Fiona said, jumping to her feet. "How did she overpower you?"

"My last clear memory is me balancing on the chair to retrieve the letters." Abbie blushed, and quickly added, "She's armed with a shotgun."

"We'll bear that in mind," Fiona said, heading towards the steps.

"Hey! What about me?" Abbie shouted after her. "Where are you going?"

"The others will be down in a minute to sort you out. That head injury needs checking at the hospital," Fiona shouted as she sped up the steps.

CHAPTER FORTY-FOUR

The track was slick with mud, and gusts of wind scattered rain across the windscreen and battered the car's bodywork as Fiona and Humphries led the dash to Field Barn. When they pulled up outside, light spilt from the house as the wind caught the front door. It crashed open only to slam shut moments later, throwing the approach back into darkness.

Fiona gave Humphries a worried look before jumping out of the car. A gust of wind caught the car door, wrenching it out of her hand.

"Should we wait for the armed response team to arrive?" Humphries shouted to be heard over the wind.

Fiona looked up at the house. No lights were on upstairs. It was only the front hallway light that seemed to be on. The house looked sad and abandoned.

"Can we have a decision? There's no point in us standing here getting drenched if we're going to wait."

"We'll go in, carefully," Fiona shouted, before sending two officers to check around the back. The remaining team grouped together before cautiously moving towards the banging front door. Humphries looked at the door catch before picking up a heavy stone to hold the door open, and with a nod, they stepped into the entrance hall.

They were greeted with a hushed silence as they entered the central hall. After struggling to be heard over the gusty winds, everything felt too still. Shouting their presence, their voices echoed around the cavernous room. Tense, they span at the approaching patter of feet. They sighed in relief when two dogs weaved around their legs, wagging their tails. Fiona moved to the central island and lifted a corner of the chequered dish towel draped over a wicker handbasket. Inside was a casserole dish and a bottle of wine. The tale of Little Red Riding Hood came to mind as she lowered the dish towel.

The house appeared abandoned, but she warned everyone to take care and keep in contact as they fanned out to check the other rooms.

Humphries received a call as they moved off. After listening to the caller, he said, "There are no lights on at the rear of the house, and the back door is locked. Should they break in?"

"Tell them to stay where they are, and we'll let them in," Fiona said, remembering the layout and heading toward the kitchen. She pointed to the other side of the hall, and said, "The rest of you head that way. Through that door is a long corridor that leads to the rest of the house."

They were startled by the crack of a gunshot. "That came from the rear of the house," Fiona said, breaking into a run, worried about the safety of the officers stranded outside the back door. She hurtled through the kitchen and raced to unlock the door. She pulled it open, shouting, "Where did it come from?"

"Over there, somewhere."

"Then why are you standing here?" Fiona said, pushing past them into the blinding wind and rain.

Humphries grabbed the sleeve of her raincoat. "You're not armed. We should wait."

Fiona pulled free. "For what? There's a risk to life. Listen. What can you hear?" Fiona wiped the rain from her eyes, listening for any sounds above the howling wind. "Everything's gone quiet."

"It's pitch black out here. Have you any idea where you're going?" Humphries shouted after Fiona, as she ran out into the driving rain. Against his better judgement, he followed her across the uneven yard. He was pleased to hear, after a moment's hesitation, the boots of the other officers behind him. They all skidded to a halt and dropped to the ground at the sound of a second gunshot. This time it was followed by angry shouting and the sound of someone running towards them.

As Fiona climbed to her feet, watery mud dripping from the front of her coat, Duncan jumped over a gate and appeared in front of them, looking crazed. The wild look in his eyes was enhanced by strands of hay sticking out of his hair. "Thank God you're here. It's Natalie. She's trying to kill me."

Moments later, Natalie appeared, standing on the other side of the gate, aiming the shotgun at Duncan. Her hair was similarly stuck up on end and looked like a bird had tried to make a nest in it. As rain dripped from her nose and chin, she shouted, "You lying bastard. Don't listen to him. He lured me out here with false promises and tried to kill me."

Duncan looked at Fiona and twirled a forefinger by his temple. "I told you. She's gone crazy. Which of us is waving a gun around?" He looked down at his arm, and seeing blood, cried, "She shot me," before promptly fainting.

Stepping over him, Fiona shouted, "Get him out of here and get him medical attention," before facing up to Natalie. "It's all over. Put the gun down."

Waving the shotgun erratically, Natalie shouted, "If I wanted to kill him, trust me, he would be dead. I'm an excellent shot."

Adrenaline countered the chill of her soaked clothing, as Fiona took a step forward. "Put the gun down."

"Not a chance. It was lucky I had it with me," Natalie said. "He's lying. He tried to get it away from me."

"Put the gun down before it goes off again, and we can talk about it."

"That wasn't me," Natalie said, waving the gun again. "It went off when he tried to grab it, even though that's not what he planned. He wanted to kill me in a way that looked like an accident, back in his hay barn. I'm not dropping it until you arrest him for attempted murder."

Taking another step forward, cold water squelching in her shoes, Fiona asked, "Why did you come out here with the gun?"

"He invited me. I brought him a lovely pheasant pie and a bottle of wine, and this is how he repaid me."

"I absolutely did not!" Duncan shouted. "I didn't want her here. She turned up uninvited and armed. You can see how unhinged she is. I don't even like pheasant pie."

Fiona glanced behind to see two officers helping a revived Duncan to his feet. She shouted, "Get him out of here," keeping her eyes on Natalie.

"He's the one who is crazy," Natalie said. "He killed my sister and lured me here under false pretences so he could kill me as well. I was expecting a romantic meal."

"So, why did you bring the gun?" Fiona asked, edging forward.

"I was doing what you told me to do. You said I was in danger, so I was protecting myself," Natalie said. "Thanks for the advice, by the way."

"You're not in danger now, so why don't you put the gun down and step away with your hands where we can see them? Duncan isn't going to harm you with us here."

"If you insist," Natalie said, placing the gun on the floor and moving to the side. She pointed at Duncan and said, "But you'll be making a dreadful mistake if you don't arrest that man."

As two officers approached Natalie, Fiona said, "Read her rights and arrest her." Turning, she said, "And him as well. We'll sort this out at the station when we're dry."

CHAPTER FORTY-FIVE

Fiona, dressed in the baggy leggings and a faded blue sweatshirt she'd found at the bottom of her locker, gratefully took a mug of steaming coffee from Humphries. It would probably keep her tossing and turning through what was left of the night, but she craved the caffeine. The initial interviews of Natalie and Duncan had given her a pounding headache, but little else. Both were protesting their innocence and blaming the other for the murders. Incredible though it seemed, she thought Natalie's version of events sounded the most plausible.

"What's the plan?" Humphries asked.

Fiona sipped her coffee, struggling to focus her bleary eyes on Humphries. Within the windowless interview rooms, she had forgotten how late it was. Now, she was drowning in a wave of exhaustion as the week of broken sleep was catching up on her, and everything ached. Making no effort to move, she said, "We probably should head home. Start afresh tomorrow after they've had a night in custody to think things over."

Similarly slumped in his chair, Humphries nodded. "Probably."

"Have they had any joy with tracking down Olive yet?"

"No, but it shouldn't take long. Cameras have picked up her car registration on the M4, and she'll be stopped as soon as she exits the motorway." Humphries blew across his coffee before adding, "It might be academic. It turned out she had an alibi for the time of Pat's murder, and it has been confirmed by several people. It looks like we should be concentrating on Natalie. She was obviously lying when she said she had never seen the letters Abbie found in her kitchen before."

"She could be telling the truth," Fiona said, rubbing her eyes with the heels of her palms. "We know from Abbie, that Duncan has visited the farmhouse several times over the past few days, and he was left waiting in the kitchen on at least one of those occasions." Yawning, she added, "I've asked they urgently run fingerprint tests. The report should be waiting for us in the morning. If the only fingerprints on the letters are Pat's, it leaves things wide open."

"So, she wore gloves when handling them."

"Or Duncan did, and she's telling the truth when she said last night was the first time she had seen them."

Abbie walked in with a bandaged head and sat down heavily beside Humphries. "What's happening?"

"What are you doing here? Shouldn't you be in the hospital?" Fiona asked.

"No, but because of the head injury, I shouldn't be left alone, so here I am."

"It doesn't work like that," Fiona said. "I take it you discharged yourself. You need to be cleared fit for duties."

"And you are?" Abbie said defiantly. "You look totally shattered. What time did you start this morning? And anyway, I'm not on duty. My shift officially finished hours ago."

"Do you want a coffee?" Humphries asked.

"I heard you've arrested Natalie and Duncan," Abbie said, shaking her head. "What happened out there?"

After receiving a quick summary of events and the explanations given by Duncan and Natalie from Humphries, Abbie said, "My memory is clearer now, and thinking back over the evening, Natalie's version does make some sense."

"Nothing about that woman makes any sense," Humphries said. "And are you forgetting that she attacked you and left you trapped in her cellar?"

"No, but that doesn't make her the killer," Abbie said, rubbing her tired eyes. "You weren't there. I was. It's possible that she was so intent on meeting with Duncan that she wasn't thinking straight."

"She hid your car in one of her barns, even if it was a pointless exercise, as we all knew you were there," Humphries said. "Why would she have done that if she wasn't planning to harm you once she dealt with Duncan?"

"She probably moved it because it was in the way," Abbie said. "I forgot she asked me not to park there the day before, because it made it difficult for her to negotiate the corner in the tractor."

"It's late," Fiona said. "Make that point clear when you write your report tomorrow."

"So, you think she might be telling the truth?" Abbie asked, leaning forward. "And you're going to concentrate on Duncan?"

Humphries threw his hands up in despair.

"I'm too tired to make sense of either of their explanations of what happened tonight. Duncan and his girlfriend, Olive, do have strong alibis for Pat's murder. We'll review their alibis for the fire and Murphy's murder tomorrow. Go home and get some sleep," Fiona said. "With fresh minds, maybe some of this will start to make sense."

Humphries and Abbie slowly stood. "What about you?"

"I'm coming in a minute. There's one thing I want to check before I leave."

"Which is?" Humphries asked.

"I want to know the location of Pat's smartwatch and the full report on its readings," Fiona said. "Do you know how far back they went?"

"I'm not sure. Why?" Humphries asked.

"The paramedics and Gibson gave a much wider range for the time of death. We accepted the time of death shown on the watch because it was within that time range. What if Natalie wasn't wearing it that day? What if Duncan was wearing it, and it stopped recording when he took it off while he was sitting in the pub with his friend, giving him the perfect alibi," Fiona said. "He put the watch back onto Pat's wrist when he returned home for *the second time* that evening."

"It's possible, I suppose, but proving it can wait until tomorrow," Humphries said, holding out his hand. "Come on."

Fiona allowed herself to be pulled up from the chair, and the three of them made their way out of the station together, in a sleep-deprived haze. The cold night air tried its best, but it failed to shake them awake as they left the building. Shivering, having left her drenched coat behind, Fiona said. "At least it's stopped raining."

"A silver lining, and all that," Humphries said through chattering teeth.

Fiona turned to Abbie, and asked, "Where are you going?"

"Home, where else?"

"Where you'll be alone with a head injury," Fiona said. "Why don't you crash at mine?"

"Or mine?" Humphries offered, before bringing them to an abrupt halt. "What's he doing here?" he asked, moving protectively toward Fiona while glaring at Stefan huddled in a coat beside Fiona's car.

"I can handle it," Fiona said. "But it might be best if Abbie stays at yours tonight. See you both in the morning." Satisfied Humphries and Abbie were walking away, she approached Stefan, questioning him with her eyes.

"I was waiting for you," Stefan said unnecessarily.

"And here I am."

"You've had a pig of a few days. Can I drive you home?"

Fiona shoved her hands deeper into her coat pockets. "I didn't want to give you my answer like this."

"I'm here to see you safely home, not demand answers," Stefan said. "But I'll take one if you're offering."

It took all of Fiona's remaining reserve of energy to look up and say, "The answer is yes." It was an effort to stay upright when Stefan put his arms around her. Her legs wanted to buckle as she held onto him. She rested her head and melted into his warmth as he tightened his grip.

Stefan pulled away first. "Let's get you home."

Fiona merely nodded as he led her to his car. She had no recollection of the journey home or how he carefully carried her inside, placed her on her bed and pulled the covers over her as she slept.

CHAPTER FORTY-SIX

Fiona woke with a start. Her duvet was twisted uncomfortably around her, she was fully dressed, and it was light outside. She kicked her way out of the tangled duvet which was reluctant to release its grip on her and threw on a clean set of clothes. She paused on the landing. She didn't look her best, but she didn't have time to worry about it.

With a mixture of relief and disappointment, she found the house was empty. Stefan had left a note, saying he was called into work, next to his car keys and the coffee machine was set up. Was he a saint? She took a grateful sip of coffee before filling her flask and heading out to Stefan's car.

She took the station steps two at a time. There was a buzz in the room when she placed her flask on her desk and picked up the fingerprint report. She skim-read to the conclusion. The only fingerprints on the letters were Pat's and Abbie's.

Humphries came over and handed over the report on Pat's smartwatch. As Fiona flicked through it, she said, "Have you read it? Summarise what it says."

"The experts say your theory is possible. The watch has been sent to see if there's any trace evidence of Duncan wearing it."

Fiona's brain was on fire as it churned through all the possibilities simultaneously, making it hard to pull out one coherent strand of thought.

"What do you think?" Humphries asked. "Where do we go from here?"

Working hard to slow her whirling brain, Fiona said, "If we're correct about Duncan murdering Pat, then we're talking about a small window of time. He was possibly at Field Barn when

Harding was there discussing the fallen down wall,"

"Harding has been asked repeatedly, and he says he saw nothing to suggest there was anyone else in the house," Humphries said.

"Well, ask again. We were all thinking about an unknown visitor. This time, specifically ask whether there was anything to suggest Duncan might have been at home." Fiona drummed her fingers on the desk. Something was niggling away at the back of her mind, tantalisingly out of reach. "I need to look at the crime scene photos."

Humphries looked over Fiona's shoulder as she closely examined each picture in turn. "What are you looking for?"

"I'll know when I find it." Fiona zoomed in on a picture of the outside of the house. She leaned back with a frown. "Has the garage door always been closed on our visits?"

"I think so," Humphries said. "I think Duncan's car has always been parked on the drive."

Looking again at the zoomed-in photograph, Fiona said, "I don't think it's electrified. We need to check, but my parents had something similar on the integral garage when I was a kid. It's opened and closed by pulling a rope inside. My dad changed it because it couldn't be closed from the outside, and he thought it being left open all day when he was at work, was a security risk. Ask Harding if the garage door was open or closed when he talked to Pat about the wall. If Duncan returned home from work *before* driving to the pub to meet his friend, it's possible he had closed the garage door from inside before Harding arrived."

Humphries thought the suggested scenario over in his head, thinking the timing would still be tight, before saying, "Why would he bother to close the garage door? Why not leave it open so he can make a quick exit?"

"He knows the recorded time of death will be whenever he removes the watch from his wrist, so a speedy exit isn't his priority." Zooming out of the picture, Fiona added, "The drive and the garage doors can be seen from the house, and he doesn't want Pat to know he's there. Or he knows she'll hear the car, and he wants her to think he's arriving home from work like every other day. Closing the doors indicates he's home for the evening, ready to relax with a decent glass of wine."

"Okay, keeping to his usual routine to keep Pat off her guard makes sense," Humphries said. "It follows that Duncan would worry that Harding might remember a small detail like the garage door being closed, but what about Murphy? As far as we know, he wasn't close enough to even see the house, let alone whether the garage door was up or down."

"But he was wandering around claiming to have seen something. Duncan heard about it and didn't want to take the risk," Fiona said. "Did you get a list of everyone who was in the Suffolk that night?"

"Yes, I'll look at it after I've spoken to Harding," Humphries said, returning to his desk to make the call.

Fiona rang Duncan's secretary. "Hi Karen, can you cast your mind back to the evening that Pat Thomas was killed?"

"I can, but I haven't remembered anything new."

"When we talked before, you said that on that evening, Duncan pointed out the time to you. Was it usual for him to prompt you like that?"

"You asked me that before," Karen said. "It was a little unusual, but I'm sure there were other occasions when he reminded me."

"Do you remember if he was looking at the wall clock?" A long silence followed, and Fiona started to think Karen had forgotten her.

"No, now you mention it. He was wearing a wristwatch."

"Was that unusual?" Fiona asked. "Did he usually wear a watch?"

"I don't know. He mostly checks the time on his mobile phone, but that doesn't mean anything."

"Did you glance up at the wall clock to check the time?"

"Goodness, let me see. No. No, I don't think I did. I would have been rushing to close down what I was doing to save my mother from worrying if I arrived home late."

"Thank you. Could you come into the station today to give a

statement to that effect?" Fiona asked. "And possibly identify the watch?"

"I can, but why don't you simply ask Duncan?"

"Oh, we will," Fiona replied, before walking over to speak to Andrew, who had just walked in. "I'm going to interview Olive shortly. Other than the witness who saw a slight person leave Murphy's home the night he was killed, has anything else come to light?"

Andrew shook his head. "So far, there is nothing else to explain his death. No forensics or anyone with a serious grudge against him. There was no change in his routine in the days leading up to his death, he didn't appear to have any worries, and there's no history of depression."

"Nothing except his boasts that he knew who killed Pat," Fiona said.

"Do you think he did?" Andrew said. "His friends dismissed it as another one of his tall stories."

"It's possible he caught a glimpse of Duncan's car on the track," Fiona said, "but if Duncan heard what he was claiming and believed him, it's irrelevant. If we can prove he's responsible for his wife's death, the fire and Murphy's death will follow."

Ending a call, Eddie said, "This might be significant. On the night Murphy was killed, Duncan kept the liaison officer talking into the early hours. It was the one and only time he wanted to talk. Before then, he had been a closed book, and the following morning, he said he would prefer she left him to grieve in private. With hindsight, it sounds like he was ensuring he had an alibi for the evening."

"Which means he knew Murphy was going to be killed that night," Fiona said. "Good work."

"Fiona," Rachael said, as she spun her chair around. "A camera picked up Olive's registration plate that evening. It's a few miles out, but it shows her driving in the right direction and going the opposite way an hour later."

"Brilliant. Send me the exact locations. Because of the remote location of the Hardings' home we didn't concern ourselves with cameras. Can you check to see if her car was picked up that evening and which direction it was heading? I'll be starting the interview in ten minutes," Fiona said.

"Can do, but it will take a while."

Turning to Andrew and Eddie, Fiona said, "At the moment, we only have one witness who saw Duncan and Olive together. When we went through Duncan's bank accounts, there were numerous payments for pub and restaurant meals. They covered a wide area, and we assumed they were work-related. Go around them all, showing photographs of Duncan and Olive. Someone else might remember seeing them together. When we get full access to Olive's bank accounts, cross reference them to see if there are any places that they both attended at the same time."

Seeing Humphries had completed his call, she went over to him. "Well?"

Grinning from ear to ear, he raised his thumb. "Harding is sure the garage door was closed and ..."

"Get on with it," Fiona said.

"They need to do some more analysing, but there was a subtle change in the vitals recorded on the smartwatch from eight o'clock in the morning onwards on the day of Pat's death. It may be enough to prove a change of user."

"That means if Duncan later confesses, he can't claim there was a surprise argument, and he lashed out on impulse, not expecting Pat to fall to her death. If he took the phone that morning, we'll be able to argue he had pre-planned every last detail," Fiona said. "We'll interview Olive now and reinterview Duncan straight after."

CHAPTER FORTY-SEVEN

Olive started her interview on the offensive, complaining they had ruined a planned visit to see her brother, they had no right to interrogate her and denied she knew Duncan or his wife. She had no alibi for the night of the fire or Murphy's death other than she was asleep at home alone. Her argument was her lack of an alibi confirmed her innocence. Why should she have one when she had never met the people before and knew nothing about any of them?

Fiona decided to start with the night they had evidence of her driving in the area. "Would a neighbour be able to confirm that your car was parked outside your home Saturday night?"

"Possibly. I don't know. I don't tend to keep tabs on my neighbours, but you never know."

"But you are quite sure you were asleep in bed on that night?" Fiona asked.

"Yes, I've already told you," Olive replied testily. "I've checked my diary, and I had no engagements. It was a busy week, as I remember. I left the club late, and as I had an early start the following morning, I went straight to bed."

"Have you ever had problems sleeping?" Fiona said, looking down to read the message that had just come through on her phone.

"No, nothing out of the ordinary. Maybe the odd sleepless night if I was stressed."

"And on those few occasions, what would you do?"

"Do? How do you mean, *do*?" Olive shrilly asked.

"Would you get up? Read a book or watch television? Maybe go for a walk to get some fresh air?"

"I might try to read a book, but that's about it."

"You wouldn't say … decide to go for a drive?"

"No… I don't think so," Olive said, for the first time sounding less sure of herself. "Hang on. I remember now. There was an evening when I did pop out. I woke up and remembered I didn't have any milk for coffee in the morning, so I popped to the local shop. That may have been around that time. I can't remember what night it was, but that's probably what the neighbour saw. Can I say that I'm appalled you have spoken to my neighbours without just cause. That's an invasion of my privacy when I haven't been charged with anything." She turned to her solicitor and asked, "Can I make a formal complaint about it?"

Before the solicitor replied, Fiona asked, "Who said anything about a neighbour seeing you drive off? I certainly haven't, but for the record, where is this local shop?"

Looking confused, Olive leaned back in her chair and crossed her arms.

Fiona pulled a matching confused face. "I didn't think the name of your local shop was such a contentious issue."

"The Spar shop," Olive forced out through clenched teeth. "It's just around the corner."

"So, that wouldn't explain why you were driving on the main road, heading toward Hinnegar Woods late that night? Where were you going?"

"How? No. I wasn't there. Whoever saw me must be mistaken."

Fiona placed her phone, showing a date-stamped picture of Olive's car, on the desk. "Is this your car?"

Olive looked at the photograph. "No comment. I would like to suspend this interview now."

"As you wish," Fiona said. "We'll come back later when you've had time to rethink how you spent that evening."

Less progress was made interviewing Duncan, who replied, "No comment," to every question from the start. Not prepared to waste time when they had so many enquiries to follow up on, Fiona said, "I'm suspending the interview now, but you should be aware we can apply to hold you here for four days from the time of your arrest." Registering Duncan's shocked look of panic, she stood and added, "So you might like to spend your time working on some more constructive replies."

Once in the corridor, Fiona said, "I'll check whether Duncan's secretary has come in and been able to identify the watch. Then we'll help out with checking the pubs and restaurants Duncan recently visited."

Rachael confirmed she had spoken to Karen. "While she couldn't confirm that the watch she was shown, was the one Duncan had worn that day, she did say it was similar. She also said she thought it was a surprising choice as Duncan's taste was usually very traditionalist."

When Fiona shared the news with Humphries, he said, "Looks like we can build a good case against them. The custody sergeant will be pleased if we can release Natalie. She's giving him an earache about how she needs to leave to attend to her farm."

"We still have the matter of assaulting and imprisoning a police officer and discharging a firearm," Fiona said. "I want to hear her full version of last night's events again, but as she's a low-flight risk, if I'm satisfied with her explanations, I'll consider releasing her on bail."

During the interview, Fiona and Humphries shared looks and raised eyebrows when Natalie insisted that she had only lightly shaken the chair Abbie was standing on, not expecting her to fall. She simply had no choice other than to restrain her in the cellar, as she absolutely had to honour her date with Duncan. He had stipulated that they keep their blossoming relationship secret, so she couldn't arrive with a police officer in tow.

If Fiona could have charged Natalie with gross self-entitlement, she would have done so but settled with assaulting and imprisoning a police officer. It was the events at Field Barn she was more interested in.

"Well, it's obvious, isn't it? I was hoodwinked by that cad,"

Natalie said. "I only wanted to support him through his grief as his sister-in-law, but he told me how he had always held a candle for me. Oh, he can turn on the charm when he wants to, and I fell for it. Then, last night he showed his true colours. All these years, and I never once realised the bumbling buffoon was only an act. Underneath, he is cruel, cold and calculating. I feel sorry for my poor sister being lumbered with him. If she had confided in me, I would have helped her escape the marriage, despite everything else. I'm wondering now if Duncan pressurised her into banning the hunt."

"Can we stick to the events of last night?" Fiona asked.

"That rogue persuaded me to go outside with him as he had something in the hay barn that he wanted to show me, and stupidly, I trotted after him."

"To the hay barn? In the middle of a storm?"

"You're not a country girl, are you?"

"Okay, fine," Fiona said. "What happened when you went to the barn?"

"He told me to wait while he climbed up the stack of hay bales to retrieve whatever it was that he wanted to show me," Natalie said. "Luckily for me, I was interested in the quality of the hay and moved to take a closer look. From the corner of my eye, I saw him laid out flat on his back, pushing a top bale with his feet. I shot out of there just in time as the first few bales came crashing down behind me, bringing the others with it. Do you know how many farmers are killed or seriously injured every year by falling bales?"

"I don't, but can we continue with last night's events?"

"I was flabbergasted, as you can well imagine and stood there rooted to the spot in the pouring rain. That is until he came charging towards me. I fired the shotgun into the air and started to run for my car. I was halfway across the yard when he caught up with me and started to wrestle the gun away from me. The gun went off a second time in the scuffle, but I managed to hang onto it. I pointed it at him, and he ran off. I was planning on getting to my car and driving home, but that's when you lot arrived. It was the first time I was pleased to see your miserable faces. Now that I've explained everything again, can I go? I have animals to feed."

"We can release you, but there will be certain restrictions, and you won't be able to leave the area."

"You clearly have never run a farm. It takes weeks of planning to go away for a few days."

"Okay," Fiona said, feeling her headache return. "We'll take you downstairs to be officially charged, and then you'll be free to leave."

Back at her desk, Fiona was reading the most recent report on the watch, when she received a call from Andrew. Two hotel workers had identified Duncan and Olive as being a couple who were intimate with one another. Following their meal, they had booked an overnight room which the woman had paid for. After thanking Andrew, she turned in her chair and asked, "Have we access to Olive's bank accounts yet?"

"Should do shortly," Rachael replied.

"When you get them, look for a payment to the Snooty Fox in Beresford. Looks like we can prove they are both lying on several counts and build a solid case against them. Two witnesses say they shared a room there last month."

"So, we can charge them, now?" Andrew asked.

"I'll keep pushing them for an admission," Fiona said. "But we've enough to charge them without a confession if necessary."

"So, once the others are back, we're all in the Squire for a celebratory drink," Humphries said. "Fiona's buying the first round." He crossed over and whispered to Fiona, "You can invite Stefan."

"Get out of here," Fiona said, trying to sound cross, but failing to hide a smile.

CHAPTER FORTY-EIGHT

Fiona arrived home tired but pleased with the progress made on the case. It had been a busy week collating all the evidence, but she was confident they had a strong case and, at last, felt like she could relax,

As proof of their lies was put to them, Duncan and Olive looked more and more like they were going to confess. She thought it likely that Olive would be the first to crack, although Duncan had started to drop comments about how difficult and intimidating Pat was. Either way, she was sure it was only a matter of time.

She kicked off her shoes and took a moment to stretch out on the sofa. As soon as the last few loose ends were tied up, she was going to take a well-earned break. Not that she would have much time to relax. Her father had chosen a care home and had agreed to give it a try. She had promised to help with the move and be around generally to support her mother. Peter was due to be released home, and she was determined to spend some time with him and be a better friend. And her living room still needed redecorating.

It all was a bit of a mess, but she felt insanely optimistic about the future. Stefan was coming around later to take her out, and just thinking about him made her smile. Where past boyfriends had tended to be a drag on her mood, he lifted it. Her mother's demands, driven by her desire for grandchildren, that Fiona hang onto every boyfriend, even the ones who hurt her mentally and physically, had been irritating in the past. She still had trust issues and boundaries to work through, but with Stefan, she intended, for once, to follow her mother's advice.

BOOKS IN THIS SERIES

A DI Fiona Williama Mystery

A Fiery End

A tradesman is set alight in his vehicle on an isolated road. His daughter is missing. And time is running out.

"I was on the edge of my seat and couldn't read fast enough."
"Totally riveting."
"Superb murder mystery and police procedural."

DI Fiona Williams is a driven detective who cares deeply about getting justice for victims and their families.
Driving home late at night, she comes across a vehicle engulfed in flames. The driver is at the wheel, oblivious to the inferno surrounding him. There is no explanation for why the vehicle was on the road or why the quiet tradesman was murdered in such a macabre way. The only witness to the fire, claims she saw nothing. Whatever she did see goes to the grave with her when she is brutally strangled. Frustration grows when the driver's daughter disappears. With time running out to find the daughter alive, Fiona is drawn into a web of powerful men determined to keep their deadly games secret. Juggling a family crisis and a growing suspicion her boss is corrupt, her judgement is hampered by her attraction to the man central to everything.

A Mother's Ruin

A single mother is brutally murdered in her garden.

DI Fiona Williams interprets the crime scene differently from her colleagues but fears her history of failed relationships taints her judgment. The wrong decision will change the lives of three children forever.

In a male-dominated department, with mounting evidence pointing in the other direction, will she find the courage to trust her instincts and narrow the investigation?

An intriguing mystery that blurs the distinction between the villain and the victim.

A Relative Death

An eye for an eye. A death for a death.
Some people will do anything for revenge.
And one detective will do anything to stop them.
DI Fiona Williams returns from a short break to a station stretched by the antics of a gang of youths, staff absences and three murders in quick succession. With unconnected victims and widely different murder methods, the only link is they seem motiveless. Forced to work in small groups rather than as a team, frustrations and jealousies flare-up between the officers creating a minefield of tension and a headache for Fiona.
As the most experienced officer, she is pulled from the initial case of a poisoned pensioner to investigate the shooting of a wealthy landowner's wife. She is annoyed the murder of a

defenceless war veteran is given lower priority and thoughts of the pensioner's last moments are never far away.

The two victims have never met, and the only similarity is their murderer was someone who knew them well. The chances of it being the same person are remote.

When a breakthrough comes in the investigation, it seems Fiona's nagging thought that the cases are connected may be correct. To fit the missing pieces together she will have to risk her life for an enemy she has worked hard to condemn.

An Educated Death

The best-kept secrets are the deadliest.

When a private boarding school pupil drowns in a lake on the grounds, DI Fiona Williams is called in to investigate. Security around the school grounds is tight, making it a closed community.

Fiona thinks the death was due to a secret society initiation rite that went wrong, but the school denies the societies exist, and her investigation hits a wall of silence.

A second pupil dies, but the silence continues.

The school is concerned with its reputation and upholding traditions, the influential parents care only about protecting their children, and the pupils have secrets of their own.

Nobody wants Fiona to expose the whole truth.

BOOKS BY THIS AUTHOR

The Skeletons Of Birkbury

Bells On Her Toes

Point Of No Return

Who Killed Vivien Morse?

Twisted Truth

The Paperboy

Trouble At Clenchers Mill

Trouble At Fatting House

Trouble At Suncliffe Manor

Trouble At Sharcott

Printed in Great Britain
by Amazon

34888303R00139